Was it her imagination, or had those guns just moved in closer?

The gun muzzles pointed at Selena, and her partner, Dobry, trapped her gaze and didn't let her look to the people beyond. Inside she raged for freedom, wanting to strike and fight and even lose rather than stand here unresisting.

Dobry's next words shocked her. "This woman is one who knows your people. She saved your homes in the past."

The pause was excruciating. The magistrate, an older man with a full, gray beard, walked deliberately around Dobry to examine Selena. She knew this man would not hesitate to order their deaths if he truly thought they were a threat. "I was here this past winter," she said. "I called for help when the Kemeni rebels attacked."

"There was a woman here," he agreed. "We know she was Selena Jones, of the American FBI. That she worked against terrorism." Then he smiled. "What we don't know," he said, "is who *you* are."

She opened her mouth. Closed it again. Eyed Dobry and found him eyeing her back.

Because of course, they didn't have any papers on them to prove their identities.

Dear Reader,

Offered the chance to go back and revisit Selena's world, is there anyone here who thinks I so much as blinked before leaping to my feet and wildly waving my hand—"Me! Me! Oh, pick *me!*" (The muse has no shame, really.) For while I had an extensive chance to explore Selena's character in *Checkmate* and to learn a little about Cole, I didn't really have the opportunity to see how they were *together.* How would they work as a team, at home and in the field? And given more "air time," what sort of fellow would Cole turn out to be?

Along with all that, I wondered, what would it be like to be Selena, trying to cope with the events of *Checkmate* as she went on with her life? The answers made for a delightful writing experience, and I hope they make for good reading, as well. Enjoy!

Doranna Durgin

DORANNA
DURGIN

COMEBACK

Published by Silhouette Books
America's Publisher of Contemporary Romance

Special thanks and acknowledgment are given to Doranna Durgin for her contribution to the ATHENA FORCE miniseries.

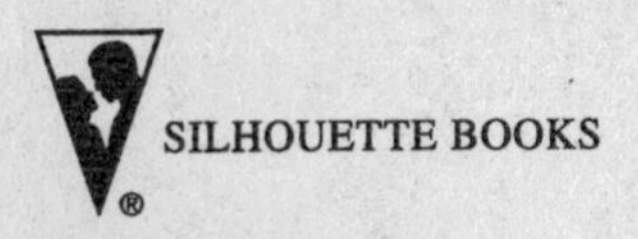

ISBN-13: 978-0-373-51416-8
ISBN-10: 0-373-51416-6

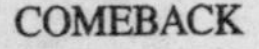
COMEBACK

This edition published by arrangement with Harlequin Books S.A.

www.SilhouetteBombshell.com

Printed in U.S.A.

Books by Doranna Durgin

Silhouette Bombshell

Exception to the Rule #11
†*Checkmate* #46
**Beyond the Rules* #59
**Survival Instinct* #85
†*Comeback* #102

†Athena Force
*Hunter Agency stories

Silhouette Books

Femme Fatale
"Shaken and Stirred"

DORANNA DURGIN

spent her childhood filling notebooks first with stories and art, and then with novels. After obtaining a degree in wildlife illustration and environmental education, she spent a number of years deep in the Appalachian Mountains. When she emerged, it was as a writer who found herself irrevocably tied to the natural world and its creatures—and with a new touchstone to the rugged spirit that helped settle the area and which she instills in her characters.

Doranna's first fantasy novel received the 1995 Compton Crook/Stephen Tall Award for the best first book in the fantasy, science fiction and horror genres; she now has fifteen novels of eclectic genres on the shelves. Most recently she's leaped gleefully into the world of action romance. When she's not writing, Doranna builds Web pages, wanders around outside with a camera and works with horses and dogs. There's a Lipizzan in her backyard, a mountain looming outside her office window, a pack of agility dogs romping in the house and a laptop sitting on her desk—and that's just the way she likes it. You can find a complete list of titles at www.doranna.net along with scoops about new projects, lots of silly photos and a link to her SFF Net newsgroup.

Dedicated to my own teammates:
Duncan, Belle, Jean-Luc Picardigan and ConneryB.

Chapter 1

Someone's following me.

Selena's heart rate skyrocketed higher than expected, surprising her with reactions left over from months ago. Reactions that came from two intense days inside the Berzhaan capitol during which she outwitted, outran and outlived the terrorists who'd taken everyone else in the building hostage. Now that familiar tension zinged through her body—a body she somehow kept walking at a normal pace. Outwardly oblivious, inwardly on high alert.

Except this was the modest little Virginia town closest to the CIA training facility called the Farm, and if the description *sleepy* didn't quite do it justice, *bustling* went too far. On a crisp early fall evening, headed from the family-owned pharmacy along the main street to the sports shop, Selena was in no danger from terrorists. Down the sidewalk, a teenage girl walked her dog. Across the street, a middle-aged couple shared an ice-cream cone. A man in running shorts headed down the sidewalk away from Selena; a woman in more sensible sweats jogged in place, waiting out one of the town's few signal lights. Vehicle traffic was sporadic, heavily populated with the practical rather than the luxurious.

And still, someone followed her.

Selena Shaw Jones didn't waste time doubting herself. Never did. Doubt hadn't gotten her out of Berzhaan alive. She'd done that on her own, using her wits and her grit… and trusting her instincts. So now, without changing her stride, she headed past the big brick structure of the sporting goods store, ducking down the alley beside it. *Choke point.* Anyone following her would stand out clearly if he so much as hesitated at the intersection, while the alley itself was dark enough to hide Selena from a casual glance.

Except she quickly realized she could go one better. The old brick building's deeply inset windows, half a story above her, offered plenty of ledge for a woman quick and nimble. The darkened panes meant an unoccupied room and no one likely to notice her or give her away. Up she went, scraping knuckles and ignoring the stinging pain as she caught her balance, crouching with her back to the brick and her eyes on the alley entrance. Her left hand crept beneath her black leather duster to her back pocket and pulled out the knife clipped there, thumbing the short tanto blade open. A blade meant for close work, with wicked angles of hard steel.

And yeah. Here they came. One at first, hesitating on the decision to enter the dark area. And then a second, meeting up with quick whispers and a few restrained gestures. One male, one female, features deliberately obscured by deep jacket hoods.

Selena wiped a trembling hand along the thigh of her

navy cargo pants. Tailored enough for casual chic, they nonetheless had the flexible pocket capacity she wanted. She'd become quite fond of the style since it had served her so well in Berzhaan, holding a plethora of small improvised weapons for her private guerrilla war against the Kemeni rebels. She wasn't so fond of the trembling. Not fear, that trembling. Just awareness. Readiness. A need to act.

Come a little closer.

And oh, they did. They tried to cover it, as the man playfully backed the woman into the darkness, nuzzling at her ear and murmuring something to make her laugh. But Selena saw the surreptitious glances, even from within their hoods. They were looking for her. They wondered if she was hidden in some dark corner or if she'd found a hidden exit. She pushed her back against the brick, waiting...

Until finally they'd gone beyond her.

She leaped down from the windowsill, cat-light, and covered the ground between them in a mere pounce. Just enough time to put the knife up to the side of the man's hood-covered neck before shoving him, hard, against both the woman and the wall. The woman's eyes widened; the man froze at the sharp touch of metal as it pierced his jacket through to his skin. Impulses left over from Berzhaan surged through Selena, urging her to be swift and final. A quick stab into the man's neck and a forward slash of her arm—messy but effective—and she'd get the woman with the end of her swing.

Get real, Selena. This wasn't Berzhaan. These two weren't good enough to pose an immediate life or death threat.

And then she recognized the woman—saw enough of her to know those rounded features, that stubby nose. Shock made her step back, but not without shoving the man aside and off balance. By then she'd recognized him, too.

Students. From the Farm, where she'd been teaching these past months.

But they shouldn't be here—not trailing her. She'd played rabbit for them before, but never unknowingly. "What the hell—"

She didn't have time to finish, not with the woman's eyes going even wider as a pair of hands clamped down on her arms. No more thinking, then, just reaction. Pure adrenaline hit. She yanked herself forward, sliding those hands down to her wrists, and then she whirled, her captured arms twirling over her head in a fast, deadly dance. They faced each other only for an instant, his now-crossed hands still on her wrists, and then she jerked back with her right hand to throw him off balance, jammed her right leg in behind his and shoved him backward. He fell over her leg—so simple, so effective—and she levered him around his own arm. He twisted to fall facedown in the gritty soil and even then she didn't stop, shoving the arm up high and landing on his back just as the joint cracked. By then her knees were on her attacker's spine and the knife at the base of his skull.

She knew better than most how little it took to kill a man that way.

"No!" The woman leaped forward as if to grab Selena's arm and thought better of it, hovering without touching. "He's with us! He's the trailing eye!"

Selena's fierce intent abruptly faded away into nothing more than a pounding heart. Of course they'd had another "eye" on the team. Why he'd been so foolish as to come up on her from behind, bodily yanking her out of a confrontation that had nearly been resolved without him, she couldn't imagine. Now he moaned in pain, afraid to move. She stabbed her blade into the ground in pure disgust.

"Goddammit, what were you thinking? What were any of you thinking, following me on my personal time?" She yanked the knife free and folded it, standing away from the man so the other two could check on him. Dislocated shoulder, for sure. She still hadn't gotten a good look at him—didn't even know which student she'd disabled.

But as pure reaction faded, thoughtfulness returned. Enough thoughtfulness to know there'd be an aftermath to this moment. The injured man would lose his place in the class. Conversations would be had, explanations demanded. She swore again, more softly this time. And finished the question she'd once started. "What the hell are you doing out here? Didn't anyone apply a sanity check to this little stunt? What did you *think* would happen if you followed me without bringing me in on the exercise?" She looked down at the injured man. The other two had carefully moved his arm so they could roll him over, and she recognized him well enough. Not a great student, but not a bad one. Not generally this stupid. She reached into the deep pocket of her leather duster—a little worse for wear, this duster, but repaired well enough after the previous spring—and fumbled for her phone.

The woman looked at her, eyes big all over again, and then going suddenly narrow. "You were supposed to know. We thought you *knew*."

A noise from the sidewalk—someone had finally noticed the ruckus. Selena snapped her head around to face the new arrival, ready to drive him off with a few snappy orders and the badge jammed into her pocket.

Instead she found Steven Dobry. The burly Farm instructor and CIA technical ops expert was older than Selena, his features and bearing an unremarkable and perfect canvas for demonstrating his disguise strategies to the students. He didn't do a very good job of hiding his own desire to be in the field, or his skepticism that Selena—younger, female and formerly FBI—had ever belonged there. Dobry said, "I've already called for help."

"Suddenly," Selena said, "this all makes a certain twisted sense."

"Nothing about this makes sense." Dobry waved at the scene before them. "What the hell is this all about?"

Selena shook her head. "No. Nice try, but no." She released the phone and let her hand settle in her pocket. There, he wouldn't see that she had it clenched. But on the outside she'd found her cool, the guise of the experienced FBI legate and specialist in international counterterrorism. She'd attended embassy balls and palace dinners; she'd negotiated with heads of state and walked through terrorist territory in more countries than Dobry could even imagine. "That's your question to answer. You knew they couldn't tail me undetected."

"Did I?" He raised an eyebrow at her, visible enough in the faint fan of light from the closest streetlamp.

Fury swept through her, along with the sudden understanding. "You thought they could do it. You figure I'm full of crap, and you were going to prove it. This wasn't a training exercise…it was an exercise in embarrassment. *My* embarrassment." She narrowed her eyes at him, her fist still clenched inside her pocket and her voice deceptively casual. "And how's that working out for you?"

The woman looked over at Dobry, anger rising on her face. "You *used* us. You set us up!"

Dobry sent a cold look Selena's way. "It's a shame you overreacted so badly. This should have been a perfectly safe exercise."

"It could have been," she agreed. "*If* you'd let me in on

it. Not to mention it would have been infinitely more challenging—I could have led them on quite a chase before I dumped them. But instead you sent them out cold and green. I'll bet you didn't even warn them not to take me on."

"He was no threat to you!"

The woman stood up, now freely glaring. "And how was she supposed to know that? She didn't even know it was *us*."

Selena heard sirens in the background, still faint and far away. "You knew my background, whether you believed it or not. You lied to your trainees. You left me out of the loop. Me? I'm just a CIA officer on my private time who reacted exactly as I should have. I know who I'd rather be when it comes to facing the DDA over this."

"Damned cold bitch, aren't you?" His sullen anger told her she'd scored a point.

"No," Selena told him. "I'm smoking hot. Too bad you're only now beginning to figure it out."

The DDA—Deputy Director of Administration, the ultimate boss of the Farm—didn't actually put in an appearance for the chewing-out phase. The Director of Training and Education handled the job just fine on his own. Equally scathing on both their counts, troweling the blame thick. Selena thought she imagined frustration when he looked at Dobry and concern when he looked at her.

On the other hand it could have just been a twitch.

But unlike Dobry, the DDA knew her background. He knew the CIA had offered her a spot high in the counterterrorist hierarchy, but that as she had healed physically from those several intense days in Berzhaan, as she had debriefed and reported and followed through on the incident, the need for an extended period of lower stress had made itself clear as well.

Selena hated it. She saw it as weakness. Yes, she'd spent two days fighting for her life—and yes, during that time just about everyone she'd seen had been trying to hurt or kill her. She'd saved the lives of the prime minister and most of the hostages. Outgunned and outmanned, even on the brink of what seemed like certain death, she'd managed to convey information to lurking rescue forces. She'd *won*, dammit.

These days, she felt like maybe they'd won, too. Instead of surging forth into her new life, she'd ended up here, instructing. De-stressing. There'd been that one clandestine meeting with Oracle shortly after her return from Berzhaan, but she wasn't of any great use to that supersecret fledgling intelligence agency as long as she was here. Recovering.

Not that the teaching position was a bad thing in and of itself. She was good at it; she enjoyed it. She just wanted *more*.

She wasn't likely to get it as long as she was doing things like turning clueless newbies into broken bits of student. At least the injured trainee would be allowed back for the next session. Small consolation, but one that Selena held on to.

So she didn't make excuses to the DDA—he knew exactly why she'd reacted with force, and he knew she'd pulled her punches or the injured trainee would be a dead trainee. She limited her responses to acknowledgments and she glared at Dobry's back on the way out of the Farm's administration building, holding her anger tightly inside. When she would have walked away, heading through the dark night and the newly falling mist, he hesitated.

"Selena—"

The anger snapped. She pivoted, glaring at him with such force that he fell silent. She said, "Don't, Dobry.

Don't even try to pretend what happened tonight was my responsibility. I'll take it like a good soldier for the director, but you haven't earned that from me. If you hadn't disrespected me and used your students to prove the point you *thought* you had, none of this would have happened." She took one step toward him, lowering her voice into the dangerous range. "And it better not happen again. Not this, not anything like it."

He paused, that sullen expression lurking and an overlay of his own anger on top of it. Finally he said, "You don't belong here. Maybe not for the reason I first thought, but you don't belong here. The CIA doesn't take on FBI cast-offs. They broke you…let *them* fix you. The rest of us here don't need your problems."

Selena let the words sit there until he seemed to give up on a response at all. What she felt underneath—half-believing the validity of his words, half-believing she couldn't be fixed at all—stayed private. Hers only. She kept her voice matter-of-fact, devoid of the intensity that had startled him a moment earlier. "Too bad that's not your decision to make."

And this time she did turn and walk away, heading for the sophisticated gym inside what looked like a perfectly picturesque barn. She hit the locker room to strip away her leather duster, the navy cargos and black trail sneakers, and replaced them with black spandex. Shorts and sports bra and attitude, all of which she took to the gym. She put on a pair of lightly padded gloves and tackled the workout bag, pounding the dust from it with fist and foot alike. She pounded out what was left of the adrenaline, chasing the unfinished feeling left from the alley encounter. Unfinished, because she'd pulled her punches even after the trainee had grabbed her from behind, invoking body memories of life and death in the hands of the rebels-turned-terrorists. Tafiq Ashurbeyli, with his gun jammed to the back of her head. With his body pressing her against the wall. With his men ambushing her when she'd thought herself as of yet undiscovered, unknown.

She wished the punching bag was Dobry, or the dead Kemeni leader, or any one of the men she'd been forced to kill.

She wished it hadn't been that poor stupid trainee.

Don't be so hard on yourself. That was Cole's voice, popping up in her head. Cole, who'd dropped everything to sneak inside Berzhaan when the terrorists struck. Who'd put up with her in the months since, just happy enough she was still alive. A rededicated marriage, and he'd meant it. And now a ghost of his voice said, *If you were as bad as you think you are, you wouldn't care so much.*

Cole.

She glanced at the wire-covered clock, eyes bleary with sweat. Eleven o'clock. He'd be waiting. He'd had a meeting this evening—something to do with his security consulting job. It was a position he'd once called laughably easy, by which she knew he'd soon be bored. But he'd taken it so they could stay together—so for once they could both be at work in the same country. In the same city. Even in the same temporary housing. Talking about children and family life and not particularly getting anywhere with either.

Selena cursed and thudded her fist into the workout bag—this time without any force behind it, and she used the motion to push herself away and head for the locker room. She pulled on the sweat suit she had stored there, transferring her badge, her knife, and her ID to the kangaroo pockets of the hoodie. She slammed the locker closed on the remainder of her things, twisting the token lock in place. The students might ply their newly learned skills on the neat row of locks, but they knew better than to actually take anything. Another time, she might have left a booby trap for them. Something involving a paint ball.

But not this time. This time she hesitated at the barn's big sliding door, squinting into precipitation now too hard to call mist. Moderate rain. Not enough to deter her.

She felt someone's eyes on her and turned to discover a figure by the corner of the barn. He stood in the shelter from the rain, just close enough to identify as the male trainee from earlier in the evening—the one who'd been lucky, and come away intact. He stood hunched, his hands in his pockets, his posture straightening as he realized she'd seen him. But he hesitated, his mouth just barely open—on apology rather than accusation, Selena thought, but she was in a mood to hear neither.

She turned away and ran into the dark rain.

Cole Jones dropped for a few push-ups, just enough to get his blood moving. Then he returned to the paperwork spread over the kitchen counter and pondered whether this particular client needed the super-duper countersurveillance electronics, or the super-duper-whooper version.

He thought the super-duper would do. But these people had money and they seemed to like to spend it. He shook his head at the papers and contemplated letting a game of darts make the choice. The countersurveillance protection, he could provide. The security, he could provide. Dealing with the people? Another mind-set altogether. He found himself constantly fighting the urge to sell them some Florida swampland just to see if he could. Not that they were stupid people. By no means.

Just not possessed of much imagination.

Cole's own imagination was getting lonely. *Time for a Selena Sanity Fix.*

He perked up at the sound of the key in the town-house door. A two-story town house, every bit as big as their own apartment in D.C.—bigger, even. But it had a closed-in feel; more rooms, but smaller ones. Not as airy. Didn't feel like home at all.

On the other hand, it felt like they were getting away with something just being here together. Cole left his papers and headed for the door, hesitating at the kitchen entry just in time to find Selena standing in the entry hall. Dripping, bedraggled, cheeks flushed and breath still coming fast. He didn't even have to ask. She'd tried to outbatter and outrun her demons again.

She hadn't yet acknowledged that it didn't really work. Like a drug, the effect wore off. Like a drug, it seemed to take more and more out of her each time.

He didn't have to ask what had triggered her this time. He'd known since receiving her phone call from town that she'd have a hard night. He held out a hand. Wordlessly, she removed wet shoes, then stripped off her soaked sweats and gave them over to him. Given his own personal clothes management, he would have tossed them on the floor of the small laundry closet—but for Selena, he hung them in the bathroom. Passing the thermostat on the way back, he turned it up a degree or two.

He found her at the darkened living room's picture window, staring out rain-smeared glass into the darkness. Still in her workout shorts and sports bra top, all long, lean muscle and more angles than most women. Unless, from this view, you looked at her ass.

Cole always looked at her ass.

He adjusted his jeans to allow for the predictable response, and went to join her. He knew enough to make noise as he entered the room, and to wait for the slight shift of her head that meant she'd heard him, lost in thought as she was. Cole had enough of his own nightmares to respect hers...and he'd seen her in action. He respected that, too.

He came up behind her, snaking an arm around her long waist to flatten his hand against her stomach. Hard abdominals met his touch, as tense as the rest of her. He kissed her bare shoulder next to the black strap and rested his chin there, as glad for her height as ever.

It made for a good fit.

She didn't resist as he snugged her back against his chest. He said, "You're not one of the bad guys. It wouldn't upset you like this if you were." And he didn't know why she snorted softly in true amusement, but it didn't really matter because she relaxed slightly under his hand, fitting in more securely against his chest and making him regret the old collared polo he had on. He kissed the side of her neck, lingering there.

She said, "If only I hadn't—"

He snorted back, right against the soft skin of her neck, and then nipped that skin lightly in apology. But his voice held no sign of doubt. "And what if some guy on the street had grabbed you like that? Do you think he'd be in it for fun and games? You reacted just *right,* darlin'."

"Then I should have stopped sooner. I should have known the guy was with the two I'd already exposed."

He shrugged; he knew she'd feel it. "Lena, they train us. They send us out into the field, and they make us who we are. They *want* us because of who we are. Dobry is the one who put his trainees at risk. Dobry is the one who's ripe for a lawsuit—from you as much as from that poor dumb kid." Not so much younger than either of them, that trainee hadn't been. Not physically. Emotionally…psychologically…just an infant.

Selena released a pent-up huff of air, amusement at the thought of bringing suit against Dobry. "Well, I *am* a lawyer."

"See?" he said, speaking the words into the satin skin below her earlobe. "He'd never know what hit him. You always have that effect on me, too." He slid his hand lower, over skintight spandex, and tugged her bottom back into his growing erection. He managed to lose half of her next words, his eyes closing, his breath catching.

"—miss it?"

"Um," he said. "What?"

Not that she was immune to his touch; she tilted her head slightly so he could nuzzle aside her wet hair, tasting salt and rain. "Being in the field."

Ah. Guilt of another sort, also on her shoulders. He'd been a contract operative for the CIA before the incident at the Berzhaan capital—before he'd been caught on film and tape and digital media, tangled up in crutches and an air cast and heading to meet his equally battered wife at the steps of the capitol.

He had one of those pictures, an eight-by-ten glossy, tucked away. It captured everything about their marriage worth saving—the intensity of their feelings, fierce and devoted and out there on their faces for the world to see. It captured Selena's grit, her triumphant emergence from the smoking, battered building—bruised and bloodied, beaten and shot and nonetheless coming down those steps on her own two feet.

Of course, it also captured his scruffy blond hair and charming all-American features, devoid of the disguise he'd worn on his way into the situation. He had, at that moment, become a liability to the very agency that found his operational flexibility to be such an asset. No more laid-back, come-what-may exfiltrations, no more flying by the seat of his spy pants.

They hadn't even picked up the bill for his broken leg. He'd come after Selena in spite of the CIA, not because of it.

So now he played at security consulting, appeasing paranoid companies and individuals whose imagined problems far outstripped their reality.

Good money, though.

And it would do, for now.

Selena tensed in his arms; he blew gently against her neck. "Relax," he said, and used all his breaking and entering skills to dip his fingers inside the waistband of that darned spandex. "Just thinking. Of course I miss it. But the leg's just now getting back to where it'll hold up to real stress." He pushed against her without thinking and nearly lost his train of thought again. It wasn't just the touching, the contact, the delicious pressure…

It was knowing what she'd do to him if she ever turned around and took him on.

He cleared his throat. "And anyway," he managed, "this is great timing. Being in the same country as each other for more than a week at a time is definitely an asset when it comes to the whole family thing."

Oops. That had been a mistake. The whole family thing hadn't gone so well. *A* for effort, not so great for results. They'd checked; they'd learned that Selena's erratic cycles were more than just inconvenient. That getting pregnant would take a lot more than what happened naturally every time they got their hands on each other. And then it came…her words soft, a little sad. "And look how well that's turning out."

"Ah," he said, regret making his throat hum. "Darlin', that's turning out just perfect." And it always did. Perfect moments of intimacy, pillow talk cementing the bond that had once been fracturing.

Not to mention the marriage counseling.

He realized he'd introduced a rhythm to his movement against her, and that the blood was fast draining from his brain as she accepted his words and matched his movement. He was doomed if he kept talking, because he would soon be babbling nonsense. "We'll find a way, but in the meantime…just…" That last word turned into a strangled noise as she offered up a little twist of her hips, her stomach muscles tensing beneath his hand. When had his other hand crept up to cradle her breast? He had no idea. He pulled her tighter, but it didn't keep her from turning in his arms and wrapping one long leg around his hips so they met properly, all the right spots in all the right ways. While he was still gasping from that, she somehow shucked out of that spandex.

"Oh, thank goodness," he said fervently. And he wasn't sure how he ended up on the floor on his back, or when she'd gotten his jeans off, or how she'd so quickly positioned herself to take him in, but it didn't matter. He gasped, and he rocked his head back, and he said, "Oh… thank—"

And she laughed, and she took him on.

Chapter 2

Selena rustled in sleek aquamarine silk and pretended the opulence of the faux ballroom didn't strike chords of the Berzhaani capitol building; she ignored the czar-like splendor, the chandelier and filigree and rich wallpaper. She smiled at the trainee beside her, stuffed into a tux one size too small and pretending it didn't matter, and she rattled off a final, emphatic Russian phrase. He frowned in concentration.

"Bzzt!" she said, imitating the *Jeopardy* buzzer. "That was a joke. The daughter of the Russian diplomat sees that you aren't charmed by her, and goes to look for better company." She turned her back on him, spotted Cole on the other side of the room wearing a tux that fit him very well indeed, and gave him a slow wink. He hiked his eyebrow just enough to let her know the dress did indeed perfectly match her eyes and turned a bored look to the young lady who was so earnestly trying to impress him.

Young. They were so young. But they were good, or they wouldn't be here. They'd learn.

Behind her, the desperate young man said, "But it wasn't *funny*."

She had pity. She turned back to him, champagne flute elegantly balanced in hand, the ambience of the staged diplomatic reception surrounding them both. "It is if you're Russian."

As this student should have done—but probably hadn't—Selena had already memorized the exact layout of the room. She knew who stood where, and which student had slyly disappeared from public view to attempt her assignment of bugging a small reception room—nothing too challenging, this first time out. She knew which of the instructors circulated, relaxed and enjoying their role-playing for the evening. She knew the location of the special guests—such as Cole—who added extra flair and a sense of unknown for the students. She'd spotted one of the other students on special assignment simply by his withdrawn nature, and knew there was a third, someone good enough to keep her or himself unnoticed so far.

The injured trainee wasn't the only one conspicuous by his absence. Others had left the Farm—dismissed, or dropped out. Those remaining were halfway through their training, and tomorrow Selena would take up the counter-terrorism classes with intent. Until now the instructors had bled counterterrorism work into the other classes—token introductions to favored weapons, to profiling, to interrogation. She'd assisted them as needed, but she hadn't put her own program into full bore. Not yet.

It hadn't worried her. Her entire career consisted of educating the right people in the right way so they could best work with the United States to prevent terrorist actions, sometimes even when those people had no intention of learning at all. These trainees, on the other hand…they could only be called motivated.

And now the young man who had been flirting with the daughter of a Russian diplomat lifted his head and said, "I get that! The joke! 'Czechs sitting in Red Square eating matzo with chopsticks'!" And as she inclined her head at him, his eyes widened slightly in a way that had nothing to do with their conversation. Just enough to get her attention, not quite enough to tell her anything.

Until someone slammed into her from behind, hard enough to knock her off balance. Never so off balance she couldn't recover, though her champagne splashed across several surprised faces as she lost her glass. Never so off balance she couldn't whirl in response, heeding the flare of fierce reaction that immediately sparked deep within her chest.

But no. This wasn't the Berzhaan capitol building it resembled. It was a group of people in a fake embassy playing fake roles with the earnestness of those who understood their lives might one day depend on it. So Selena clamped down on the fierce impulse to do fierce harm and drew herself up into her most offended huff, spewing Russian invective even as she turned around.

And came face-to-face with Steven Dobry.

She knew in an instant that this had been no accident at all. That Dobry had known just what he'd been doing—this venue, this moment—and that he'd meant for her to turn on him. To prove she'd overreacted several days earlier when his trainee had gone down at her hands. To prove that she'd do it again.

Except he'd lost this chance. She'd done only exactly as she should have. She saw in his eyes that he knew it, too—but he didn't have the wherewithal to stammer an apology in character. She spit a few more Russian words at him and turned her back to stalk away.

No one in the room was stupid. They'd all know he'd acted deliberately, even the students who had no real clue about her days with the Kemenis. She'd be lucky if there wasn't speculation…if someone didn't sort through rumor to find truth so they'd all know.

It's what they were training these young men and women to do.

As Selena huffed toward the exit of the grand ballroom—stairs that led to a richly appointed hallway and then out the door to the very ordinary eastern Virginia countryside—a dashing figure cut her off. Deliberately dashing, with that very charming, that so irresistible look on his face. Extreme self-confidence—cockiness, even—and a lick of bashful charm. He offered his elbow and said, "May I find you conveyance?"

She said, "That would be most kind."

"And may I kick yon gentleman's balls up into his throat on your behalf?"

Selena pretended to consider. "Why, yes," she said. "Yes, you may." And then she glanced at Cole and said, "Just don't get me fired."

Cole cast a regretful look back into the theater of the evening, finding Dobry in discussion with someone by a side exit. "Maybe not, then," he said, and led her up the short, wide tier of steps. "Maybe another time, when my perfectly justified response might be less easily traced to my perfectly reasonable self. I do like that dress, by the way."

"I wore it for the poor young man who received most of

my flying champagne. Easily distracted, I'm afraid." But as they turned into the hallway, Selena hesitated, her hand still on Cole's arm. Hmm, a nice welcoming committee, the Director of T&E himself. And coming out a more discreet exit into that same hallway, Dobry and the supervising instructor. A third man, unknown to Selena, seemed to mean something to Cole. Tension hardened the muscle of Cole's arm under her fingers, and she gave a little squeeze.

The director looked at Dobry and said, "Are you done with this?"

"For the record—" Dobry started.

"No," said the director. "I mean, *are you done with this?* Because I *am*. These scenarios are to train our incoming employees. They are not springboards for your own clumsy whistleblowing. If I have a concern, I'll handle it. If you have a concern, then you tell me and I'll handle it."

Selena listened with remote respect, showing no sign of the surprise she felt; Cole's arm relaxed under her touch. "Sir," she said, when the director turned to her after receiving immediate assent from Dobry.

"And you? Are you done with this?"

"I was never part of it." Simple words, sincerely said.

The director considered them a moment, then nodded. "Good. Now, I'm expected inside. I believe we're just about to reveal one of our evening's operatives. Always a dramatic moment. In the meantime, I believe you two—" and he indicated Cole and the unknown man "—have something to talk about." He nodded at them all and walked briskly down the hall. After a hesitation, Dobry followed.

"Walk with me," the remaining man said, the only one of them not dressed for an evening of high entertainment. Not even in a suit, but khaki pants and a thick sweater and warm ankle-high hikers. He cut his gaze toward Selena, and Cole laughed as he ran his hand along the neatly hung coats on the hall rack, stopping at Selena's.

"Nope," he said. "She comes with me. We'll walk together."

And that's how Selena learned the CIA was pulling him back into the fold, back to black ops and back to the intense risks they'd both so recently left behind.

Away from everything they'd been trying to build.

Chapter 3

Thousands of miles and several weeks away from that CIA training exercise, Selena hit the three-mile marker of Goat Camp Trail and stopped to tip her head back and slug a generous amount of water. With the late October dry heat and three thousand feet of altitude in the stark, majestic White Tank Mountains of the Arizona desert, she knew better than to short herself on water.

One of her first lessons at Athena Academy, as it happened.

If she turned south to Black Canyon, she could close her eyes and imagine the terrain beyond, all the way to the five-hundred-acre tract of private land where the academy tucked in against the base of the White Tanks. The stables snugged up closest to the stark, scrubby wilderness, a place of majestic saguaro cactus and startlingly beautiful flowers, with stunted, scattered paloverde and ironwood the closest things to trees that the area could offer. The saddle of land held more than its share of them, giving shade to students who habitually pushed themselves hard both physically and mentally. Science labs, survival hikes, group bonding exercises, rock climbing, endurance swimming…Athena knew how to turn out a well-rounded young woman. Young women such as Selena, who had started her prelaw work long before she actually hit college, or such as her fellow Pandora group member Kim Valenti, code-breaker extraordinaire before she found her niche with the National Security Agency.

Yep, she could just about see it from here, even if only in her mind's eye. In fact, if she really wanted, she could easily cut through the rugged terrain and approach Athena from behind.

But today she stayed to the public trail, honoring park rules and moving fast and light for her morning workout—a quick jog along Goat Camp where the terrain allowed, confident climbing where it didn't. On to Mesquite Canyon, where the steep ground offered up plenty of loose rock to send the unwary tumbling down…no thank you. She'd gotten her quota of cholla spines within her first year at Athena. Not to mention prickly pear, creosote bush and that close call with a bark scorpion. Everything living in this alienesque landscape seemed to sting or stab or prickle.

And yet she loved it here.

Not so surprising she'd heard the call of it even from across the country at the Farm.

Especially not surprising with the conflict now constantly roiling through her head and through her heart. She'd hoped to calm her mind, to let her strong early foundation reemerge, eliminating the self-doubt that had grown since she'd accidentally pulled a man's arm out of joint.

Accidentally.

"Who does *that*?" she asked herself out loud, muttering through a nearly closed mouth to keep the sandy grit out of her teeth when a sudden gust of wind hit her hard enough to flap her shirt.

It hadn't been too bad until Cole had been whisked off to do whatever it was the agency thought only he could do, even after they'd washed their hands of him in Berzhaan. Then she'd had more time to think—more time than she could fill with workouts in the gym and on the running path. More time to worry about what this separation would do to them, and why Cole had agreed to go in the first place. They hadn't had time to talk before they snatched him away; nothing but a quick good bye kiss and separation right there at the Farm training exercise, the Russian princess left on her own. But she'd made it through the end of the training session and then she'd known just what to do. She'd come here.

She picked up the pace, anticipating the slowdown on the Mesquite Canyon trail. No good came of taking such footing for granted, and she didn't. Once she hit the ramada at the end of the trail she picked up a jog, finishing off the ten miles when she reached the borrowed bike parked at the Goat Camp trail head.

Four miles back to Athena...long enough for her trail-cleared mind to clutter up again. Full of self-doubt, full of concern. Pedaling was no distraction at all.

When Cole was here, she'd turned to him for her strength. He believed that she'd be able to leave her Berzhaani demons behind, and for a while that made a difference. Several precious months of being in the same house, in the same country, and now he was gone again. They hadn't started their family; they hadn't resolved their future.

They'd damned well convinced each other that they had their *now*. That their *now* was good.

Selena heard her own harsh breathing and realized she was doing it again. Her legs burned as she sped along the closest thing to a main road in the area and she forced herself to straighten on the bike, one hand lightly keeping it on course as she swooped around a turn, coasting. Even in this dry air she'd worked up a sweat, and she pulled her water bottle free of its clip and squeezed lukewarm water into her mouth.

By the time she reached the school, cruising past the dorms to reach the paved circle through the staff housing, her flushed face was dry of sweat, but her hair under the helmet was still soaked. Selena parked the bike at the little bungalow that principal Christine Evans had offered for the visit. She went straight inside for a shower, then grabbed a protein bar as she combed out her hair, squinting at the length and contemplating a cut. Done, she glared at herself, giving her flat lower belly a resentful poke. Selena was long and lean from head to toe, and it seemed nothing so curvy as pregnancy would ever even temporarily alter that theme.

She wondered if Cole had truly considered that possibility.

She pulled a wide-toothed comb through shoulder-length hair to tame it into order, and clipped it carelessly at the back of her head, up off her long neck. It was a severe look for the strong bones of her face—long and lean like the rest of her—so she pulled a few tendrils loose to soften her jawline and take attention away from the little cleft in her chin.

Cole liked that cleft. But Cole wasn't here.

Selena straightened the shower curtain and hung the bath towel and went out to the little kitchenette to grab some more ice water. Handy thing, this bungalow. Small but complete. Trust Athena to have extra housing on hand for alumni visits. Trust Christine Evans to understand how visiting the school could provide the grounding needed by its graduates, so many of whom had gone on to excel in the high-stress, high-risk jobs for which Athena had so ably prepared them.

Trust Christine to be waiting outside her door with a handful of letters and an invitation to walk around the campus. "Slowly," she added. "You've already had your workout for the day, if I don't miss my guess."

Selena accepted, slipping on a pair of leather Teva sandals and slipping out the screen door. When Selena had attended school here, Christine had been mentor and supervisor; in the intervening years, her visits had allowed that relationship to mature into mutual respect and affection. They weren't close—but then, Selena had very few people she would call *close*. Not her divorce-scattered and complicated family, not the fellow students at college who'd been intimidated by her acumen with law and language, and not her coworkers from her years of traveling overseas as an FBI legate. Trust, yes—that had been necessary to function in her role of building counterterrorism relationships in the tumultuous regions in which she worked. But not true, deep friendship.

Only Cole.

Now for the first time she looked at Christine with a friend's eyes and realized that the older woman actually looked her sixty-plus years. Though her shoulders were as straight as ever, reflecting her army officer's training, her short gray hair had gone almost entirely white. Her stride didn't hold quite the assurance it had just over a year earlier.

Of course, getting shot in the abdomen would do that to a person.

"Are you well?" Selena asked, and they both knew the deeper question behind it.

"You should ask the students," Christine said, raising one wry eyebrow.

Selena laughed. "They wouldn't dare suggest otherwise."

"Then there's your answer." Christine held out the letters. "From some of your classmates. I have permission to share them, of course. It's one way we can all keep abreast of one another's lives."

Selena felt a stab of guilt. When was the last time she'd written such a letter?

Christine might well have seen it on her face, for she waved away the moment. "You were a Pandora, Selena Shaw. None of you turned into letter writers. Holiday cards will suffice."

Selena laughed, short as it was. The Athena students matriculated in seventh grade, starting in a class of thirty, divided into small groups. By the time they graduated, they'd learned to live as a team, work as a team and compete as a team. The Cassandras had been one of those groups, legendary under the leadership of Rainy Carrington—and cohesive enough that when Rainy had died two years earlier, the remaining Cassandras had rallied and proved not only that she had been murdered, but that her death was part of a larger plot, one involving the international crime magnate Jonas White.

Jonas White. The same man who had masterminded the hostage snatch at the Berzhaani capitol eight months ago, trapping Selena inside the building with the rest of them. The man Selena had killed in order to save Berzhaan's prime minister, and one of the few deaths that had failed to haunt her in the months since.

But Selena hadn't been in the Cassandras. She'd been

in the Pandoras, where instead of one-for-all, the girls had decided that they could most effectively serve their group by being the strongest possible individuals. *I work alone first and best* was the Pandora motto. Kim Valenti, Diana Lockworth, Ashley Sheridan and Selena made it to graduation, and all four had gone on to make an international difference in recent years.

Interesting, then, the circumstances under which she'd recently seen Kim and Diana.

And because she was thinking of that meeting, Christine startled her by smiling—as sentimental an expression as Selena had seen her display—and saying, "It's nice to see that you do manage to work well as a team when necessary."

Selena hid her startled reaction at Christine's apparent synchronicity with her thoughts. After all, that recent Oracle meeting had been beyond clandestine. In fact, she still didn't know who played the role of Delphi, the Oracle contact. Delphi had been the one to warn her about impending terrorist action in Berzhaan right before the hostage crisis; Delphi had been feeding her such tidbits for years, mining information from various security agencies in a highly secretive effort to overcome the interagency turf wars. And though Selena knew she was far from the only one at the receiving end of Oracle's information, she'd been startled to discover that her fellow agents were also former schoolmates. Kim Valenti had been at that meeting, as had Diana and few more recent graduates. An unofficial Athena force.

And then there was Allison Gracelyn, the meeting's facilitator—daughter of Marion Gracelyn and currently an NSA programmer. While still at Athena, she'd developed what turned into AA.gov, the Athena Academy Web site, but she'd kept a low profile since then. Selena couldn't help but wonder just what she'd been up to behind the scenes… and just what she was up to now.

Selena's reaction, checked as it was, must have given something away, for Christine's eyes narrowed slightly. "Whatever you wandered off to think about…I was referring to you and Cole."

Oh. Right. Work well as a team. That they did.

When they had the chance.

"We're trying," Selena said. "Maybe we'll get another chance to work in the field together." She realized that their rambling pace had taken them toward the stables, forty stalls worth of well-trained horseflesh. Arthur Tsosie had been the stable master here when she'd been enrolled, a quiet man with a lilting tenor voice and full of as much people sense as horse sense. It was nearly impossible to recall riding here and not think of the Navajo Codetalker, and how he so quietly and ably shepherded such prodigies as Athena encouraged. "I should take a ride," she said, a total non sequitur that Christine accepted almost as if she realized that the most important parts of their exchange had indeed just happened in Selena's mind.

"Feel free," she said. "Just after dawn is still best. Tomorrow the girls will be back from their visit to the base, so you'll want to beat them to the best of the trail horses."

Luke Air Force Base. Along with trips to the Indian nation reservations, the weeklong survival course in Yuma, a week of study at the Flagstaff observatory, Christine made sure the girls got out to the base, to hospitals, to police stations…to see how people and organizations worked together.

And how they didn't.

After all, there'd be no need for Oracle if the CIA, FBI, NSA, or recently created Homeland Security actually shared their intel as effectively as they all claimed to. But Selena knew better than to let her thoughts wander there again, not with Christine's sharp eye on her. She changed the topic to inquire after the latest crop of Athena freshman, and led Christine to the barn to point out a few horses Selena might enjoy. And Christine let her do it, which Selena took as the gift it was.

Dawn brushed the mountains a pale taupe as Selena rode out—borrowed boots, borrowed helmet, but her own schooling tights with leather knee patches and bright lime racing stripes up the outside leg. The horses might have changed since her time at Athena, the stable master might have changed, but the trails were the same, and she knew right where she was going—a zigzaggy route through the clumpy brittlebush, skirting the various cacti and looking out at terrain unobscured by any significant presence of tree or shrub. The odd paloverde, a few scrubby creosote bushes. Low desert mountains: skeletons of the earth. She took her dun gelding through a series of switchbacks to the summit as the light turned from diffuse to etchingly sharp, and after forty-five minutes of rugged riding, she came to the three-thousand-foot summit.

There she dismounted, loosening the saddle girth a notch and sitting cross-legged with the reins loosely in hand, a process that let her know how much her body would pay for this particular emotional exorcism. Didn't matter how fit she was…nothing used riding muscles but riding muscles. The gelding bobbed its head a few times to see if she really meant it—they were really just going to stand here—and then snorted loudly into the morning air, mouthing the bit a few times before finally settling into a hip-shot stance of equine patience.

"Just watch," Selena told it. She waited, the southern part of the Phoenix valley spread out before her as the sun rose. The earth warmed and soon enough she saw the first of them—dust devils borne of a cold night followed by the desert sun on flat, hard earth. They spiraled sandy dirt into the air, creating miniature funnels that curved into the sky and danced capriciously across the ground, lifting tumbleweeds high into the sky. Selena grinned, watching them, remembering her younger self doing just this thing. Back then, she'd appreciated the power of the things—compact, giving way before no man, rising and subsiding on a whim. Now she saw their freedom and imagined that feeling in herself. Free from the impact of her past, from her unfulfilled future…free from herself.

Oddly, she thought about Oracle. She thought about her self-doubts, and how it surprised her that she'd been invited to the recent meeting. A meeting called not because of any particular current crisis, but because Delphi, the code name of the person behind Oracle, thought it was time to be proactive instead of reactive. They'd discussed the potential ramifications of the fall of Lab 33, the organization that had been behind Rainy Miller Carrington's death among so many other things. *Be ready*, the carefully prepared notes had told them all. *At any time, you might be needed to follow up on the information still being gathered in the wake of Lab 33's downfall.*

For starters, there were the Spider files. One of Oracle's agents had been at work deciphering them, discovering a collection of incriminating records against highly placed people. Prime blackmail material. *We need to know more about the person behind these files,* the agenda stated. *Be alert for any references to the code name "A"—now possibly known as Arachne—or events related to anyone on the attached eyes-only list.*

She could do that. No problem.

High alert: there are indications of imminent terrorist action on U.S. soil. Current priority is to pin down the details.

She could do that, too.

Except that she, like Cole, was now a known face, a highly recorded face. And she was damaged goods, already relegated to teaching duty while the CIA waited to see if she got her act together.

Not that she wasn't good at teaching; in a way, it's what she'd been doing all along, albeit with the foreign dignitaries with whom she'd been trying to establish counterterrorism partnership programs and not in a classroom. Pulling together the material was second nature, starting with the U.S. counterterrorism policy. *First, make no concessions to terrorists and strike no deals. Second, bring terrorists to justice for their crimes. Third, isolate and apply pressure on states that sponsor terrorism...*

And she knew firsthand how those policies translated to real-life action, so who better to explain it?

But it wasn't what she wanted to do, was driven to do. She didn't want to teach others how to deal with terrorism...she wanted to deal with it herself.

Damaged goods.

She hadn't been damaged goods when she'd been here at Athena. She'd been young, with the confidence of the young. She'd been...

Strong. Capable. Gulping down the learning she'd been offered, the self-defense and sharpshooting and athletic training along with the languages and politics and peeks into the inner workings of law-enforcement agencies.

Looking forward, not back. Not tied down by family, by relationships…by experience.

Selena closed her eyes, felt something in her chest swell and open, reconnecting to that younger version of herself. The unscuffed version, still bright and shiny new and full of all the fervent intention Athena could nurture to the fore. It was still there. *Just remember to look for it.*

When she opened her eyes, it was to another budding dust devil in the sere valley below. She smiled at the sight, and told her gelding, "See that? I told Jonas White that I was the Road Runner. But I think now I'm the Tasmanian Devil." She watched a dust devil grow, sweeping up dirt and debris. Then she nodded, getting to her feet and dusting off her behind, but not ever taking her eyes from the churning column of air. "Yeah. I like that. Somehow I don't think Taz carries a lot of baggage."

As if to prove the point, the dust devil spit out a tumbleweed. Selena laughed out loud at it and gave her surprised horse a pat. "I think I'm on to something," she told the gelding, and reached for the girth billets of the close contact-saddle. Not that she thought she'd find herself suddenly, miraculously unaffected by those days in Berzhaan or by what she'd done there.

But it was a start.

Chapter 4

Oops.

One really Big oops.

Cole yanked the defector—his defector, now, after weeks of hunting—out of the line of fire, and they both stumbled into a tiny doorway alcove. A tiny *Berzhaani* doorway alcove with a securely locked door. How the hell had he ever agreed to come back to Suwan?

As if there'd ever been any question. *Cole, would you like to come back to black-ops fieldwork for this one job, after which we'll say wham, bam, thank-you ma'am and drop you like the hot potato you are?*

Of course he'd said yes.

A shot pinged against the pale stone of this old home, showering them with chips and dust. The defector's hand tightened on Cole's arm. "You have a plan. You must have a plan."

"For this?" Cole laughed, short and entirely mirthless. "Sorry, Dr. Aymal. This isn't your lucky defection."

For the man had made it out of Afghanistan without incident, escorted and flanked by CIA exfiltration experts, and then they'd handed him over to the Berzhaan team—who should have seen him onto a plane headed for the States. But a little bobble here, a little bobble there...they'd lost him. Cole didn't yet have the full story on that, but if the guy's luck held true, he could well see how it had happened.

Because who'd have thought Cole would be under fire from his former fellow CIA contract employees? Dark ops men of superhero proportions who hadn't re-upped, but who instead had come to the Middle East to work for a security consultant. Until now, Cole had thought they still worked for that man.

He'd been wrong.

Boy, had he been wrong. *Walked right into this one, didn't you?* Whoever they worked for now, they weren't on Cole's side any longer. And they were bold. Bold enough to open fire in the narrow streets of this dignified old neighborhood on the edge of Suwan.

"C'mon, Jox!" The voice of a man who'd once worked beside Cole shouted out from behind cover across the street. Worked beside Cole closely enough to know the nickname based on his CIA station name. Definitely not working alongside Cole any longer. "Get real! Give it up. We'll even let you walk away."

But not Aymal. That was a given.

And Aymal was too important to risk. He carried a mental map of weapons-exchange locations—and key pieces of intel regarding an impending terrorist strike. None of which he had divulged so far, nor seemed inclined to divulge until his feet hit safe ground. U.S. ground.

Was his fake nose slipping with his sweat? Cole gave it a firm nudge, as though he were pushing up glasses; there was no give. Just the expected itch. Without turning around, he said to his defector, "Tell me that if I manage to get you through this alive, you'll put half the terrorists hiding in Afghanistan out of business."

"Most certainly," Aymal assured him. Eagerly, too. The guy spoke some English; he had to know the offer Cole had just received. "I'm certain your government considers me a valuable asset."

"Oddly, I consider me a valuable asset, too," Cole muttered, scanning the roofline across from them. Two-story stone buildings lined the street, butted up side to side. A woman's balcony jutted out of the second story, elaborate scrollwork framing the screening that allowed ventilation but kept the women out of sight. Seemed like there should be some way to use that...but no. Too far to the side.

Then he caught a glimpse of movement on the roof. Hmm. *Give it up? I don't think so.* To his once-friend-now-enemy, he finally shouted, "I don't see that happening."

"Trust is such a fleeting thing," the man shouted back. "Too bad you don't seem to have much choice." He unleashed another shot at them to prove his point and it skipped over the corner of the stone and across Cole's side, right through the leather satchel slung over his shoulder. He flinched, cursed, and didn't give it so much as a cursory inspection. If it burned that damned bad, it was a surface wound. Behind him, Aymal, too, flinched—away from the solid impact of the bullet in the wooden door.

Cole really hoped there was no one home.

To their pursuer, he said cheerfully, "There's always choice."

But he wasn't looking at the car that hid the two men,

and he wasn't about to return fire in this populated neighborhood. Instead, he looked up.

Yup, there was someone on the roof. Three little figures, clutching a stick bat and a big red ball and a—okay, he didn't know what that last thing was. Didn't matter. It would do the trick. He waved at them, a wiggle of his fingers. Selena would smack that hand just for bringing the kids into this—*what if they were our own?*—but they were safe enough. To his newly sworn enemy, he called, "They *do* have cops in this neck of the woods, you know."

"I happen to know they're busy right now," the man said, all too confident.

Dammit. They must have arranged a diversion. Cole looked at the kids again, made up his mind. "Get ready to move," he murmured to Aymal.

"Where?" Aymal's voice held a desperate note. A not unreasonably desperate note.

Cole nodded at the car currently serving as shelter for the two men who'd chased them this far. "There."

"But—"

"Look, you do your thing with your defector stuff, and I'll do mine with the getting-us-out-of–this-alive stuff, okay? Be ready." And he looked back to the roof, motioning to the kids. *Move to your right.* Universal gesture language, carefully performed by the hand not holding his semiautomatic pistol. Clearly puzzled but just as obviously curious, the kids shuffled over until he stopped them. Right over the bad guys, they were—bad guys who were running out of patience, and who fired off a couple of shots to express their displeasure. "Seriously," Cole told Aymal, not taking his eyes from his new allies, "we're gonna move. Any minute…" A new gesture for the kids, then, though *drop your toys* was a harder one to convey.

But then understanding dawned, and the kids looked to one another and to the toys in their hands. Also clear enough in any language. *Are you sure? Do you really mean it?*

Cole gestured more emphatically. *I really, truly mean it.* And grasped Aymal's abaya with the same hand that held the gun, careful to keep his fingers outside the trigger guard.

"Jox, last chance!" Still behind the car. Still beneath the kids, who shrugged at one another, not frightened as they might be. They were up on the roof, out of sight of those below.

And gunfire was clearly not a new experience for them.

They released their toys. Bat, ball and unidentified dropping object, plummeting down just behind the men who had Cole and Aymal cornered.

Aymal yelped, "*Na baba*!"

A defector with a wealth of languages at his disposal. Cole didn't speak Barzhaani as well as Selena, but knew the equivalent of *you've got to be kidding*! when he heard it. "Not kidding," he said, cheerful enough as he watched the toys fall—timing his move, waiting for the inevitable curse or shout of surprise—

There. Now. He gave Aymal a jerk of a jumpstart and sprinted all out for the car, crouched low, ignoring the burn of his side and the hot trickle of blood there. First things first...he slid in behind the car, yanking Aymal close and holding his finger to his lips in what he hoped to be an unnecessary warning.

Their diversion quickly ran its course. The operative-gone-merc snarled, "Damn smart-ass kids." And then he raised his voice, full of annoyed impatience. "Time's up, Jox. We're coming in!"

A pause. A second man said, "What the hell does he think he's doing? If he could get into that house, he'd have done it already. He's got to know he's outgunned. And the rest of our people will be here before the cops even get close."

"I don't know, but I'm getting bored."

"Jeez, Hammer, get *down*! What do you think—"

"Relax, Buzz. Don't get girly. Looks like we got lucky."

Yeah, pretty much in your dreams. Cole kept his hand up, cautioning Aymal to silence, and listened carefully. His leg ached mildly under the strain but held strong—good and healed. And then the brush of cloth against metal told him what he needed to know—the men were creeping around the front of the car, still slow and cautious, still waiting for Cole to spring to life. As Cole intended to do…just not how they expected. He gestured Aymal around the back of the car and by now Aymal had caught on, moving silently with a glimmer of hope. Cole peered around the back bumper to make sure the far side of the car was clear, then hauled Aymal around with purpose. A quick peek though the back windows of the diminutive Zaporozhets sedan revealed the Dolph Lundgren look-alike and his unwieldy sidekick to be engrossed in their approach of the alcove, a situation that wouldn't last long. Like Cole, they wore hooded abayas over western pants, and wouldn't stick out in a crowd. But even after several days in the long robe, Cole still found maneuvering in it to be unwieldy.

Such as when one had the need to spring full bore along the street, running as lightly as possible and waving back over his head at three small co-conspirators, not looking back but hearing just a hint of a giggle drifting down in the still air. As soon as he found a gap between buildings he ducked in, bouncing off the far building with one hand and checking behind to make sure he still had Aymal.

He did. And Aymal looked astonished. "We're still

alive," he said, and patted himself as if to make sure he was still all there. He looked much more at home in his own abaya, which covered the same white kurta and pants Cole wore. Once out of sight they could pull off the abayas and continue with their new looks—the one thing about the day's plan that hadn't gone awry.

Yet.

"Alive so far," Cole agreed. They jogged as fast as they could through the narrow space and popped out the next street over, where Cole spotted an old Russian Niva transport and headed straight for it.

"*Na baba,*" Aymal muttered.

"Relax." Cole checked the door handle on the way by. If it had been locked he would have kept right on walking but no, luck was on his side this time and he stopped, smoothly opening the door and sliding into the driver's seat to drop his gun by the stubby transmission hump gearshift and immediately twist down under the dash of the diminutive—*really* diminutive—SUV. "Try not to look conspicuous, okay?"

"I *am* conspicuous," Aymal said, reaching for dignity. "So are you. And you bleed."

"Yeah, I bleed. Not a big deal. Just don't *hover.*"

Aymal decided to lean against the wall to check a convenient problem with his foot and by then Cole had the vehicle started and straightened to find Aymal staring. "What're you waiting for?"

"We can't just *take* it."

"You're not really up on this terrorist-defector stuff, are you? Of course we can just take it. You heard the man—the police are at a convenient diversion. And we'll be careful with it. Very careful." Cole didn't wait for Aymal to close his door before shoving the gear stick into First and peeling away into the street, using just enough restraint to avoid telltale tire squealing.

Aymal twisted to look out the back window, and when he was finally satisfied there was no immediate pursuit, he straightened, assessed their route, and said, "We should be heading for the airport."

"To the pickup?" Cole shook his head. They were already out of Suwan, heading south in a land that almost immediately looked uninhabited, arid rocky steppes without so much as a forlorn little hut to speak of civilization. "We missed it, buddy. They're long gone. We're going in deep until I can arrange something new." Something he could *trust*. He shifted gears to turn, pushed the speed back up until he hit the low cruising speed of this road just south of Suwan, and fumbled in the satchel lying across his thigh. The newly perforated satchel. "Dammit," he muttered, and took his second hand off the wheel, holding it steady with his knees as he flipped the satchel open.

"*Dawana*!" cried Aymal, grabbing the steering wheel.

Cole narrowed his eyes for a quick glare even as he pulled his cell phone out and reclaimed the wheel. "That wasn't very nice."

"*Bebakhshid*," Aymal said, but he didn't sound very sorry.

"You aren't really comfortable with the whole notion of guns and action, are you?" Cole pulled the phone antenna out with his teeth, flipped the thing open, and had his thumb headed for the pertinent speed-dial number before he realized the phone had no signal. Big surprise, given the way this had all gone so far.

"I worked at a *desk*," Aymal informed him. And then, at Cole's surprised glance, he added, "Someone has to."

True enough. And Cole's briefing had focused more on the particulars of getting the man out than the particulars of who the man was. He jammed the antenna against his chest to collapse it and left the phone sitting between his knees.

"Where—"

"Two choices," Cole told him. "We can drive around in circles hunting a solid cell signal, looking obvious and pathetic. Or we can hole up somewhere and ask around until we find someone who knows where to pick up a good signal, at which point I will venture forth and bravely make some phone calls."

"Hole up…you know this area?"

"You'd be surprised," Cole said, feeling cheerful again. The distinct lack of pursuit turned out to be quite a mood enhancer. "More choices—we go south and hit silkworm people territory, or loop around to the north and see what can be done in Oguzka. I happen to know they have no love of people who solve their problems by shooting other people."

"How—" Aymal stopped himself with a shake of his head.

"Faith," Cole said. "Have faith. Do you think they would have sent me if I couldn't do the job?"

"Your first attempt to make contact with help put us in this stolen car, fleeing bullets and leaving a blood trail."

Cole glanced down at the blotch of red seeping through his abaya. "*Trail?* That's just a single footprint, and we're bringing it along with us. Anyway, intel didn't know those guys had done a flip-flop on us. They're *gonna* know, though." And he said no more, for of the village he was comfortably certain.

They had, after all, been extremely grateful when his wife had saved their collective butts eight months earlier.

Chapter 5

Selena settled into the saddle, ready to head back to Athena—and from there, back to work. Back to Virginia, to prepare for her upcoming evaluation—and after that, either back to the Farm or back to Langley. Either way, she'd deal with it.

She'd just lifted the reins when her cell phone rang, the Looney Tunes riff she'd installed upon returning home from Berzhaan. Her horse startled, head raised and ears swiveling, and she shifted seat and leg just enough to reassure him. The Velcro closure of the pommel bag yielded to her grip and she slipped the phone out just as it was ready to give up on her and switch over to voice mail.

She didn't bother with much of a greeting. Very few people had this number. "I'm here," she said, without hesitating to check the caller ID.

"Miss Jones."

"Shaw Jones," she corrected the man, hunting her memory for a name to go with that familiar, gravelly voice.

"We need you back at Langley."

She stilled. The DDO, that's who she had on the other end of this call. Deputy Director of Operations. The man who would make the ultimate decision about her readiness for working counterterrorism.

Except he wouldn't be calling her himself if that's what this was about. In fact, she couldn't think of *any* reason he'd be calling her himself.

Without asking any of the questions bouncing around in her mind, she said, "On the soonest flight, sir."

"We'll have a chopper pick you up in forty-five minutes. I assume you can get down off that mountain by then?"

She didn't even ask. He'd talked to Christine. He had the best GPS tracking system in the world and the tech to latch on to her protected phone…it didn't matter. He knew what he knew. "If this horse is as good as advertised," she told him, already heading toward the trail and mentally calculating where she could cut downhill between switchbacks.

But his next words stopped her short. "You should know," he said, "JOXLEITNER missed his pickup."

Selena froze in the saddle, her world spiraling in around those words. No sight, no sensation, only the barest awareness of the horse prancing sideways beneath her. Not Cole. Not now. "He—"

"You'll be briefed on the plane." The man hesitated—not out of uncertainty, that was clear enough. Out of courtesy, to give her more time to process the news. "We're sending you in to bring him back."

Chapter 6

Selena handed over the reins as the helicopter approached, calling back her apologies for bringing in a hot horse even as she sprinted off for her bungalow and the lightweight suitcase she'd brought.

The young woman working the stables—what was her name, Teal?—this morning didn't seem surprised. In fact, she grinned widely and waved as Selena left her behind. Typical precocious Athena student. Christine didn't seem surprised by the turn of events, either, and as Selena came bursting back out of the bungalow, Christine met her with an electric golf cart, gesturing for Selena to toss the suitcase in the back.

Selena almost said, *How—?* but Christine preempted her. "I got a call. No, I don't know why. I just know that chopper's here for you."

Selena said, "Cole."

It was enough. Christine's mouth set in a grim line as she revved the little cart up to its top speed, not waiting for Selena to settle into place. They zipped past a line of young women running with light packs, gleaming with sunscreen against the desert morning sun. *"Athena!"* the girls shouted after them.

Selena knew how fast information spread here. The girls, returned from their field trip, knew who she was, what she'd done in Berzhaan, and what she was doing at the Farm—and all before they'd finished brushing their teeth. She grinned, for an instant lost in flash memories of her own days here.

And then suddenly she was clasping Christine's hand in a goodbye, climbing into the massive Bell 430 helicopter while ducking rotor wash and dragging her suitcase along behind. Christine stood by the cart at the edge of the wash, her short white hair whipping in the wind and her hand protecting her eyes. Selena pointed at her borrowed boots as she reached for the door. "I'll send them back!"

Christine waved off her concern with a *you must be kidding* look and Selena settled back into the seat, buckling up as the pilot lifted off. Better to think about boots than to think about Cole.

Briefed on the plane. No kidding.

Selena sat in the luxurious Bombardier Learjet, slowly realizing that no amount of ventilation could obscure the results of her hasty downhill ride. Selena sweat, not so bad. Horse sweat...definitely lingering. "Sorry," she'd said to the pilot of the lightweight craft as he'd greeted her upon boarding. "I was—"

And he'd already been nodding. "So I see. Well, make yourself at home in a different kind of leather seat. There are materials waiting for you on the table."

Selena jammed her suitcase into the overhead and dumped her shoulder-slung leather briefcase—worse for the wear since Berzhaan, but she wasn't about to give it up—on the window seat as she plunked herself into the aisle seat at the executive table. The folder waiting there was red, sealed with official stickers, and shouted *I'm full of secret stuff*. She instantly broke the seal, somehow restraining herself from dumping the contents wholesale onto the table. At some point the plane rolled down the runway and lifted into the air, but she couldn't have said when.

There wasn't all that much material in the folder. A summary, for her benefit: Cole had been called back into the field because they'd seen a perfect opportunity to use the Berzhaani reporter persona he'd established during the hostage crisis before he'd removed the disguise and ended up blazed across the front page of national and international newspapers. *Au naturel*, so to speak.

She took a moment to absorb the irony of that. Cole had come to Berzhaan unauthorized, on his own time, and ultimately had been released from his contract because of it. The agency hadn't even paid for treatment of the leg he'd broken in the process of helping to defeat the terrorists, although the state department had happily picked up the bill. But now the CIA had called on Cole to use the very persona he'd developed during that incident.

These are your people now, she reminded herself, and went on to read the mission brief.

Cole Jones had gone to Berzhaan to locate and retrieve a Afghan man lost in mid-defection—Dr. Aymal. Selena went hunting for a first name and didn't find it, and then realized the man must be Pashtun—a culture that generally took on surnames only to make dealing with Western nations more convenient. Aymal was this man's lone name, and he didn't appear to have any need for such convenience.

Feeling the pressure of the allied hunt for terrorists across the Mideast, Aymal had made the leap to the other side, reaching out to the States with promises of information about both Iran-to-Iraq weapons sales and impending terrorist strikes across organizations. CIA officers had gotten him from Afghanistan to Berzhaan...and then lost him and nearly one of their own in an ambush. Aymal, it seemed, had gotten away but still had nowhere to go.

Cole had gone in to find him. To do what he did best, which was to navigate his way through high-stakes circumstances that couldn't be planned to the last detail. Going into Berzhaan, he'd had only a number of contacts and pickup arrangements.

And this time, he'd missed one.

What were you thinking, to leave me? To leave us?

The brief didn't make any suggestion as to what might have happened. It noted only that no Westerners had been reported as killed or jailed since Cole's arrival in Suwan, Berzhaan's capital city.

A city Selena had recently come to know all too well.

And that's why she was here—in this plane, on the way to Langley in her riding tights and boots and aroma. Because she was Cole's wife, and the only person who had the barest chance of anticipating Cole's moves. Because she knew the city.

And because the city knew her. It *loved* her.

And it owed her.

By the time they reached Langley—setting down on a private airstrip, hustling off to the McLean campus in the waiting car—Selena was more than ready for a shower and change of clothes. But her clean-cut escort indicated there was no time for such luxuries. The young woman smiled pleasantly and said little, walking Selena through the lobby of the Original Headquarters Building, expediting her passage through security, stowing her luggage in a small locked room. They headed up to the fourth-floor main entrance to the New Headquarters Building, moving too quickly for Selena to catch the view of the OHB from the sky-lighted entry corridor. But when they hit the atrium, Selena dug in her heels just long enough to take in the four stories of airy windowed space, to get a good look at the three suspended aircraft models overhead. She recognized the Blackbird and squinted up at what looked like a drone of some sort.

"I'm sorry," the young woman said. "But they're waiting for us. We really can't linger here."

Nor did she want to. Not with Cole's fate in question.

Odd. Until the previous winter in Berzhaan, neither of them had ever seen the other in action. Even then, they'd merely passed each other in the midst of chaos, hesitating long enough for a quick exchange of information across the room. Before that they'd gone their separate ways while working, aware of what the other was doing only through vague hints and innuendos.

Now suddenly Cole's life depended on her, and unless she was mistaken, they would very much see each other in action before this was over.

She wondered if it would feel as strange then as it did at this moment.

Her guide led her through the atrium to the six-story tower on the other side, and they entered the glass-sided elevator to ascend to the fifth floor. The door at which they finally stopped opened into a room lined with windows and a view of the landscaped courtyard, fish pond and manicured trees.

Selena noted those things only absently. For sitting around the table of this little briefing room with its high-tech presentation options and Aeron chairs were several people she didn't know…and one she did.

Steven Dobry.

He looked her up and down, pausing visibly at the lime seam stripes on her schooling tights. "Nice."

She didn't respond. She suspected that were their situations reversed, Dobry would still be up on the mountain, and it was enough. Nodding a greeting to the others, she pulled her eyes-only folder from the briefcase and dropped the briefcase to the floor, sitting in the empty chair with a pad of paper and pen neatly waiting for her. Then, since everyone else had ice water at hand, she poured herself a glass from the pitcher in the center of the table and helped herself to a croissant. The sandwich she'd had on the plane hadn't nearly done the job.

The busywork gave her a chance to assess the others in the room. Just three of them: Dobry, the man she belatedly recognized as the individual who'd pulled Cole out of the training event at the Farm, and a woman she didn't know. "All right, I'm here," she said. "And the sooner I get back to Berzhaan, the better."

"That's the idea," the woman said. "My name is Janet, and this is Randy."

Selena raised an eyebrow as she bit into the croissant. No last names, even for this? Janet smiled at her. "You'll be working with the station chief in Berzhaan. There's no point in cluttering the situation with distracting details."

Selena swallowed without chewing. "Cole is over there somewhere," she pointed out. "You can trust that I won't be distracted from that." *Whatever he was thinking when he left, I intend to put us back together.*

"Really?" Dobry said. "I thought the whole reason you were teaching at the Farm was that you couldn't be trusted at all."

The woman aimed a disapproving look at him. "This operation will depend on teamwork. We chose you, Mr. Dobry, because of your expertise with disguises and your familiarity with Ms. Shaw Jones, although your language skills for the area are only passable. We expect you to go in under a subtle cover, and to be available to obscure both your identities when necessary—the instant it's necessary. If we've made a mistake, we can rectify it before we waste any more time."

Dobry was smooth enough, Selena would give him that. "My words weren't well chosen, but this is something we really should put on the table."

"That's fair enough." Randy No-Last-Name put down the pen which had only hovered over his pad. Dobry's pleased nod disappeared fast enough when the man pinned him with an unwavering look. "But you should keep in mind that if we find it necessary to shuffle the team, you're the one who'll be going back to the Farm."

Janet didn't let the words linger before moving on. "We've considered the circumstances which sent Ms. Jones—"

"Shaw Jones," Selena said. "Or better yet, Selena."

Janet nodded. "Selena, then. Monthly evaluations have shown satisfactory progress. The details of last month's incident at the Farm and the aftermath actually played a significant part in the decision to move forward with this ops plan. Selena's reaction was an excellent example of a trained field officer reacting to a perceived threat. And we trust enough time has passed so that any awkwardness resulting from the incident is gone."

In other words, we're all adults here. Let it go, Dobry.

And Dobry considered it. He looked at Selena, chewed his bottom lip for the merest instant, and nodded. "Right," he said. "Let's not waste any more time."

Right, Selena thought. Because if they looked any more closely at the incident, he might have to answer questions about his own judgment that night. Up until now, he'd covered his ass by standing by his original response, that he'd simply been taking appropriate initiative to assess what he saw as a potential problem. But scrutiny wouldn't do the claim any good.

Randy said, "Your station chief is Stan F. TRAMMEL. Selena, your station name is now Elaine P. BLUEMAN, and Steven will remain George M. FLEAGAL. All communiques will come to you via the station at these names. Selena, I assume you know that overseas case officers refer to one another by their station names alone."

In fact, Selena knew this wasn't always the case, but close enough. She nodded. She'd had months to learn the ins and outs of her new alphabet family, and she'd absorbed much of it from Cole long before now, including the convention of using all-caps for a case officer's last name. But she raised her hand, just briefly—interruption rather than a request to speak. "I think I've missed a step." She sent an even look in Dobry's direction, weighed his probable reaction and went ahead anyway. "I don't understand why I'm being partnered with anyone at all. I'll have the backup of the local station, and I'm sure Langley's resources will be at my disposal as well." *Not to mention Oracle.* Although that last wasn't a fact that anyone here could know.

Janet looked at her with her agency face on, but Selena thought she saw a gleam of understanding. "Although you have significant Berzhaani government and security contacts and we expect you to work this op under the cover of your own name, there's a good chance you'll also end up working the streets. In fact, we assume that'll happen. When it does, you'll need a man on your team."

Selena winced at the thought. Under those circumstances, Dobry would have the initiative.

But the man had no agenda in Berzhaan. Had no reason to do anything other than his best, grabbing the opportunity to return to the field on a permanent basis.

And the hell of it was, the CIA was right. In the business section of the city, she could wear Western clothes and a modest attitude and get by just fine. But without the cachet of the embassy behind her, without official business to wear on her sleeve, she'd have to be much more careful in the outlying areas.

And if she knew Cole, he'd dug himself a little hidey-hole for Dr. Aymal so he could then go sniff out his options. A hidey-hole she'd have to find, and that she had no chance of finding if she was hanging out in the embassy trying to pull strings.

Dobry's expression had turned earnest. It wasn't one she'd seen on him before, and she wasn't quite sure what to make of it. "Look, I don't have exactly the same stakes as you, but this man is a CIA operative in trouble and the asset is carrying invaluable intel. I'll do everything I can to get them out of there."

Selena nodded an acknowledgment, but Janet was the one she looked to. *Don't make me ask it.*

Janet was no dummy. She volunteered the information. "Because of Selena's experience in Berzhaan, she's to be the senior operative." She raised a hand as Dobry's mouth opened. "However—Selena, I trust that you understand this is an unusual situation. FLEAGAL is an experienced officer. Take advantage of that fact."

Selena nodded. "Gratefully," she said, and meant it. She'd use anything that would help her find Cole and get them all out of there alive. She shifted in the chair—Aeron or not, she'd been sitting for far too long, especially in the wake of that wild ride down the mountain.

Janet's mouth pursed; she tapped the closed file folder in front of her. Red, like Selena's. "Do more than tolerate one another," she reiterated. "Work together as the team we know you can be. Because there's more to this asset than you know—information we received right before this meeting. Aymal's former case officer briefly regained consciousness. He doesn't remember much, but he does know that Aymal mentioned the terrorist attack will be *soon*—and that it will involve a school."

God, no. Not kids. She'd have to tell Delphi for Oracle as soon as possible, although the Oracle system probably would soon have the intel. She closed her eyes, trying to assimilate the additional urgency—another layer on top of her concern for Cole. For a moment it all mixed together, her remembered fears for the schoolkids she'd ultimately saved from the hands of the Kemeni eight months earlier, her instant protectiveness of any child, her ongoing efforts to have her own children with Cole.

But then, none of it was anything new. She'd been working for the next generation from the start, creating cooperative counterterrorism programs in allied countries as an FBI legate. She hadn't thought she'd ever be in that particular position again, but the responsibility suddenly clicked into place, as snug as the shoulder harness for her Beretta. "When do we leave?"

Randy must have been the go-to guy, the details facilitator. He smiled, and looked satisfied. "I've reserved a couple of spots on a Starlifter leaving Bolling within the hour. BLUEMAN, you can pull things from the suitcase you had in Arizona, and you'll also find a suitcase already packed. It has both Western and Berzhaani-style garments, as well as your personal effects."

Selena stopped short of reacquiring her croissant. "You went to the town house."

"While you were in the air," he agreed. "And there's a travel outfit in that overnighter by the door."

She opened her mouth, then decided to fill it with a torn piece of croissant rather than words. Just doing his job...and doing it well at that. After she swallowed, she said, "Thank you. Do I have time to change before we leave?"

Dobry frowned in doubt. "How fast can you do it?"

At that moment, she thought, *What would happen if I ditched him and showed up alone at the plane?*

Tempting. So tempting.

Taz would do it.

But Selena wouldn't.

Not yet.

Instead she left her chair for the overnight bag and zipped it open with economical purpose, pulling out a deep turquoise shirt knit in a chunky, exaggerated weave, and a pair of her black cargo pants. She nodded approval at Randy, and then grabbed the bottom of her shirt—she was halfway to pulling it over her head before Janet laughed, a quietly amused sound.

Randy glanced at Dobry and said drily, "Point taken, but there's a bathroom just down the hall that will do. I think we can spare the thirty seconds it'll take for you to reach it. Not to mention it has a mirror—there's makeup and jewelry in that case, too."

Selena dropped her shirt and grabbed the overnighter. "Works for me." She looked back at Dobry on her way out. "Faster than you can flush a urinal."

When she returned just moments later, she found them up and waiting. She grabbed her croissant and a cream-cheese bear claw, wrapping both in a napkin and shoving them—along with a bottle of water—into her briefcase. At Dobry's raised brow she said, "I don't know about you, but I'm still making up for breakfast. I get cranky without my corn flakes."

"Can't have that," Dobry said, trying to make it sound lighthearted and failing. Selena left the overnighter in her chair—let the CIA have the horse-imbued riding tights, and she'd buy Athena another pair of boots—and breezed out the door ahead of him, close on Randy's heels. Once in the hallway, Janet said, "Randy will see you to the plane from here. Good luck, FLEAGAL...BLUEMAN."

But it hadn't taken luck to get Selena out of that embassy alive the previous winter. It had been persistence and a determined exploitation of all the tools she had on hand, from a sheaf of flying papers to decorative marbles and dry ice. It had been teamwork with Cole—an unusual remote teamwork where they'd each simply trusted the other to do what was necessary.

And now she was just as determined to do it again.

To judge by the action of the Starlifter crew, they'd been holding off departure. As soon as Selena and Dobry set foot on the plane, the pilot and co-pilot started takeoff procedure, assisted by the two flight engineers. One loadmaster double-checked the security of the pallets as Selena and Dobry settled into aft-facing seats, their gear stowed by the other loadmaster.

Selena waited for the crew to button up and take their own seats; takeoff wasn't far behind. Once they were in the air one of the loadmasters offered them some MREs, and Selena was glad to supplement the pastries. She found herself with beef enchilada and used half the water from her appropriated bottle to trigger the flameless chemical heater. The loadmaster just grinned at her as Dobry ate his beef ravioli cold, shaking his head at Selena's offer of the rest of her water.

After they tucked the resulting garbage away, Dobry cleared his throat and said, "I meant it, you know. I'll do what I can to make this work—I want to stop that terrorist attack as much as anyone. Schoolkids? No way. And you've got Cole—JOXLEITNER—to worry about, but I've got my own motivations."

"Motivation enough to get over how you feel about me?" Selena asked, and the loadmaster who'd been sitting with them suddenly found the need to inspect the pallets again.

"I don't—" Dobry started, and stopped with a frown. No point in pretending, and he'd seen that.

Selena didn't even try. "I took a lateral leap to a position you don't think I deserve. Now I'm out in the field and you don't think I'm good for that, either. Don't even try to tell me those things don't matter to you."

He frowned, shaking his head. "I won't. But other things matter more."

She looked steadily at him, waiting for any sign of doubt, for his eyes to shift away from hers. They didn't. She said, "Just keep that in mind. Whatever you think about me, getting Cole and Dr. Aymal out of Berzhaan is all that matters."

"No arguments," Dobry said, and when he saw her

doubt, he added, "Look, I just want to get back in the field. I'm not going to do anything to jeopardize that. *Anything*."

And that, she believed.

Chapter 7

The U.S. embassy in Berzhaan seemed strangely like home. Its exquisite Sekha carpets crafted from native silkworm, old-world light fixtures, rich inlaid woodwork...wonderfully familiar. Even the smell of the place—strong coffee mixed with wood polish and a slightly dry smell of age, reminiscent of old attics everywhere—spoke to her. Selena took a moment to breath deeply of it, ignoring Dobry's impatient hovering and the emerging soreness from her hard ride down the mountain. Then she turned to the marine on guard desk duty and said, "We're here to see Dante Allori."

The young man returned her an inscrutable look, as if the statement wasn't the least bit outrageous. "Do you have an appointment?" He knew perfectly well that she didn't.

"Call Bonita," Selena suggested. "See if she wants Selena to come up for a quick visit."

Doubt sneaked out. "Selena Jones?" Maybe a little respect, too.

"Selena *Shaw* Jones." She pointed at the desk phone and smiled, a little too sweetly. "Give it a try. Or don't, and see what happens when she learns I was here."

That got through to him—as did the fact that she knew Bonita, the ambassador's personal assistant, well enough to say it. He reached for the phone, eyeing her as it rang through, and spoke a few quick words.

Selena smiled as he stiffened and held the phone away from his ear slightly. When he hung up, she offered, "Bonita has a way with words, doesn't she?"

"Yes, ma'am," the young marine said, putting some starch back in his shoulders as he nodded at the sleek, latest and greatest metal detector arch.

"New toys," Selena observed. She pulled out her weapons, which had conveniently bypassed customs security checks as they slipped in through the States-occupied airfield west of Suwan—an airfield that provided operations support for the limited U.S. presence in Berzhaan and through which she and Dobry had entered the general population to reach the CIA station, emerging complete with a convincing set of papers. First her sturdy Beretta Cougar, meant for strong hands and long fingers. A variety of knives—the short tanto blade she'd had at the Farm, a lock blade Buck and a tiny stiletto she'd adopted after her previous Berzhaani adventures with the ice pick. She had a length of braided monofilament in her pocket, but left it there; the detector would ignore it.

Still, the young marine muttered something about "worse than a Klingon" as he secured her batch of goodies away in their own little lockbox. Even Dobry looked at her askance as he handed over his Smith & Wesson snub nose.

"The point," he said, "is to avoid conflict by avoiding detection. Or weren't you paying attention to the classes we taught?" He certainly had. His new identification had included pictures in which he looked subtly but significantly different, and by the time they'd left the local CIA station, his appearance matched those photos—darker brows, colored contacts, a mole, a pair of distracting, trendy glasses with thick frames, and padding around his torso that turned his fit, burly frame into an entirely different shape. Five minutes to apply, two minutes to rip away.

But Selena had grown used to his barbs; over time she'd decided it was the only way he knew how to be. The marine had not, and bristled as he took the little revolver. Ah, youth. Selena felt old at twenty-seven, but she only smiled at Dobry. "Been there, done that," she said, waiting for him on the other side of the detector. "A good backup plan or two never hurt anyone."

The marine said, "I only wish I'd been here when you took down those terrorists last winter."

"No," Selena said gently, "you don't."

"Ma'am," he said by way of apology, and made Dobry go through the detector three times.

"Selena! You look so much better without the blood. I've never considered it a suitable accessory." Bonita actually rose from her chair, leaving her powerful domain—the phone lines, the scheduling tools, the custom-sized petite chair—to greet Selena. Her lips were stained their usual power-red, and today her nails matched. Such touches seemed out of place on a mature, gray-haired woman, and Selena knew darned well Bonita did it on purpose just to see who'd fail to take her seriously.

"Blood?" Dobry said, and eyed Selena as she drew back

from the hug Bonita gave her. "From the hostage situation. Of course." He already seemed tired of hearing about it. Poor Dobry. He didn't look like the kind of man who took well to having his assumptions challenged, and his assumptions that Selena had arrived at the CIA overbilled, underexperienced and fading fast were taking a good hard hit.

"Goodness, no." Bonita turned to him as if only then noticing him. "From the incident in Oguzka that morning." She beamed at Selena. "I was so proud to hear you shot that one terrorist in the ass, my dear. Entirely appropriate. You didn't mention on the phone that you'd brought a friend."

Selena bit back a grin. Bonita in full *keep 'em off balance* mode. "This is Steven Dobry. We're working together on this one."

"This one *what*?" Bonita returned to her chair to survey Dobry over her neat desk. But Selena only waggled her eyebrows, and Bonita laughed. "Can't blame me for trying," she said. "The ambassador is waiting for you. Lucky you—you were the perfect excuse to delay a meeting he's been grumbling about for days."

"He's doing well, then?" For Dante Allori had been shot during the hostage incident, and although it had seemed a minor wound at the time, a man of his age and physical condition didn't always come back from the simple things.

"I've said as much in my e-mails, so I don't see how repeating myself will do any good. You'll just have to go see for your own eyes."

"Yes, ma'am," Selena said, and led Dobry to Allori's office, knocking gently even as she opened the door.

"Selena!" Allori rose from his desk—bigger than Bonita's, and nowhere near as neat—and smiled hugely at her. "What, no blood today?"

Dobry muttered, "Good God."

"He means the hostage thing, not the village thing," Selena assured him. "Dante, you look well!" In fact, the man had lost a significant amount of weight, and although his face held more lines and his hair more gray, he exuded a new vigor where before he'd only exuded dignity.

"Let's just say I recently had a life-changing experience," he told her. "New priorities. New tailor, too." He patted his sleek suit lapels and leaned forward to take her hand, drawing her around the desk into a fatherly hug. "You, too, look well. A little thin, perhaps. A little ragged around the edges. Could be we took different lessons from those days?"

"Could be I'm still learning mine," Selena said, all too aware of Dobry's presence. "Dante Allori, this is Steven Dobry. We're working together. I wanted to drop by and let you know I was here...and that I've got my ears open."

"What can you tell me?"

"Just that we're missing some people."

Allori sat in his massive leather chair and tipped it back to regard her, then Dobry. "Mr. Dobry," he said, and nodded an acknowledgment of Dobry's presence. "I don't suppose this has anything to do with the interesting little incident yesterday—wild west gunplay in one of the quieter old neighborhoods of this dignified city, involving several children?"

Selena recoiled at his words. "Children?"

"Not to worry. They're safe. They somehow got it in their heads to drop their playthings on the heads of the Clanton brothers from the roof of their building."

Selena smiled, brief though it was. *Cole*. Who else? Cole, through and through. Finding the unexpected, using every opportunity at his disposal. Trapped by the terrorists, she'd found she had a lot more in common with him than she'd once thought.

And it gave her a place to start.

"I'm not sure how I can help you," Allori said, though he'd been watching her face and knew he'd said something of significance to her.

"You already have," she told him.

Dobry cleared his throat and said, "Anything you can tell us that doesn't quite seem ordinary could be of help. We'd also be pleased if you could advise us on the best locations for acquiring local information. We have some information, of course, but—"

Allori cut him off with a frown. "Your best source of that information is standing beside you."

Selena trod lightly. Carefully. "We haven't had much opportunity to put our heads together," she said, saving face for Dobry—for if he'd listened to her, if he'd truly believed her capable in her legate posting here, he'd have known better.

"Ah." Allori nodded his understanding. "As for the other, you have my complete cooperation. Things out of the ordinary it is." He drummed his fingers on the desk, one quick riff and then silence. "As delighted as I am to see you, Selena, I'm surprised to find them asking this of you. And without official cover, unless I'm mistaken."

"Don't worry about me, Dante." Selena couldn't hide her grim response, not entirely. "I would have volunteered for this one, given a chance."

At that, Allori's perceptive gaze narrowed slightly. He knew Selena chose her words with care, and that they were to be plumbed for significance…and that whatever was happening, it was of personal importance to her. So again he nodded, and then he turned on his public persona for

Dobry's benefit. "Have you eaten yet? I know of a place you might find interesting."

Dobry would have bowed out—his mouth was open, his polite regret in place—when Selena overrode him. If Dante wanted to steer them toward a particular establishment, then by all means they would be steered.

Cole sat on the roof of a jouncing bus, turning it into a de facto double-decker. He wasn't alone—Aymal kept him company, along with a handful of other content travelers, tucked in amongst the luggage of the clattery old vehicle.

"How many times?" Aymal asked him, keeping his head close enough to Cole's that they might not be overheard, but not so close that an unexpected bounce might cause them to smack skulls.

A lesson hard-learned, that one. For while Cole knew their best chance of going unnoticed was to speak a decently local language—in this case, he and Aymal had Russian in common—and speak it normally, Aymal insisted on skulking and whispering at every opportunity.

He probably hadn't been a very subtle insurgent, either.

Now Aymal rubbed his eyes with one hand, careful to place his fingers so accidental poking during their jouncing would be unlikely—another lesson hard-learned—and said, "My head aches like fire, and I'm certain I have whiplash. Do you truly think it was necessary to trade our comfortable vehicle for this?"

"I think," Cole said, summoning patience, "that the comfortable vehicle was as hot as they come."

Aymal presented equally obvious patience. "This is the autumn season."

As if Cole could think of the Russian idiom with his own brain going whocka-whocka-whocka inside his head and his side burning. Not bleeding anymore, because it had been fairly minor after all, an in-and-out under the skin just behind his hip that squeamish Aymal had sparingly cleaned with makeshift supplies. But skin was fussy like that; it didn't like to have gaping open spots. He said, "The circumstances under which we acquired the vehicle made it of interest."

Aymal got it that time. "Still," he said. "Why this back and forth, back and forth? Why not go where you intend for us to go?"

Oh, for Selena's patience. "Because we might be of interest, too. This gives me a chance to see if anyone has acted on that interest." If anyone got sloppy, following a bus from Suwan to the west-side village of Qundan and back.

His news reporter persona—a disguise that would have to be reapplied or removed before too much longer—could also have walked into the building that ostensibly housed the newspaper. Did house the newspaper, but was also so much more…an underground highway, a sanctuary…a sly first step to reaching the actual CIA station. *To reaching help.*

But having been betrayed on one level, Cole was not inclined to trust established underground options—not until he had some understanding of what had gone wrong. Best to bounce around on the top of this bus a route or two, establish they were in the clear and stash Aymal so he could poke around for some answers.

It could be as simple as connecting with the local station chief.

Or it could be that the station chief had been the one to sell them out.

"We don't have time for this," Dobry said, not even looking at the restaurant's opulent decor as Allori put his head together with the young man who was handling seating requests. Russian architecture surrounded them, left over from earlier occupation and overlaid with the Berzhaani sense of style—elaborate scrollwork given more corners, complex patterns made more geometric. Clashing seemed to be of no concern; in someone's eyes, more was clearly better. Layers and layers of more.

But Selena found herself tired of arguing with her erstwhile partner. "What did you have in mind?" As long as it involved food…

"Standing out in the middle of a restaurant like two sore thumbs definitely wasn't it."

She glanced at him, honestly surprised. "Don't tell me you're concerned that we won't be able to fade into the woodwork when we want to." She shook her head. "I've seen your work. *Where's Waldo* has nothing on you."

He looked back at her, just as surprised at the compliment, and whatever he'd been building up to had been defused. But defused was one thing; in accord was another. "I just don't see the point in making this any harder."

"If we'd been given an ops plan, I'd agree with you. But we're not breaking cover…we're creating it." Selena lifted her chin in acknowledgment as Allori gestured to them, *follow me*. "Looks like I'm coming back to Berzhaan to face what happened here so I can get on with my life."

That should suit him, and to judge by his thoughtful expression as he moved past her to lead the way to the table at which Allori waited, it did. In the States, Selena would have found his assumed dominance to be offensive; here, she—

Okay, she still found it offensive. But for all they'd clashed, Dobry hadn't pulled sexist crap on her, and she knew he was only settling into the culture here. Doing what he did best, which was to blend. As he pulled a chair out for her, he said, "Then who am I?"

Allori gave no indication that this was a strange conversational development. "Complimentary tea will be here soon. I hope you still like it sweetened with jam."

"Very much," Selena said. "I've been a complete scandal at work."

Dobry eyed her. "So this is where you picked up that habit."

"Something from every place I've worked, that's my goal." Selena didn't bother to look at the menu. "Botsarma for me today—you should try it, Dobry. Lamb stewed with plums and veggies. It'll stick to your ribs and still leave room for pahlava."

"Stuffed fish for me," Allori declared. "And you had best be a friend of Cole's, eh? A very good and trusted friend."

Dobry's look turned sour, and Selena suddenly recognized it—the look that meant he'd be disagreeable because he felt threatened. And he felt threatened because he didn't have the background material on Cole to pull off such a role. She caught his eye. "Who better than me to prep you for that? And it's not something we'll spend a lot of time holding together. We're here, we're establishing ourselves with this meal, and if we need to fall back on this, we've got it."

"Think of that on the plane?"

She had to admit not. "Between the embassy and this place." She added, for Dobry's benefit, "I wouldn't have kept it from you if I'd thought of it before this. And I'm still open to alternatives."

"And just maybe I'll think of something." For where Selena had emerged from the unprepossessing maintenance building on the embassy grounds that served as the station house with more ammo for her Cougar .45 and a variety of conservative women's clothing, Dobry had gladly gotten his hands on the case he had so reluctantly just left in Bonita's care. Makeup, latex, mold material and dyes, even a wig or two. Selena had no doubt they'd make use of it all on top of Dobry's already misleading appearance. If nothing else, her skin tones were too fair to pass on the streets without a second look. Dobry flashed her a look that said he was thinking it through, and said, "You need to be yourself, but there's no reason I should dangle myself out there naked. I've got papers for Kenneth Goff—I'll use 'em."

Selena nodded, unconcerned that Allori overheard it all. He was often an unofficial participant in such things.

The young man returned with a gorgeous lacquered tray that held their tea—a small pot and the special pear-shaped *armud* glasses. And the jam pot, of course, just as intricately decorated as the other serving pieces. He served them with a careful flourish and took their orders. As he left, Allori's expression changed, a barely perceptible smoothing of his features. "Over there," he said, and his eyes directed Selena's quick glance to an older man, a Berzhaani in a formal Turkish three-piece suit, a dignified blend of East and West with a knee-length jacket and loose-fitting pants under the vest. "Davud Garibli."

Selena nodded. "He replaced Amar bin Kuwaji." Bin Kuwaji, the deputy prime minister who had been executed on the same steps where Selena had almost lost her life… and where she'd eventually emerged victorious.

Allori nodded. "Conservative, as you might guess from his dress, and yet supportive of Prime Minister Razidae and his efforts to modernize and move forward. But he doesn't appreciate Western interference, and would not be pleased to know of U.S. activity in Suwan. Stay off his radar."

"Any other changes I should know about?"

"I would consider him the most crucial. Your legate successor is having quite the time with him."

"I don't envy my successor, then." She'd have to do more checking on that one.

Allori nodded at a woman who'd combined traditional with modern, wearing an elegant thigh-length tunic over an ankle-length skirt that moved like tencel and shimmered like silk. Her hijab was of matching material, and her makeup so expertly done as to be invisible. Dobry took one look and his eyebrows shot up to maximum altitude. "Good luck with that," Allori said. "She's one of Berzhaan's rising stars."

Selena's brow set at a more skeptical slant. "You're kidding. Bollywood, Berzhaan style?"

"All part of the new Berzhaan—especially since the Kemenis were more or less decimated by your actions last winter." Allori seemed quite cheerful about it all.

"Great," Selena said. "Just what I had in mind when I did that."

"And ah," Allori said, "here's someone you should meet." He raised his hand, to whom Selena wasn't sure—not until a harried man made his way over to their table—in his fifties, fit but obviously stressed, he nonetheless greeted Allori with pleasure and hesitated just long enough for introductions. "Scott Hafford, I'd like to introduce an old friend of Cole Jones, Steven Dobry. And this is Cole's wife, Selena." To Selena, he said, "Mr. Hafford works in security consulting, and has had occasion to associate with Cole in other locales, through some of his employees."

Scott Hafford. Selena kept her reaction from her expression, her mind flashing back to that recent Oracle meeting—to the Spider files and the names of those influential people Delphi suspected of being controlled through blackmail.

Hafford was one of them. And she was willing to bet the chances of finding someone else with that name—especially someone in an influential position—were mighty slim.

Hafford looked at Selena and smiled in sudden comprehension. "Selena!" he said. "Jones never did stop bragging on you, but I never knew your name. Now that I do, I can see he had every reason to be proud." He nodded at Dobry, and added, "I'm working with Razidae's people to rebuild the capitol with the best possible security. We certainly hope they never face a situation similar to what you went through, but if it happens..."

"Be prepared," Selena said, and smiled back at him. She wondered what he'd done to end up in the Lab 33 files, and whether he knew, yet, that someone had him listed for a little undue influence. And then it occurred to her that he might have just the resources she could use—that, in fact, they were just the resources Cole might use, given the chance. "Cole knew your people, too? I'd love to be able to tell him I had the chance to say hello."

Hafford's mouth twisted ruefully. "I've got a new team. I'm afraid most of the people Cole knew have pulled away to form their own organization after we got here. They were down and dirty guys, always interested in the thick of things. I'm working more with the technical tools of the trade these days, so..."

Damn. She didn't try to hide her disappointment; it suited the moment either way. Hafford said, "You know, I wouldn't suggest this to just anyone, but you might find Bill Betzer's guys at the Plush. It's a bar...actually has a different name, but none of us can pronounce it, so it's nicknamed the Plush—which I can assure you, it is not. As much as I respect your ability to take care of yourself and perhaps everyone in this room, I wouldn't suggest that any woman go there alone."

"Not a problem," Dobry said, and his Kenneth Goff voice turned out to be all gravelly. How'd he even do that? "We can give it a visit."

Excellent. Already a potential trail to follow.

They exchanged a few more polite words and Hafford moved on. Selena sat back as the server brought their order. "And that," she told Dobry with satisfaction, "is why we had time for this."

Chapter 8

They stood outside the Plush as Selena deciphered the faded Arabic script scrawled along the side of the door. "Grout," she finally said. "Who would name a bar 'Grout'?"

"Whoever first started calling it the Plush had a permanently warped sense of humor."

"British, probably," Selena murmured. "One of their rhyming slang things. Probably started out as *Flush,* because they knew the place was a toilet. Although if they were hoping for actual flush toilets, I'd say they were disappointed." She adjusted her hijab, unaccustomed to the full-coverage scarf. Her clothes, too, were modest—a traditional feminine salwar kameez with loose cotton pants beneath a tunic, easy to move in even if it did lack a surfeit of pockets. She found the loose, ankle-length cotton coat over it all to be more confining, but it warded off the fall chill and offered plenty of opportunity to bring along a knife or two.

Dobry stuck with western clothing, but his shirt was loose-fitting and long, as close to a tunic as he'd get without actually putting one on. He drew no notice; there were enough Western men in the city that his modest clothing let him blend in with the crowd, especially in this neighborhood. Selena was the one who didn't belong by virtue of her sex, no matter how she dressed.

It was the reason Dobry had come to Berzhaan with her. Or rather, that Kenneth Goff was here. Selena had had no problem during her legate days here; she hadn't been trying to keep a low profile, and it had suited her to be noticed and remembered. Likewise, plenty of Berzhaani professionals were women—but even then, business attire wasn't necessarily suitable outside the workplace.

And Selena was definitely outside the workplace. "If we're really lucky," she said, "Cole's already made contact with these guys."

Dobry took the straight line. "And if we're not?"

"Then he probably *will* contact them. We're ahead, any way you look at it." One step closer to bringing in a valuable asset...and one wayward operative. She'd already done her best to alert Oracle to the impending terrorist attack, pausing in an Internet café to send an anonymous, veiled e-mail warning to Delphi. She'd follow up when she could...but she wanted to see what she could learn this evening first.

"As long as we come out of there with our heads intact," Dobry agreed, but Selena took it to be a classic Dobry grouse and allowed him to lead the way.

The interior was smoky, smelly and double-smelly, incense on top of cigarette fumes. Selena let her hijab fall around her shoulders, not concerned about keeping up appearances here inside. In fact, the sooner they understood she would take care of herself, the better. She let Dobry hit the bar to murmur discreet inquiries while she sized up the place and the occupants and summed it all up with an *ugh*. Tough, scrappy, and capable, but *ugh* all the same. Small tables, crowded corners, dark frayed decor, not-so-friendly arguments and an entire population of men who looked like they'd made a study of mean and ugly.

A hand landed on her arm, firmly enough to halt her in her tracks. Her pulse shot up into the triple digits, fight or flight zinging along her nerves. *Kill before being killed…*

But she fought past the instant body memory, *hands on her arms before they threw her against a wall—before they overwhelmed her no-holds-barred attempt to escape and escorted her into captivity—*

Instead of going for her Cougar, she grabbed the thumb—hairy knuckles and all—and gave it an expert twist. Not a gentle one, but a painful move that resulted in a bass squawk. "If you thought you could touch me," she said, her deadpan voice the only way she could balance her internal chaos of reaction, "you were wrong."

The man was big, more-burly-than-thou, and as darkly hairy as his knuckles had suggested. He drew his hand back to put her in her place with a mighty slap. "You little—"

Too predictable. Selena stepped into the opening and jabbed her little stiletto—so easy to palm from the wrist cuff that held it—against his armpit. Groin would have been better, but men like these learned early to protect themselves on that front, especially when facing a woman.

That's okay. Armpits were tender, too.

"Read my lips," she told him, as he froze in his awkward position. "Still wrong. No touching."

From a corner table, a man spoke up. "Buzz," he said, "you're going to give this place a reputation."

"No one's bleeding yet," Selena offered. "We'd still just be talking if Buzz hadn't tried the touching thing." She spoke to the man at the table, but didn't take her eyes off Buzz. When he shifted slightly to adjust his balance, she let the stiletto draw a pinprick of blood, staining the man's shirt.

"Talking about what?" the man said, and by then the rest of the room had quieted to listen in—and, Selena thought, to dive in. They might not even care that Buzz would get spitted on her stiletto, not if they were bored.

"Looking for Bill Betzer," Dobry said, coming up behind Buzz and positioning himself between Selena and the room. She gave an inward blink—he'd put himself in the line of fire for her. But he was still his same dour self as he aimed a remark over his shoulder at her. "That didn't take long."

"His arm is still in its socket," she reminded him, a comment that made Buzz flinch in spite of his obviously lurking temper.

The second man at the table stood up, a Dolph Lundgren kind of guy with the hard eyes that Dolph had never learned to fake. "I hope you're looking for work. If you do me out of a man, I'll need a replacement." To Buzz, he said, "That's what you get for making assumptions, bud. Now go find yourself a place to sit. The beer's on me."

Rather than trust him, Selena nudged his shoulder hard enough to make him take a step for balance, and as he did it she slipped under his arm and behind him. After a glance at Betzer, he growled, "Damn right the beer's on you," before he stalked off to his own rickety table.

Selena discovered her hands shaking from reaction, the internal conflict of restraining herself. Of holding back. *It was never Defcon 1,* she reminded herself. Her body had only thought that it would be. She closed her hands into fists, nails biting into her palms and one hand weighted by the cold metal of the stiletto.

"Have a seat," Betzer said, nodding at the nearest table. The three men currently sitting around it rose without comment. "That could have gone badly for you."

"It could have gone badly for him," Selena responded, but she knew all too well he was right.

"And was it worth all that to find me?" Betzer shoved his own drink around the table, a mug of kvass. Nonalcoholic, malt based, known for its vitamin B content and freely available throughout Berzhaan. A careful man's drink.

"Let's find out. I'm looking to meet up with—"

"Cole Jones," the man said, startling Selena right into hope.

"Have you seen him?" She couldn't keep that hope from her voice.

He dashed it with a grunt and a shake of his head. "Just know who you are."

She narrowed her eyes at him, but Dobry was the one to voice skepticism. "You just happened to know—?"

That got them a snort. "I do read the papers. I even tune into a news station now and then. For a while there, the whole world knew Selena Jones."

"Selena Shaw Jones," Selena muttered, an interruption Betzer barely noticed over a gulp of kvass.

"I had more reason than most to pay attention." He set the mug down in its previous condensation ring. "Cole was in some of those photos, too. Former teammate and all that."

Dobry made a noncommital noise; Selena didn't even do that much. She'd been in the news, true enough. But that had been months ago, and these men hadn't been in the country at the time; Hafford had brought them in afterward. They'd presumably been busy elsewhere, probably in Iraq. Busy enough so Selena's appearance wouldn't be more than a blip on the radar.

Besides, she knew Cole. He'd have discovered this hangout even faster than she had. And he'd have come here to see these men. So Betzer had either seen Cole or he expected to; his mistake was in revealing that the contact had refreshed his memory, making her so easily recognizable. "You don't trust me," she surmised.

"I have no reason not to trust you," he responded, and when she just watched him he smiled a small wry smile and added, "You might well be able to fight your way out of a besieged building, but that doesn't mean you're good on the streets. Different skill set." Meaning, *No, I don't trust you.*

"I can't argue with that." She shook her head at the scantily clad—by Berzhaani standards—young woman who stopped by the table with a drink tray. After all, she didn't trust him fully, either. She certainly had no intention of mentioning Aymal. "It doesn't mean I'm *not* good on the streets, either. And I'm obviously not alone."

Betzer squinted up at her, his gaze shifting briefly to Dobry. "When it comes to that, I don't recall hearing any introductions."

"If you want a name, I can give you one," Dobry said, and for once Selena applauded the hard note in his voice.

Betzer smiled back at him. "I don't see the point, do you?"

Time to get things back on track. "If he hasn't been here yet, Cole will show up once he knows you're in the area. I hope you'll at least tell him that I'm staying at the Park Hyatt."

"You've lost him pretty thoroughly, have you? Don't tell me I've ended up in the middle of a lover's spat."

She refrained from rolling her eyes. And far too close to what felt like it must be true. Now he was just plain being a smart-ass. Playing with her. "When I find him," she said, moving away from the table, "I'll be sure to mention how helpful you were. In fact, I know a number of people who would be interested in how helpful you were." It was a veiled threat, just enough to show him she could play games, too. With her contacts at the embassy and intelligence communities, she could well make things difficult for him.

His smile turned thin. "If I see him, I'll let him know. But I wouldn't wait for it. Check out—"

"Agabaji's?" She turned that smile back at him. "It's where I'd be right now if I hadn't heard you were here."

He held his hands up in a universal *backing off* gesture. "Just trying to live up to my helpful nature."

"Maybe you'll have another chance," she told him. She discovered the path to the doorway was unnaturally clear, and decided to take the hint. These guys might have Cole's confidence, but they clearly were a closed group. She bid Betzer and crew a good evening, and preceded Dobry out onto the street.

As soon as the door closed behind him, Dobry eased out a tense breath. "Waste of time."

"Not as useful as I'd hoped," she agreed. "But it may turn things our way before we're through. And Agabaji's is just a few blocks away." She eased the hijab scarf back over her hair, although she was bound to attract attention walking in this part of town after dark regardless. She touched the little LCD pressure light in her pocket, with no intention of using it unless she had to. It would only broadcast the presence of unusual visitors with unusual toys.

"You knew about this Agabaji's place?"

She glanced at him in the light of the half-waning and barely risen moon, bright enough to gleam off the occasional glossy stone edifice and the worn cobblestones.

Enough to mark the inevitable byproducts of the horse-drawn carts that still frequented this area. Selena carefully avoided such spots. "I know about a lot of places in Suwan. This particular place is a good one to pick up information, but it's a little rougher than the Plush. It's worth walking in with a little attitude already showing."

"Great."

"Cheer up," she said, wondering if his glass was ever half-full. "I'll be recognized. We won't have to go through that little butt-sniffing ritual again."

All the same, she set a purposeful pace. At Agabaji's she didn't expect to find news of Cole, but there were those who would talk to her—in exchange for U.S. cash—and who would know the recent activity of the streets. Dobry matched her pace and they walked in silence, listening to the sounds of the Suwan night. In this quarter, that meant the occasional faint honk of a car horn, the random shout in the distance. Those on the streets either walked with purpose, as did Selena and Dobry, or else staggered under the influence.

"You can't even smell the sea," Selena murmured, thinking of her old embassy apartment with its view of the sea…how it sometimes turned bright in the sun and reminded her of Cole's eyes. The last time she'd had those thoughts, she'd been uncertain of their future together, uncertain if she carried their child. Odd how events could crystallize the truth of one's feelings, as the hostage incident had done for her, solidifying their partnership—turning them into a couple now trying to become a family. And now their future was once more uncertain, and this time Cole was the one in trouble.

Cole and a man who could save a school full of lives.

For she couldn't think of any circumstances under which it was a good thing that Cole hadn't made contact with his former teammates. He more than anyone knew how to take advantage of the unexpected.

Something she'd unwittingly learned she had in common with him.

A scuff of sound scraped the night and Selena broke stride, drawing in a sharp breath as the skin across her shoulders tightened. They were only a block away from Agabaji's, a literal hole-in-the-ground establishment that drew trouble simply because it also drew those who lived on the edge. Mercenaries of all nationalities, Berzhaani men who lived on the edge of the law, sometimes even a terrorist or two—at least until that unlucky man realized that terrorists were no more welcome in Agabaji's than child abusers were welcome in prison.

Dobry hesitated as he realized Selena had fallen back. He turned and, in the darkness, she thought he reached for her arm and then thought better of it. "Don't make something of nothing," he said. "We don't want to linger—"

The faint whiff of body odor, of alcohol...of gun oil.

Selena was the one who grabbed Dobry's arm, hauling him to the building at the edge of the narrow street, pushing him up against the cut stone.

"What the hell—" His protest cut off in a grunt of surprise as something hit him, followed by the clatter of metal against cobblestone streets. *A blade.*

Selena crouched and scooped up the fallen knife, then dragged Dobry down after her. "Down," she muttered as he resisted. "They don't expect us to be low." No need to ask if he was okay; the man hadn't been able to compensate fast enough for their changed distance and the knife had bounced off hilt first.

And now Selena had it.

In a moment, she'd have the man who threw it.

Chapter 9

He ran. Hard soles smacked the cobblestones with heavy steps and Selena smiled a hard little smile as she took off after him, slipping out of her long coat on the run and leaving it collapsed on the stones behind her like an empty person suit in the moonlight. Dobry shouted something behind her but she didn't heed him; she knew from Farm experience that his fierce sprint couldn't hold up to her sustained effort. The man ahead of her ran so heavily that she suspected the same.

If nothing else, she wanted a good look. A mug-shot kind of look, a memory she could take to Station Chief TRAMMEL and his identification resources.

For this was no random attack. No mugger profited by starting the screaming early, and most women watching a companion knifed in the dark would certainly commence to make noise. No, this was someone who didn't want them here—*them*, as in she and Dobry. Who'd even had the time or opportunity to learn they were in the country?

Her prey turned a corner, breathing harshly now; his steps took on an uneven, leaden quality, his feet thudding dully instead of smartly slapping the cobblestones. Selena pulled her tunic up far enough to reach the gun snugged against her side, ripping the material along the way.

Ahead of her, he grunted loudly, snarling a barely intelligible curse right before a dog yelped—and right before he fell. A weapon clattered off the stones to spin away—with luck, right out of reach.

Selena didn't slow her pace. She spotted him, a dark form against moonlight cobbles, and she turned him into her own personal launching pad. The back of his thigh, his ass, between his shoulder blades and then a special effort to thrust off his head, spinning in midair so her other foot could snap his head back on the way down. She landed in a crouch and no fool he, he heaved himself up with such purpose he could only be hunting for his weapon.

She bared her teeth and leaped in front of him—and this time she had her gun out, the big solid semiautomatic reflecting modest moonlight, close enough to his face to get his complete attention, far enough away so he couldn't reach her. She rapped out, "Who sent you?"

"I—"

"Gijdyllah!" She gave him a moment to absorb that rudeness. "Don't even try to convince me you just had a whim." She fished out her little LED flashlight and shone it on his face, directly into his eyes. Let his night vision adjust after that. And she had a perfect impression of his features, a heavy face over that barrel-chested body, starkly painted in the harsh, narrow beam of light. His shirt caught her eye, an olive fatigue shirt, and her already pounding

heart did a triple beat, a trill of recognition. She flicked the light down to his pants and quickly back again. "Kemeni," she said. She didn't mean for her voice to come out in a harsh whisper, but it happened anyway. "Who leads you, Kemeni? You've got a brain somewhere—it's damn sure not in this body."

He drew back, enough to shield his eyes with his hand, squinting at her dry words in rebellious bafflement. And then the night exploded and he stiffened, his eyes losing focus as his hand fell and his head followed, hitting the cobbles hard enough to break a nose he no longer breathed through.

"Selena!" The voice sounded a little tinny in the aftermath of the gunshot.

"Goff?" she looked into the darkness, feeling entirely exposed. She could just as well have been the one dead on the cobbles. "What the *hell*—? I was—"

Closer now, close enough so her eyes fastened on the two approaching figures and she lifted her Cougar without thinking, wary of such fast approach.

"Whoa," said Betzer's voice, sardonic as it had been in the bar. "Thought you'd be grateful, with him about to go off on you and all." But he stopped short, holding both hands out from his side in a wide, unmistakable message.

Go off on me? She'd been *talking* to the man. She'd also temporarily night-blinded him. She'd been standing out of reach, and she'd had a big pistol to keep things that way.

But Betzer was saying, "Just thought I'd keep an eye on you—for Cole's sake. I wasn't far behind when this guy popped out of the woodwork. Or stonework, in this place. Just as glad for it. I'd hate to have to explain to Cole that I let his wife get killed on my turf."

"It's my turf, too," Selena said tightly, but closed her mouth on more. The man may have acted like a jerk in the bar, but she could believe he'd watch her back just to avoid Cole's wrath. Slowly, she lowered her weapon. But she didn't holster it, and she moved into the shadow of the nearest building.

"Looks like someone's not happy about your search for Cole," Betzer commented. He'd come closer—not so close as to alarm her, but close enough to talk more quietly.

Not that his shot hadn't gathered enough attention—lights were going on, and soon enough the local law would arrive.

And not that she really thought this attack had anything to do with Cole. A man in Kemeni colors, on her tail already? When she'd only moments earlier tipped her hand that she was looking for Cole in the first place? If there was a leak, it had dribbled down from on high.

And that, she didn't even want to contemplate.

"Lighten up, Selena," Dobry offered in his Goff voice. He'd cleaned up after her; when he gestured, her coat flopped in his grip. "We didn't get off to the best start, but the guy just saved your life."

She took only an instant to decide her course. "I guess he did at that," she said, being good. Not making waves.

Keeping her thoughts to herself.

She added, "Thanks, Betzer. And I hate to live and run, but I don't think we'll be alone here much longer." She returned to the body long enough to pat it down one-handed, hauling it over to check the front pockets and avoiding the spreading stain at the crotch. Nothing. No surprise.

Betzer said, "I'm guessing this isn't going to put you off your hunt, but be careful." He gave a brief, sudden grin, a Cheshire cat gleam of tooth in the darkness. "We may be a little prickly on the surface, but Cole's one of us, and we take care of our own."

But she was none of theirs, regardless of what he thought. And he'd killed a man she'd meant to question, *had* been questioning, and now wanted to paint himself the benevolent hero.

She couldn't think of Betzer as a benevolent anything.

"Thanks," she said again, and tipped her head at the distant sound of sirens. "I'll let you know if I hear from Cole. I hope you'll do the same."

And they parted ways with Dobry's additional thanks hanging in the air, as Selena mulled the fact that where Betzer and Dobry saw straight lines, she saw curlicues.

This situation had just gotten much, much more complicated, and she was the only one who seemed to know it.

Danger.

Selena's eyes flew open, her heart already pounding, her mind instantly reviewing the location of her Beretta—the nightstand directly next to her head—and her nearest knife, the short tanto blade she liked for its precision. Its sheath straps were snug and comforting above her ankle, right there under the sheets with her.

Her tension ratcheted a notch as the sound came again, unidentifiable, and her pulse surged so loudly in her ears that she wouldn't hear it again if it came. *Stupid*, she told herself. *Breathe*.

The soft grunt from the twin bed on the other side of the room let her know that Dobry was doing just that. Thank God, the man didn't snore, but the little grunt came regularly enough that waiting for it as she'd tried to fall asleep had turned into a bizarre form of Chinese water torture. She'd finally stuffed tissue in her ears, but it had fallen out as she slept.

Klink. Soft, and just outside the hotel room. Selena

eased out from beneath the covers, scooping up the pistol—it slipped into her hand, comfortable and heavy, her fingers curving around the big grip to welcome it home.

It shocked her to realize those fingers were trembling. She thought she'd handled the evening's encounters with aplomb, that she'd found a piece of her old self. The part of her that didn't overreact, didn't fight internal battles over threat levels, but simply *knew*. Instead she discovered adrenaline overload, lurking in wait. Her knees had gone loose, and she struggled with a moment of doubt, still unable to identify the noise and not at all sure she wasn't just plain overreacting.

Well. She wouldn't know until she tracked it down. She eased to the door and put her ear to the crack; after a moment she opened it and after another she stuck her head out into the hall.

There she discovered a Berzhaani maintenance man halfway up a ladder, fiddling with one of the fancy wall sconces. Her sudden appearance caused him to startle, drop his screwdriver, and clutch at the ladder, staring.

She realized that her pj's set of loose T-shirt and low-slung boxers covered with tan and green dinosaurs probably wasn't considered modest by Berzhaani standards. And that the gun up her shoulder, ready to come to bear, was likewise not a common sight.

Selena found a handful of curses from as many different languages, but none seemed quite right for the moment. So she brought her free hand up to waggle her fingers at the horrified man, and retreated back into the room.

"Smooth move," Dobry said in the darkness, and then the light by his bed clicked on.

Be casual. It's the only way out of this one. "The room arrangement can be changed if you'd like," she told him, and returned—casually, of course—the pistol to her bedside table. "Probably even tonight."

Propped on his elbow, Dobry regarded her in silence, one dyed eyebrow lifting over heavy features. In response to what, Selena wasn't sure. Her midnight prowling, her trendy chick pajamas—ones she wouldn't have packed had she been doing the packing—or maybe even the residual tremor of her hands. But if he had something to say, he'd have to say it out loud—she wasn't going to give him a freebie opening.

Too damned bad they'd both agreed, when they couldn't get adjoining rooms, that it would be best to stick together.

Selena slid back into bed; he courteously waited until she'd done so before turning off the light, offering no further comment. *Checking is better than not checking*, she told herself. *Knowing is better than wondering. Overreacting is better than dying*. The sick feeling in her stomach washed in anyway.

She closed her eyes and remembered the reason she was here, the reason she'd been thrust into the field when everyone knew she'd found herself a permanent edge to live on since her days in Tafiq Ashurbeyli's hands. *Aymal*, with intel that would save lives. *And Cole*. Cole, with that sloppy grin and that devil-may-care attitude that often hid how much he truly did care. But she'd figured him out. She'd *finally* figured him out.

And she wasn't about to lose him now. If that meant holding it together, then so be it. She'd hold it together.

Cole's eyes flew open, already narrowing with intent, his hand closing around the checkered black grip of his Browning Hi-Power, solid 9 mm readiness. He held his breath, listening…trying to filter out the various snorts and heavy breathing of his nighttime companions—the humped Zebu cattle who lived on this small family farm and who sheltered under this three-quarter pole barn at night.

Breathe, he thought at Aymal, fully aware that the man had slept only fitfully and now had stopped breathing—not, as with Cole, listening for a repetition of what had woken him, but simply because he'd forgotten to breathe in his fear.

The cattle shifted below the half-width storage loft Cole had appropriated—three of them, warming this small space and perfectly content to share it.

Scuffle…

There it was again. Not far from here. Cole pushed away the dirty blanket he'd taken from the bus, no doubt from someone who hadn't deserved to lose it. His side burned; he bit down on a hiss of annoyance and stood anyway, slowly so as not to spook the cattle. When Aymal shifted beside him, Cole used his free hand to press down on the man's shoulder, a silent command to stay still.

A man less prepared to face the trials of defecting through troubled territory, he couldn't imagine. Then again, he still couldn't imagine Aymal as a terrorist at all, though he supposed someone had to balance the checkbook—a highly trained mathematician turned accountant by circumstances.

Aymal had assured him that the accounts with which he'd worked would be closed by now, the money shifted to uncompromised banks. But he was equally certain that no one realized how much information he'd picked up simply by being there.

Cole wasn't quite so certain. Someone had disrupted the initial exfiltration…someone had turned Cole's own ex-buddies on to the attempted recovery and paid them to intercept. Someone, it seemed, knew *something.*

So he wouldn't assume that they didn't also know he and Aymal had hidden out on the very western edges of Suwan, just along the long slog of arid nothingness between here and the nearest village. He eased out to the edge of the loft and flipped over it, lowering himself in a gymnast's move to touch down between two sets of long, lyre-shaped horns. This time he was prepared to set his teeth against the stretch of torn flesh, and possibly even to admit that the tentative first aid and disinfectant Aymal had applied hadn't been quite enough.

Later. He patted a bony bovine hip and the animal didn't even bother to shift away from him. He squeezed by, keeping the gun well away from her, and hesitated at the edge of the small structure, staring into a night lit by a gibbous but waning moon, the pistol loaded, cocked and ready to go. The thrumming in his side distracted him; his eyes seemed too gritty to focus in the limited light.

Scuffle...

Hell. Just another cow, dark shape against dark background. Cole snorted softly to himself and eased the thumb safety back into place. *Smooth move, Jox*, he told himself, and grinned into the darkness with relief. *Yeah, smooth moo-ve.* But he was no less careful in returning to the loft, and he settled himself into place with doubts surfacing in his thoughts. This was their second night on the run, and he'd just interrupted his first few hours of sleep since it all started. Aymal was no better off—worse even, worn-out from days of intense spy games before Cole had found him, and riding the ragged edge of nerves that had come pre-frayed.

As if to emphasize that last, Aymal's hand closed on Cole's arm, a contact with just a little too much clutch in it. "Are we safe?" he whispered, if a voice that loud could ever truly be called a whisper.

"As safe as we've been since this started," Cole told him, his own voice perfectly normal if a little roughened by circumstances. "Just one of the cows…must have gone walkabout while we weren't paying attention."

"You're sure?" Aymal asked, still clutching. "Because I didn't sleep. I would have heard if one of the cows moved away."

Gently, Cole peeled away Aymal's fingers. "That's my gun arm, Aymal…you really don't ever want to get in its way." Before he'd finished speaking, Aymal had snatched his hand away entirely. One of the cows offered an editorial comment, the kind that came with its own unique odor, and Cole sighed. "Definitely a cow." And when Aymal offered nothing but a muffled sound of dismay in response, Cole said, "Hey, could be worse. Lots worse. We could have found ourselves hiding in a silkworm farm."

Aymal chose not to respond. Probably wise.

And Cole…

Cole closed his eyes and determined to get some sleep. They'd bumped around watching their tails long enough. He'd head for Oguzka to stash Aymal, and then he'd feel his way around, determine who he'd trust this time…and hope he wasn't wrong again. For now…sleep. He deliberately fed a slow smile with thoughts of Selena, of those blue-green eyes that always spoke deeply and truly to him even when she could hide her feelings from so many.

And now they trusted him, those eyes. They hadn't always, but things had changed during the hostage incident. They were partners, now…partners trying to become a family.

Never mind Aymal…it was Selena he wouldn't let down.

Chapter 10

Selena dozed her way through the rest of the night and woke early. She spent a few moments breathing deeply to reset her body's mood for the day. *Not strung tight as a wire, thank you.* Dobry looked to be a slow and grumpy riser, so she headed for the gym to get some endorphins kicked into gear. Just a light workout—some stretches and warm-ups, a mile's jogging on the treadmill, a few reps of toning weights. As much as she'd like to throw herself into the exercise and banish the night's demons, she needed to leave plenty of herself in reserve.

No telling what the day would bring.

She returned to the room for a quick shower and found a message from Allori. Clean, her hair still tousled and wet, she sat on the bed in the oversize hotel bathrobe and dialed Allori's number as Dobry spread the contents of his metal goodies case on the otherwise cleared work desk, his expression as gleeful as she'd ever seen it. Bonita put her through without comment, and Selena greeted Allori with just a little too much cheer. "Hi," she said. "This hotel is great—thanks for recommending it!"

He'd done no such thing, but he'd know she was calling from a public line—the same way he'd initially called her, which meant he wasn't too worried about the content of the call. "I'm glad it suits you," he said, using the deep, ringing tones of his public voice. "I wanted to make sure your lunch yesterday was sitting well."

"Excellent lunch," she said. "Got a little spicy—Kenneth and I had a little heartburn later in the day. But we're fine today."

"That's good to hear." Innocuous words, but his dry tone let her know the message was received. "I trust you'll avoid those dishes in the future."

"That's the plan. Today we'll try a little marketplace food." At least, that was her intent—to get out into the city, to the marketplace gossip zones she knew from her legate days, and see what info she could pick up. Allusions to the defector, any hint of what had truly happened the evening that Cole had enlisted three children in his attempts to evade a gunfight. Any hints of who the other men might have been.

For Selena was quite sure they hadn't stopped looking for Aymal.

She and Allori exchanged an additional pleasantry or two, until interrupted by an incoming call on his end. She counted herself lucky to have gotten straight through to him in the first place, and reached for her comb to tackle her hair. Dobry didn't look up from his kit, but she felt his attention nonetheless.

"You know, you're CIA now. It's the station chief you should be calling."

Half-a-dozen sarcasms rose to mind; Selena squelched them all. Could be she'd just never get on this guy's good side. "I thought we'd discuss moving forward first."

This time he turned to look at her. "Sounded to me like you've made up your mind."

I had a lot of time to think last night while you were grunting. "I've got my preferences, yes. If you'd rather just go with that, it's fine by me."

He flashed her a look that said she couldn't play him that easily. "And what's that? Information shopping?"

"Gathering HUMINT," she agreed. Human intelligence, i.e. gossip. "We know Cole was at that shooting scene a day and a half ago—"

"Do we?"

She encountered a tangle in her hair and stopped the comb. "That's why I'm here, remember? I'm the closest thing we've got to being inside Cole's head right now."

For that she got a grudging nod, and Dobry turned back to his kit, pulling out the pencil and spray with which he'd gruff up his eyebrows. He added, "We also know he hasn't checked in with his friends here. Could mean he's not in the area any longer."

"Could mean Betzer was lying," Selena countered. "Can't say as I think he really trusts me."

"Fighting off terrorists isn't the same as keeping secrets," Dobry said, in tones of significance.

Bah. Selena felt a little Tasmanian Devil rearing up inside, ready to roar out of here and conduct business in Berzhaan as she'd always done. She didn't need Dobry for this; she only truly needed him if she went to the outlying areas and wanted to keep a low profile.

But it would probably annoy the station chief if she dumped her erstwhile partner.

So she said, "Between Aymal, his pursuit and the very public encounter between them all, there's the potential for a lot of people to be interested in this situation. The more they've been digging around, the more chance they've stirred things up...the more chance we've got to gather up details that might mean something to me. Since our other current option is to go on a door-to-door search of Suwan, HUMINT seems like a good place to start."

His sideways glance sent a clear message of dissent. "We can go back to Betzer. You seem so sure Jones will connect with him—if he hasn't already—it seems worth the trouble to convince him *we're* worth the trouble. Money talks to mercs—"

She shook her head, short and sharp; wet hair gently slapped her cheek. "He doesn't trust us. That means I don't trust him. And I don't trust anyone who's only doing it for the paycheck, either."

That silenced him a moment, but only a moment. "You don't know enough about him to know why he does what. He proved himself last night when he thought he was saving your life—"

Right. Taking advantage of the moment to win her trust after a bad start, because he, too, wanted to be in on helping Cole. Noble enough as a goal, but if that was an example of his methods, she could do better to keep him at a distance.

"You're right," she said. "I don't know enough about him to know why he does what. That's why I want to take the time to scope things out a little more fully."

Dobry pulled off his shirt and picked up the body padding that came along with Kenneth Goff. The eyebrows were already what could only be called wildly successful—anyone looking at that face would hardly notice eye color or nose size or even whether Goff had any teeth left. He said, "If you weren't so blinded by your conviction that Jones has already been there and that Betzer is holding out on us—"

"He is," Selena insisted.

"—then you might be able to see he can be a useful tool. You don't have to bring him into your family, Selena. Just use him."

His patronizing tone cut through her determination to play nice. "Do I have to remind you I've got plenty of experience with using judgment in the field?" she asked him. "This very field, in fact." She dropped the comb onto the bed, stood up to stalk over to his table as he looked up from fastening the padding. "I can do this without you...can you say the same?"

His face darkened, a deep flush that told her how close he'd been to annoyance in the first place. "If you think I'm just here to parrot your opinions—"

"I don't." She snapped the words out, and made herself take a deep breath. "I don't give a flying fig if you disagree with me. But you'd damned well better not imply that because I disagree with *you*, I'm suffering emotional blindness." When he glanced up and met her gaze, she held the prickly connection longer than she really wanted to. "You've got your own baggage. I know how badly you want to get into the field again on a permanent basis. Wouldn't it be just great if you could turn this assignment into some sort of coup with you as the headliner? Well, here's a newsflash for you—you can have all the credit you can grab as long as we find Cole and Aymal. That's why *I'm* here."

Dobry was silent, steady under her regard until his curt nod broke the moment. "We'll try your sources this morning," he said. "And then we'll see."

And this is why I was perfectly happy to be a Pandora. But Selena took the tiny victory and turned her attention back to the process of finding Cole.

* * *

The Suwan marketplace bustled around them, a scene straight from *Indiana Jones*. Selena bit into a fresh fig and surveyed the area, contemplating their next step. After a morning of veiled and not-so-veiled questioning of once-established informants, she had little to go on. No one was aware of renewed Kemeni activity, though many were aware that international games were playing out on their turf. Some even knew it involved a defector. They knew of the incident surrounding Aymal's first failed extraction, and they knew of the street firefight Selena was sure had involved Cole—but not any of the details. Not who had done what or where to find anyone now.

"That was a waste of time," Dobry muttered, sticking to his gravelly Kenneth Goff voice even in their quiet conversation. He was good, she had to give him that. He talked differently, moved differently, and gave an entirely different impression as Goff. Goff was a man at home on a golf course, but not particularly good at it. A self-absorbed, currently uncomfortable man who was here out of a misplaced need to watch over Selena for his poker-game friend Cole.

"We didn't get anything out of the station chief this morning, either," Selena reminded him, tucking a strand of hair back into her scarf. She wore her own clothes this day—she wanted to be recognized. But even as a legate she'd always worn a respectful scarf when she was out and about in the general population. She tied it at the nape of her neck rather than fastening it under her chin, but her shoulder-length brunette hair was covered and her three earrings were just tiny studs. It was how the people here knew her, even two seasons later. Stylized cargo slacks, a sturdy tailored pullover sweater against the late fall chill, a heavily pocketed vest. It'd be better if she had her leather duster, but she wasn't the one who'd done the packing. "No confirmation of Kemeni activity, no word of Cole."

Dobry looked no more happy about it than she.

"Look," Selena said, "we've planted seeds. My sources know I'm trying to make their city safer—they've always known that."

"The payoff promises don't hurt."

"No, they don't. And they know I'm good for it, too." Selena itched to return to the hotel room, to grab a few moments alone with the laptop. Problem was, it wasn't *her* laptop—it was a company machine, built and configured to interface securely with the CIA network.

But not with Oracle. Not securely. She'd have to pick up the phone and deal with the sexless artificial voice at the other end of the Oracle number. She licked her fig-sticky fingers and checked her watch. "Too early for Agabaji's, but we'll give it a try later. By now they'll have heard that I'm here and hunting Cole—anyone interested in unloading details in exchange for cash will be looking for me there."

Dobry shrugged, not disagreeing and not approving. She thought about asking for suggestions—anything besides going to Betzer so soon, although she had no doubt they'd end up back at his doorstep eventually. She just wasn't ready to bring him into the fold. Trust went both ways, and she had the feeling the previous night's "rescue" had been to gain her trust as much as he truly thought he'd saved her hide.

Not that she blamed him. Cole would take Betzer apart if he learned of her reception at the hands of his former mates.

But before Selena could open her mouth and actually ask Dobry if he had any particular way he'd like to spend the time until Agabaji's opened, someone bumped into her back. At the same moment a distracted middle-aged man brushed into her from the front. Classic bump-and-grab.

Oh, no you don't! Selena all but bared her teeth and instantly kicked into fight mode. She didn't wait to feel the pluck of her vest—her hand dove for her roomy pocket, finding it already occupied. A yank and she had the man's hand clear, a solid grip on his thumb. A twist as the man tried to jerk away, and the thumb bent back far enough to make him cry out, his fingers splaying. "Not your pocket!" Selena told him fiercely, not bothering to use the Berzhaani language. Her meaning came through clearly enough and by then the man who'd first bumped into her had backpedaled away, turning to run as Dobry reached for him. Selena released the pickpocket and let him bolt, as those closest to the confrontation pulled their belongings more tightly to themselves and shifted away.

"What the hell—?" said Dobry, and at first she thought he meant the pickpocket team but then she realized he meant…

Her.

"Are you *trying* to attract attention? You probably dislocated his thumb!"

"Probably," Selena said, shifting into the deep breathing that had helped to get her through the night. She crouched, her fingers gently picking between the cobblestones to retrieve what the man had lost. "Consider it a message."

"What? The *I'm here causing trouble in your country* message?"

In a way, she couldn't blame him. He excelled in the covert, in the quiet. In going unnoticed. He'd been trained to accomplish his assignments without leaving fingerprints, footprints or a trail of broken bones behind him. But the CIA had had its chance to do things quietly. With two very public if not yet identified incidents related to this defection already, quiet had made way for *as fast as possible*.

Because Cole was out there, somewhere. Hiding his invaluable defector. Assessing the situation. Waiting for help. And if refusing to slink around allowed her to find them, to stop the imminent school attack one moment sooner, then leaving fingerprints and footprints was worth it.

Except there was Dobry, still frowning at her. A frown, she noted with abstract detachment, that looked truly disturbing underneath those eyebrows. So she held out her hand with a hasty order that it not tremble as long as he was looking, and let him see what was nestled in her palm.

Small. Discreet. Efficient. And surprisingly high tech.

"Is that—" He reached for it, and the device was all but lost between the meaty pads of his thumb and forefinger.

"Tracking device," she confirmed. "That particular pickpocket was more than what he seemed. And I just sent his people a message."

He gave her a sour look. "And if he hadn't been? If he'd been a run-of-the-mill thief?"

What was it about this guy that made her want to roll her eyes so often?

Maybe it was just her. She'd done well in the hostage incident…but she'd been working on her own. She'd specialized in developing teamwork as a legate, but maybe when it came to fieldwork, she didn't have the teamwork gene. She didn't try to hide her annoyance this time. "Then maybe he'll stop targeting Western women."

Dobry looked around the marketplace as if common sense had finally warned him they were making just as much of a scene as Selena's confrontation with the pickpocket. He turned to face the same direction as she and took her arm, moving them out of the limelight.

She noticed he kept his touch light enough to be interpreted as a request, and not a demand. No dummy, anyway.

"Okay," he said. "Let's get an early dinner, and we can hit Agabaji's on the early side. If you're right and we're lucky, there'll be a line of people waiting to get paid for what they know."

Selena disengaged her arm, but she did it gently and kept pace with him. Fine with her if they left this place now. They'd planted their seeds...and she'd learned that, instead of killing her as had been tried the night before, someone would now try to use her to find Cole. *Good luck with that*, she thought at the nameless, faceless foe. *You're gonna need it.*

"Selena." The one-size-fits-all unisex voice of Delphi at Oracle's direct contact number greeted her with assurance. "Things are still messy in Berzhaan, it seems."

She didn't bother to ask how Delphi knew it was her, or knew where she was. She'd only just been issued this phone and it wasn't supposed to be traceable, but...

She'd be more surprised if Delphi *didn't* know she'd been yanked to Berzhaan to find Cole and his defector.

"Very messy," Selena said. First things first. "Did you get my message? It turns out this defector has a lot more than weapons intel for us—there's a strike set for one of our schools."

"We got the message." The computerized voice actually sounded brisk, even a little anxious. "No other details?"

"None. I've got feelers out but I'm not sure we have that kind of time."

"I agree," said the voice, completely impersonal again. "The Berzhaani police just found the vehicle that was stolen from the neighborhood in which the most recent gunplay of interest took place." That matter-of-fact voice made no attempt to soften the next words. "There was blood on the seat."

Selena couldn't reply. After a long moment she realized she'd stopped breathing.

"Not a significant amount," Delphi continued, "but it could be an important factor."

"It could be Aymal's blood," Selena murmured, reassuring herself out loud.

"Would Cole Jones let Aymal do the driving?"

No. No, of course not. Cole wouldn't be free to plan on the fly if someone else was at the wheel. Selena glanced through the glass doors of the hotel balcony, able to see only Dobry's stocking feet as he sat with his legs splayed, reading news headlines on the laptop.

"Do you have anything else for me?" she asked, the brusqueness coming back into her voice.

"Only that the man found dead last night was a Kemeni, but there's no sign of Kemeni reorganization."

"So he's either working on his own, or he's got an enabler." Selena shook her head, looking out over a striking sunset above the Caspian Sea. "I need more than that. Nothing here is coming together. Two interrupted extractions, that smacks of inside information. And you don't get inside information unless you're good...and unless you've got money behind you."

"We concur on all counts," Delphi said, sounding particularly impersonal. "We'll keep looking. Check in soon."

That was a dismissal if she'd ever heard one. Selena didn't mind it; she didn't bother to say goodbye any more than Delphi did.

Cole was hurt. He was hurt, and she was no closer to finding him than she'd been before she'd left Athena

Academy a day and a half earlier. No closer to stopping those terrorists.

And dammit, she had a real thing about stopping terrorists.

Selena looked through the glass at Dobry's feet and murmured, "If you thought I was making waves before, Dobry…you ain't seen nothing yet." For along with the constant impulse to overreact, the worry for a fellow operative who just happened to be her fiercely loved husband, the Taz in her was ready to strike out. To strike back.

To do everything it took.

Cole's eyes watered. *What an incredible smell you've discovered.*

The stench from the public bathroom was amazing, even a dozen feet away and tucked into a little alcove between stone buildings. A unisex building crammed in at the edge of a tiny Oguzka marketplace, it was just wide enough for two holes in the floor and plenty of evidence that not everyone found success in aiming for those holes.

Cole had seen worse. Aymal as well, or surely he would have had some comment about them, the same sort of comment he'd made about sleeping over cows, the endless double-decker bus ride, or the need to ditch the nice trucklet they'd first stolen.

Cole was sure of it by now. He'd found himself a defector insurgent wuss. He was sure of something else after these days of thought, too.

He didn't trust the local station. The chief, yeah—even if the man was dirty, no one canny enough to be a double agent at that level would mess up two interceptions. Mess up *badly*. And Cole had no reason to suspect the man was dirty. But someone, somewhere along the line…it might even be as simple as a compromised communications system. Whoever'd gone for Aymal hadn't had much time to plan.

Communications then. Probably.

And therein lay the problem. How to communicate without...communicating?

For starters, he wasn't going to do it with Aymal by his side.

With Aymal tucked away behind the toilets, Cole had scrounged some meat-wrapping paper from the marketplace, and found a stubby pencil next to the cash box of a man selling kvass. The cash he left alone, but the pencil went with him—all the way back to Aymal, who waited with sulky impatience. "Here," Cole said, and thrust the writing materials at him. "Write down what you know about that terrorist attack." High-tech CIA communications procedure, to be sure. But no one could eavesdrop on it.

"Na baba!" Aymal stared in disbelief. He was practically already his own disguise, with stubble filling in the skin around his neatly shaped beard and his eyes hollow with lack of sleep and an overdose of fearing for his life. "What reason would you have to help me reach the States if you already know what I know?"

Cole hit him with a steady gaze. "Aymal, old buddy, if I was that kind of guy, I'd have already pinned you to the inside of a building similar to this aromatically attractive structure and tickled you until you turned colors and blabbed it all."

Aymal returned him a skeptical look, not such the defector insurgent wuss when it came to the bottom line.

"Get real," Cole said. "We're in trouble here. We need a pickup, and I don't think it's safe to arrange one. And you know, I don't really think you cleaned my little war wound very well and it hurts. A lot. It's starting to shorten my patience."

Aymal's expression had taken on a stubborn cast.

"Either you trust me with your life, or you don't. If you don't, then hidey-hey, we're done with each other. You can find your own ride out." *As if. Not without that intel.* "If you do, then fork it over. Because I'm not sure we'll both get out of this alive, and I don't want either of us to die for nothing. I especially don't want *me* to die for nothing."

Aymal took the paper. He took it and he tore it in half, complacently returning a piece to Cole. "Fine," he said. "Then you write here that you trust me, and that if something happens to you it won't be because I caused it to happen. Because if I'm the one who gets out of this alive, I don't want your compatriots to think I had something to do with your demise."

Huh. Fair enough. Cole took the pencil and scribbled a few words, and then carefully placed his thumbprint next to his signature. Invisible to the naked eye or not, it'd be found if this note made its way to the Agency. He folded the paper so as to keep the print intact, and handed it over to Aymal along with the pencil. "Look," he said. "I've got to go see about getting us a ride. I don't want to be anywhere near here when I do it, and I don't want to be anywhere near *you.* So grab yourself a seat and write out your homework assignment, and I'll be back before tomorrow morning."

The paper crinkled in Aymal's suddenly tightened grip. "All that time? I have no…I am prey even for the most ignorant of thieves and muggers!"

Not to mention the jerks who were no doubt still looking for them. But Cole looked at the Browning's grip protruding from his pocket and then looked at Aymal, putting his doubt right out there. "You'd shoot yourself in the foot, guy."

"You offend me! The only reason I don't have my own gun is that your people wouldn't let me bring it."

Wise people. Cole pulled the Browning free and said, "It's Condition One." At Aymal's blank look, he added, "Locked and cocked." And when that produced no enlightenment, finally, "It's a single action. There's a round in the chamber and the hammer is cocked. The safety is on. If you take the safety off and pull the trigger, bullets are gonna fly."

"Of course." Aymal took the gun with gingerly respect and examined it.

Cole used one deliberate finger to move the muzzle so it pointed at the ground and not at him, and sent Aymal a most meaningful look.

Aymal ignored him. "Safety off," he announced, and confidently thumbed the mechanism behind the trigger.

The magazine hit the ground.

"Na baba!" Cole muttered between clenched teeth. He took the pistol back, retrieved the magazine and shoved it home. Then he held the gun out so Aymal could see and flicked the thumb safety. "Off. On. Off. On. You got it?"

"Of course," Aymal repeated, sounding heartily unconvincing, and held his hand out for the weapon.

"Oh, no," Cole told him, and put the Mark III on the ground beside the convenient pile of rocks Aymal had claimed for his seat. This whole country had more rocks than it knew what to do with, including the rocks that were almost certainly rolling around in Cole's head. "You write your little weapons memoirs first, *then* you can touch the gun. Don't pick it up unless you have to—I mean, really *have* to—and before you do, you'd better know where you intend to point it. Don't wave it, gesture with it or threaten with it. If you need it, you pick it up, take that safety off, and shoot without hesitation. You got me?"

"Again, you insult me."

"Yeah," Cole agreed, turning away to leave their little hidey hole. "That's me. Always looking for a new insult. It keeps me going." Good God. What was he even thinking?

Don't overthink it. Just do it. That's your specialty.

Cole wished for his disguising nose appliance, the one that had come off on the bus and which had once turned his mostly straight nose into something more profound. The mustache had held on better than he'd thought it would, too. But neither had been meant to last longer than it took to scoop up Aymal and get him to the airport for exfiltration. Cole sighed, not bothering to hide it. He still had black hair; he still had altered skin tones and dark contacts. Those things should last another several days at the least.

He also still had a deep furrow under his skin that should have been nothing but which had, he was pretty certain, contrived to become infected. He should have known his squeamish defector hadn't done a thorough job of cleaning and wasting alcohol on it, but he hadn't been able to see it.

He turned back suddenly, startling Aymal with his hand creeping for the gun. "Don't! Touch! It!" Cole told him, and they stood frozen a moment, staring at each other. Finally Cole turned away for good, hiding the roll of his eyes. Aymal would do what he'd do.

And Cole would hurry.

Chapter 11

Selena didn't wait for evening. She almost didn't wait for Dobry. She downed a large salad with plenty of cheese and meat and then she headed for the door, having announced her intent long before. Dobry scrambled to keep up, throwing his padded vest into place. The eyebrows were still lurking on their own.

They took a cab to within several blocks of Agabaji's and walked in, giving themselves time to be seen. Then they picked a table and settled in.

Or rather, Selena settled in. Dobry volunteered to walk the neighborhood, heading for the Plush to see if he could pick up any scoops there. Selena was more than glad to encourage such initiative, and put her back to the wall to drink bottled fizzy water until the light faded and the usual crowd began to ease its way into action.

Tonight, she thought. *Tonight we keep looking until we find something.*

* * *

Cole made his way around the edge of the city, hunting a good, functioning cell signal and thinking that for his next job, a satellite cell would be just the thing. He could have had one this time if they'd all been willing to wait an hour longer to wade through the ops tech snafu they'd encountered while simultaneously briefing him and hustling him to the private plane that had flown him in as cargo.

But no. They all hadn't. So he'd had this one turned off to save the battery until he found a signal worth trying—and, in this case, a signal far enough away from Aymal so he wouldn't lead anyone straight to the man he was protecting.

For he had to assume it was possible—he'd *been* assuming it was possible. Otherwise he'd have taken a more direct approach to the local CIA station, a small printing house affiliated with the very paper for which he'd created his reporter persona. The bad guys were probably waiting to hear from him as eagerly as the good guys, however those bad guys were tapping into local CIA communications.

Bad guys he'd once trusted with his life.

But before he could call at all, he'd had to wait until he knew they weren't being tailed—and until he could safely stash Aymal for up to half a day. Now, sitting on a large rock formation with the city at his back and the sun setting before him, he had the almost undeniable urge to call Selena—just as she had called him all those months ago. Just to say *Hi, I'm in trouble and I need you to know that I love you.*

Except the local station would be watching for calls from this phone, and so were the bad guys. They'd learn his location. And if the worst came of it, then Cole damn well didn't want Selena to live with the guilt that she had been the cause.

She was like that, his Selena. Cool and calm, a fierce

lawyer warrior, all full of emotion on the inside and never sure what to do with it. Never quite seeing that it was her heart that allowed her to make such an impact on him. On others, when it came to that. Would that fool Dobry have even thought to hassle her if her intensity didn't come through? Cole snorted softly to himself. *I don't think so.*

So he wouldn't call her. He wouldn't hear her voice, or the way it got husky when she was emotional. He wouldn't swap family *what-ifs* with her, tossing around baby names as if their efforts had already paid off. No, he'd sit on the rock and compose a text message to the station chief's Bat Phone. He thought briefly about pleading for rescue from Aymal, but decided on the more circumspect. *Have package, need transportation, 20:00, here.*

Heaven forbid if they couldn't trace his signal.

But Cole didn't expect that to be the problem. He was more concerned about leaving Aymal for all this time, even though he'd warned the man it would be a while. For he had no intention of retrieving Aymal to wait for the pickup; he had no intention of being out in the open when someone came this way to look for him. Nope, this was a test, pure and simple. Before he exposed the defector again—before he exposed *himself*—he'd see who came along for the ride this time around.

The station chief wouldn't be happy with him, of course.

Oh, well.

Cole took a deep breath. Finally, he was doing something other than running and hiding. Finally time to move out…even to strike back, if he got a good look at anyone this evening. He stood on top of his rock formation—the square, chunky rocks everywhere to be found in this part of Berzhaan—and stretched, a defiant see-if-I-care move that let the cold night air rush into the warmth of his enveloping abaya.

The red- and salmon-washed horizon tilted.

Whoa. Rather than fight his suddenly precarious balance, Cole jumped from the rocky pedestal to control his landing. *Whoa.* His side burned, cranking up the dizzies, and he bent over his knees to let it pass. After an endless moment, he straightened and gingerly slipped his hand beneath his abaya to hold it over the absurd flesh wound that suddenly didn't seem so absurd at all. Just behind the bone of his hip, where he'd never been able to see it, only feel it. Hoo, boy, could he feel it now.

Great.

Cole knew better than to take any infection for granted, even an absurd little flesh-wound infection. Not when it flared up while he was on the run in an undeveloped area—not when it flared up on a part that couldn't be cut off if things went really bad. *You couldn't have been a splinter in my finger?*

Aymal's time-sensitive information wasn't the only reason he needed to hurry.

Agabaji's had turned raucous and rough, the playground of bad boys who figured they'd earned themselves some fun. The whores there were clearly used to it, although they were modest by American standards. Decently covered, they rarely did more than peer out from behind the ornate and torn old screen that "hid" the way to the back rooms. Selena tipped back her second bottle of lukewarm fizzy water and stopped herself from making a face out of sheer willpower. *God, I hate this stuff.* But ask for plain bottled water and you might well end up with tap water in a reused bottle. Right now the last thing she needed was intestinal difficulties. Her stomach was touchy enough under emotional stress.

"Hey, S'lena!" One of the regulars hailed her from across the room. He'd started early tonight, and it hadn't been with fizzy water. "C'mon over here and be sosh'ble!"

She waved back at him, hardly more than the wiggle of her fingers. "Busy!"

"You don't look—" But that was as far as the greasy little man got before his friends hauled him back to their own table, jeering him and sending Selena sideways glances just to see if she'd taken offense.

Hmm. She should have come back to Berzhaan sooner. It seemed the respect factor had gone up a notch or two since she'd taken on the Kemenis and won. *Go, Taz.*

Another man moved away from the bar and invited himself to sit at her table, his movements steady. "You're buying?" He could have been Berzhaani, given his coloring—or, with that accent, just over the line into Russia.

"Information, yes," Selena told him, shifting to Russian. "Drinks, no. Everyone here is drunk enough without my help."

He grinned. No, he wasn't nearly as far gone as the rest of them. His gaze was sharp when it met hers and he easily replied in Russian. "The Kemenis aren't the only ones who want Americans out of this place."

"No!" Selena affected shock. "You're just trying to hurt my feelings."

"If there are Kemenis left over and nursing a grudge, they might connect with like-minded people."

"There's one dead Kemeni who might have done that," Selena allowed. She'd know for sure if Betzer hadn't rushed in to save the day, dammit. She'd have to tell the station chief that the man had interfered, however good his intentions—if he made a habit of tangling with the area ops, he'd need encouragement to stop.

"I might be able to get you more information about such men."

"And this has what to do with the man I'm looking for?"

Her erstwhile informant shrugged. "Maybe nothing. Maybe something. Sometimes these things are all tied together."

"Sometimes they are," she agreed. "I'm looking for something a little more immediate, however."

Another grin, showing a tooth going bad amongst what could otherwise have been a Colgate smile. "Americans. Instant gratification."

"We are a sadly spoiled people." Selena nodded at this thoughtful truth and then abruptly thumped the glass bottle on the table, splashing fizzy water and not caring. "You got something for me? Or you just want to play?"

He did a good job of covering his quick startle at the sudden movement and noise. "Play games, I think. Go back to where it all started, American lady. If you can find him, then maybe I'll trust you with what else I know."

She considered pointing out to him that if she found Cole, she'd be gone; he'd have to hunt up someone new to sell his information to. But she didn't want to put him off entirely. She might need to come back to him.

Cole, who'd left blood on the seat of his getaway vehicle.

Cole, who held Aymal's life in his hands—and by extension, the lives of a whole school of children.

She opted for the noncommittal. "If I come back looking for you, I'll need a name."

"No," he said, and gave her that jarringly almost perfect smile. "You won't. I'll find you."

Oh, be *like that then.* She shrugged, an implication that the loss was his, and returned her attention to the fizzy water. Yuck, she still hated it. The Russian nodded—an exchange of dismissals, everyone saving face—and pushed away from the table.

It was an opportune time for her phone to ring. Not so long ago a cell phone ring tone would have caught the attention of everyone in the place, but times they were a-changin'. Of late, Berzhaan had seen a high-tech trickle to its freelance "security specialists" and terrorists alike. Sometimes she liked to image the actual content of the calls she saw come in to these rough men. *Mujaahid, get back home this instant! Mujaahid Junior has a Young Terrorists Class in forty-five minutes. And bring home some eggs!*

Or not.

She flipped her phone open and didn't even have the chance to offer a greeting before the station chief's brusque tones. "Ms. BLUEMAN," he said. "JOXLEITNER has made contact. We'll have him and his companion in friendly hands before the evening is over."

Selena almost couldn't take it in. She'd been so focused on *doing* something, on finding him...the Taz in her whirled right on ahead, unable to stop. Focused. *Find Cole. Find him now.*

Then her inner Taz hit the end of her psychic leash and yanked to a disorienting stop. "You *have* him?" she repeated, knowing she sounded vacant and unable to stop herself.

"We will. He'll be going straight to continued transportation. You have that option as well."

Hell, yes.

"Just tell me where and when." It was all she could do to keep from running out of the bar right then and there—but she still had to connect with Dobry.

Although Dobry might well want to hang around and ingratiate himself to the station chief, make sure the man knew that he and Selena were on the right track and had accomplished much already.

"Return to your hotel," the man said. "Once we've established possession, we'll let you know." From the tone of his voice, he was about to end the call.

"Wait!" Selena took a deep breath. "If he had the means to reach you, why not before now?"

For the first time she heard irritation in the man's voice. "That's something we'll be asking JOXLEITNER when we have the opportunity." And he did hang up.

Selena flipped the phone closed and stared at it, so irrationally filled with euphoria that she dared not move at all. *He's coming home.* It didn't matter that she hadn't been the one to find him, or even that she'd been hauled out to look with no apparent need. He'd gone underground for his own reasons, and she'd know them eventually.

He's coming home. A deep breath, and another.

Abruptly, common sense intruded. She needed to call Dobry, let him know she was heading out and make sure he had the chance to come along. She reached for the phone again, and this time she didn't care that her hand wasn't quite steady. Trembles of joy…totally allowed. But before she'd even hit the fast-dial number she'd assigned to Dobry's phone, he came striding through the entrance. He still moved in character, and he still greeted her in his gravelly Goff voice. But his demeanor had changed—had become frustrated and more purposeful at the same time.

Selena caught the implications immediately. He'd been called before she had. Never mind that she was the lead operative, or that she had the most at stake. They'd stuck to the old boy's network, hadn't they?

She stood before he reached the table. "You heard."

"I was on my way back," he said, by way of acknowledgment.

His irritation was evident enough that she couldn't help but say, "This is a good thing, yes?"

It took him by surprise. "Of course. I just...I thought I had a lead. I don't like getting pulled off the trail."

And oddly, she found she could understand him for once. "I guess I know what you mean." She capped her fizzy water and stuck it in the voluminous side pocket of her long coat, shrugging the coat on. Never waste safe water. "I just had the feeling...I think we would have gotten somewhere tonight. But now we don't have to." She'd report Mr. Russian to the station chief and let him follow through if he wanted.

Because she and Cole would be on the way home.

Together.

Shortly before eight and well after dark, Cole left the phone, tucked away in his pile of rocks, turned on so the GPS would lead the pickup team right to it. He'd found himself a nice little vantage point, a truly excellent alley that the proprietors of both little market booths on either side had turned into additional storage space. It came complete with rickety old metal shelves that definitely looked G.I. surplus, an oddball of an old metal desk and haphazard stacks of produce crates. Plenty of places to hunker out of sight, and he'd already stashed his courier bag.

Though he'd given up hunkering some hours ago, and now sat with his butt on the hard ground, straightening first this leg and then that from his cross-legged position just to keep the blood flowing. Had he been anywhere else he could have found himself a glass of whiskey and a private corner to pour it over his side, but this little edge of Suwan was mostly Muslim and as dry as any eastern Kentucky county.

So instead he waited, feeling the moments tick by as the dull, steady throb of fever invaded, as Aymal was up to who-knew-what with Cole's gun several hours of travel on foot and by bus away. *This better be worth it* moments, because they cost so much in the big picture.

And here came some motorbikes. Suspiciously stealthy, those little road bikes, their engines purring more than putt-putting. They would have made for a crowded ride to the exfiltration transport, but they'd also weave easily through these streets, making steady progress instead of getting jammed up in the tight spots. Not that this particular area had a problem with traffic, unless one counted foot and bike traffic.

For a moment he thought they looked clear, that they'd managed to get here without any parasite problems. But of course he should have kept those thoughts locked away, for moving more slowly came a small produce-carrying vehicle not much different from the Russian Niva he'd recently stolen.

Okay, so the vehicle came from a different direction than the motorbikes. There was plenty of reason for a produce truck to inch along the streets of this area. Two tiny family restaurants, a lawyer's office and the two fresh-food markets between which he'd chosen to camp out...it had reason to be a busy little place, which is exactly why he'd chosen it rather than the residential neighborhood that started just one street over.

But not quite enough reason for such vehicles to be in the same place at the same time as Cole expected his connection to show up. *Tsk,* he mentally admonished the motorbikes. *You were followed.*

The bikes turned down an alley parallel to the one Cole occupied and purred right up to the rock formation, circling it. They stopped long enough to shout a few words at each other, and one of them got off his bike.

He had an unpleasantly familiar form, even in the partial-moon darkness. A silhouette suitable for a B-movie action star.

Betzer. Aka Hammer. Aka the guy who had led the ambush two days earlier.

Well, frog guts on a stick. They weren't followed at all. They were the followers*—and they'd somehow gotten there first.*

As if to emphasize the significance of the situation, the motorbike twins reacted to the sight of the trucklet headlights by mounting up and scooting off—but their superbly tuned, overpowered engines cut suddenly rather than fading, and Cole knew they were still nearby. By then the truck was parked and two men in local dress eased behind the buildings to cast a wider circle in the vague area of the rock formation. Now and then they called out, but not loudly. Surreptitiously, as you'd expect from good spooks.

Cole squelched the impulse to go to them. They were compromised, and he didn't know how, or in how many ways. They were being watched by men who were perfectly capable of picking off the two agents, hauling Cole in to some slimy little HQ for questioning, and then going after Aymal. Or they might just bide their time and hang back, ready to ambush yet another exfiltration.

No, he'd bide *his* own time. Stay hidden. Get back to Aymal and take them to Oguzka where they could dig in and Cole could scare up a little antiseptic and maybe even medical care. A good solid meal or two wouldn't go amiss, either. Maybe he could even blame his wooziness on too many missed meals—though he wasn't sure which was a bigger blow to his ego, going tilty for missing a few meals under trying circumstances or because a damned little nothing of a flesh wound had gone bad. He mustered up his most stoic, John Wayne–sounding voice and muttered to himself, "It's just a damned flesh wound."

So far.

Chapter 12

Selena wore her loose Berzhaani tunic and flowing slacks and had hastily packed the rest of her things into the carry-on the CIA had so thoughtfully prepared for her. Practicality demanded the cargos and a warm shirt, but practicality be damned. Her work here was over, and soon she'd see Cole. There was no need to wear anything other than what she thought would make his eyes smile, crinkling slightly at the corners in a mix of amusement and appreciation.

Dobry took the wait more restlessly than she, checking the laptop for e-mail every five minutes and fitfully staring at the hotel phone as though it might leap up and bite him.

"Are you expecting a call?" Selena finally asked him, her tone making it clear that she meant other than the one they both expected—but that particular call should come in on one of their two cells, not the hotel phone.

She herself had done her wrap-up communicating already, letting both Allori and Delphi know that she was outgoing, and dropping Delphi the scant tidbit her Russian friend had left her with at Agabaji's.

Dobry responded with a blank look, then shook his head. "No," he said. "Just wishing we were done with this." He'd kept his padding and his eyebrows and contacts, having decided to maintain his cover appearance until all was truly said and done. He'd arrived with and briefly worn his own Dobry-face and not drawn any attention, but with Goff now firmly established as Selena's companion, he might well draw notice if he changed back.

"*Done with* would be good," Selena agreed, feeling the twitter in her own stomach. She needed busywork; she thought about going back down to the Plush to see if Betzer had stirred up any information, just for the heck of it. He'd been out when Dobry was there earlier, and Dobry had made himself content to gossip and nurse drinks with a few of the other regulars. Or maybe Dobry knew more about the implications of the Russian's words—

No. Sit. Stay.

Patience.

When her cell phone rang she grabbed for it in the most undignified manner possible. The phone identified the caller—Station Chief TRAMMEL—and she flipped it open. "Do you have him? Them? Where—"

"No." The man's tone was flat and cutting, and stopped Selena short.

She floundered for a response, and then didn't have the chance to make it. TRAMMEL said, "He wasn't there. I don't know what the hell kind of game he's playing…his phone was there, turned on only a few moments before our people got there—and off again just as they arrived. He had plenty of time to make the connection."

"He wasn't..." She couldn't quite finish the question and, as she glanced at Dobry, saw understanding cross his face.

"Not there?" he asked, and she could have sworn she saw hope rising in his features before he shuttered down into anger, cursing in emotional punctuation. Or maybe not, not with her whole world revolving around the angry voice in her ear.

She interrupted it. Not wise, but she did it, driven by sudden comprehension. He'd called for help, and hadn't shown...but his phone was there. He'd done it on purpose. *Because he didn't trust them.*

"It was a test," she told him, nearly blurting the words.

"A test?" The words came rife with unspoken meaning, things like *I hope you're kidding* and *this better be damned good* and *he wasted my resources on a test?*

"Aymal's travel plans have been interrupted twice, and both times the Agency got the raw end of the deal. Why *should* Cole trust that it wouldn't happen again?"

Silence. And then more irritation. "If he'd been there, this would be over. There was no interference this evening."

Whoops, she'd stepped on his Agency pride. So she was careful when she said, "Cole was there. He would have come out if it had been safe."

The silence this time came across as more thoughtful. "I'll debrief my people when they return. If you're right..."

Selena didn't need him to finish the thought. If she was right, then Cole was right. There was leakage somewhere. The station chief had best do more than brief his people...he'd better start looking for a double agent.

And Selena would look for Cole. She was already up, already unzipping her suitcase while Dobry watched, gleaning everything he needed from her reaction to the conversation. "Where?" she asked. "Where were you supposed to meet him?"

And after TRAMMEL told her, she hung up the phone and sank down on the bed, thoughts tumbling around inside her head.

"We're staying?" Dobry demanded, and looked eager for it.

"We're staying," Selena confirmed, absent in tone and her mind hunting the elusive memory that tickled at it. Just north of west, the station chief had told her.

It wouldn't have been where Cole had stashed Aymal. It would have been somewhere within hours, but a position he didn't mind exposing.

Except she had a sudden moment of self-doubt, an inner quailing. *What if I'm wrong about that?*

If she proceeded on those assumptions and she was indeed wrong, she could well search everywhere but where Cole had hidden himself and his human package away.

What if I can't predict him at all?

What if her wants and needs and mixed-up, shell-shocked condition had scrambled her inner sense of things? If she had no sense of self, how could she have a sense of Cole?

Stop it, she told herself, hunting that teeth-baring confidence she needed. And *north of west*. And then, trickling in as though they belonged, her Russian friend's words from earlier in the evening: *Go back to where it all started, American lady*.

He hadn't been talking about Cole. He'd been talking about her. Where *her* story had all started, here in Berzhaan eight months earlier.

"Oguzka," she said to Dobry. "We're going to Oguzka."

* * *

Boy, did he want a drink.

Just water, sweet water...or warm bitter water, or rotten egg-smelly water or...

Okay, maybe not flat-out scummy water.

Cole waited for the Agency operatives to quit poking around, and then he waited for them to move off to the side and call in a report that would no doubt also end up in unfriendly hands. He didn't have to be in earshot to know the content of that report. *No sign of Cole Jones and his human package.*

Yeah, no kidding. Figure it out, people. You weren't alone.

He'd trusted the Agency to be secure. He'd trusted his old buddies to help, not betray. He'd trusted Aymal to clean a stupid little bullet tunnel that shouldn't ever have been more than an annoyance.

Gah. That'd teach him.

He shifted behind his stack of crates. Selena had never mentioned his butt being bony, but to judge by the feel of it against the cold ground after all this time, it most certainly was bony at that.

He'd have to encourage her to do a hands-on examination once he got out of this.

For a few moments he pondered just how he might manage that. He had Aymal stashed in Oguzka—not securely, not yet. And there was a road leading west, heading for the border. If he could round up some transport, his best chance might be to make his own run for that border—a rocky area of low, rugged mountains notorious for the ease with which people moved from one side to the other. Just people living their lives, mostly—visiting relatives, grabbing up the most convenient supplies—but in recent months there had been plenty of leftover

Kemenis straggling away from the government that hunted them.

If he could get that far with Aymal, he could check in with a different station chief, bypassing the leaky communications problem altogether.

Yeah, that's a plan.

His disguise wouldn't last that long…the temporary contacts were on the way out, and sweat had already leached some color from his hair, hidden as most of it was under a sand-colored cotton kufi. A few days out in the sun without sunscreen and his skin would peel away the dye now staining it a light tea-brown.

It wouldn't matter, as long as his old pals weren't on his tail.

His side gave a warning kick of pain, and he put his hand over it. *No, I haven't forgotten you. I'm just ignoring you.*

He realized that the murmur of conversation had stopped, and shifted to peer around the crates, catching only the faintest motion in the darkness to confirm that the Agency guys had left. Yep, he was really on top of things tonight.

New first priority—after returning to Aymal, find a place to sleep. It looked like they'd have a long haul before them, and he'd do neither of them any good if he started out on three days without sleep.

Three days? Well, no fucking wonder he was woozy and stupid. Genius spy guy, that was Cole Jones.

He might have poked his head out then, but he didn't. He waited. The mercs, whoever the hell they were working for, had been interrupted. They might well return. So he waited a little longer, and indeed they came slinking back—without the bikes this time, and with no worries, apparently—not given the thorough way they searched over the area in which he'd left his GPS-enabled phone.

When they stopped to confer, Cole let himself creep closer, barely still under cover. A little turnabout eavesdropping seemed like fair play, all things considered.

"He's gone," said a voice Cole didn't know—a new member of the merc gang. Cole found himself wondering darkly whether this was a replacement for someone who'd dug his feet in over the new arrangement.

The tall one was Betzer, all right—with Betzer's lazy, deceptive voice and Betzer's confident stance, conveyed even as a dark blot in the night. "I doubt it," he said. "But I also doubt that he has Aymal anywhere in the vicinity. This was just Jones being cautious. If he ever intended to show, he meant to take the Agency to Aymal and not the other way around. No...he's here somewhere. Probably watching."

Closer than you think, dirtwad.

The other man made a noise of frustration. "We're running out of time," he said. "We need to get things in place for the capitol building."

The what? Something in Cole jerked to attention, fatigue forgotten. *What about the capitol?*

"You think Hafford'll come through on his end?"

Betzer snorted, a soft sound in the night. He rustled, struck a match, and briefly but clearly illuminated his face as he lit a cigarette.

You always were too quick to declare a situation clear so you could have your damned smoke. But this time, Cole welcomed it. *Advantage, me.*

Betzer inhaled hard enough to turn the end of the cigarette into a hotly glowing ember, then spoke around it. "Hafford will come through. Something's put the fear of... not God, I'd say, but the devil—into him. Have you seen him lately? Looks like he sees a ghost every time he passes a mirror. Whoever's behind the scenes on this one has their stuff together Good thing we went indie when we did."

So Betzer didn't even know who their new contract employer was. But Cole heard the respect in his voice, knew it was no one to take lightly.

And what was this person planning for the capitol? The formerly besieged, newly restored capitol?

"Anyway," Betzer was saying, "it'll be fast and easy to put together. The Kemeni are for sale these days, or hadn't you noticed?"

His companion said drily, "The bastards don't seem hard to find, true enough."

"Anyway," Betzer grunted around the cigarette, "in this case, failure is good enough to be success. Practically all they have to do is get through the door."

They? The door of the capitol? What the hell...was Hafford in on the security renovations for the building? He was a decent guy. Cole couldn't imagine that he'd—

Then again, he hadn't imagined that Betzer would play him, either.

Life lessons suck.

The world chose that moment to swoop around him, and he dropped a hand to the ground to steady his crouch—not soon enough. He brushed a crate, cloth against rough wood.

Betzer wasn't stupid. Cole didn't even have to see the man's change in posture to know he'd hear that faint noise. Cole faded back into the darkness of the alley, intending to come out on the other side and scale the rickety wooden ladder up the side of the building, a roof dodge he'd scoped out when daylight still washed the old stone walls of these buildings.

He hadn't counted on stumbling, or on putting so much effort into breaking his fall in silence, rolling into it with every muscle in control. And that was it, that was his escape time gone with Betzer's cigarette already ground into the dirt behind him and both men coming on.

He scrambled around the end of the desk and dove into the footwell, pulling a basket of smelly old burlap sacks in after him and then tugging the top sacks free to spill over him.

It wasn't terribly clever. It wasn't even terribly convincing. But it was all he had left this moment, this evening, after these past three days.

Which meant whether or not Betzer discovered him depended on his conviction that the faint noise had been a basic random nighttime noise. Rats. Cicadas. *Anything*.

The two men advanced in silence, splashing a pencil-thin beam of light over the ground, the crates, the buildings. Cole caught glimpses of it through the warped desk backing. They eased around the contents of the alley—all to the good, because it meant they didn't want to leave trace of their passage. They found the desk, found the basket…kicked it. It jammed into Cole, smashing up against his side—not much of a blow, but somehow it made his senses reel, made him clamp his jaws just to keep from retching his nonexistent lunch onto his knees.

He lost track of them for a moment, knowing how fatal such a lapse could be and yet powerless to do anything about it. When he could sort out the outside world again, they were nearly on top of him, returning from a fruitless search of the street. They kicked the basket again on the way by, this time out of frustration. An involuntary tear of pain leaked from Cole's eye; he put everything he had into controlling his breathing, turning that gasp into a slow, even—*silent*—exhalation.

"It doesn't matter," said the man who wasn't Betzer. "I

saw that woman of his take down Buzz at the Plush. She'll find Jones if anyone does, and then we'll have them."

"Selena." Betzer snorted. "Now there's a piece of—"

Watch it, Cole snarled silently, his pain momentarily forgotten.

"—work." But there was a leer in his voice all the same. And warning, too. "She'd best watch her step. It's one thing to get lucky...another thing to see action in the big league."

"Yeah? I kinda hope she doesn't watch her step at all. I'd like to take her on, all right."

Sonofa—

Yeah, that's thinking straight. Burst right out of hiding and throw yourself into a fight because of insults and implications at which Selena herself would merely laugh. *Down, Cole.*

And by then they were headed away, off to wherever they'd stashed their bikes. Cole waited, and waited some more. His legs cramped, and once more he gave thanks for his modest stature. As much as he moved like a larger man, he barely topped five-ten, making him of a height with Selena. He'd found it an advantage in tight scrapes like this one, but he still needed to stretch his legs now and then if he wanted them to function when called upon, so eventually he emerged from his dark sanctuary to discover the streets abandoned and the moon halfway to overhead. About ten o'clock, he decided, opting not to give away his position with the LCD flare of his watch face. He retrieved his satchel, made his careful way through the crates, silent this time. Slower, too, he noted. *Excellent. Just what he needed.*

But upon reaching the open ground and then the rock formation, he made an unexpected discovery.

Not that he could call the local station anyway, given the evidence of a leak somewhere along the line. But now that he knew Selena was here, now that simultaneous relief and worry washed through him at the thought that she was hunting for him right *here*, right *now,* he might have chanced a call to her. Even if Betzer's group had a descrambler working the CIA phone frequencies, no biggie—he and Selena could have talked around it. She'd catch on right away; she'd keep up with his hints of eavesdroppers and she'd cover his ass.

He just hadn't counted on the fact that Betzer might take his phone.

Chapter 13

Amazingly, she slept.

For Cole's sake, she slept hard and fast, knowing she couldn't do anything with a middle-of-the-night arrival in Oguzka. But several hours before dawn she rose, carefully folded the silk salwar kameez, and pulled on sand-colored cargos over silk long underwear and a black waffle-weave shirt in a fatigue sweater cut over a snug silk camisole.

She had to hand it to whoever had done the packing…they knew the Berzhaani fall climate. She'd bought a mid-weight jacket to use under her vest but otherwise wore her own clothes. Dobry had been less fortunate—his torso padding and overall beefy build left him few options in this region of small, wiry men. He wore a tunic over his own dark pants and a bulky, shapeless canvas jacket over that. She did find herself appreciating the way the body padding concealed his sleek SIG Sauer, if not the delay he caused by pulling it all together.

For Selena didn't intend to wait for the station chief to get through his debriefing and come to conclusions about whether she was right—that Cole had been there, that they'd had unwelcome lurkers as well. And if she was right about Cole's tactics, and Cole was right that the Agency was compromised…then she couldn't tell the station chief where she was going, either.

She just needed to go there and take care of it herself.

Believe in it. Believe that her jitters and elevated pulse and readiness to *move now* meant something. At the very least, that the gut reactions she'd so recently come to doubt were indeed taking her in the right direction.

For once, Dobry seemed to think so. He was as willing as she to cut loose from the station chief, at least for now.

Of course he is. Less credit to spread around.

She trusted that gut feeling, too. She simply believed that Dobry's motivation would drive him to do the best possible job, and that's all she could ask from him in any event.

They met at the hotel door and assessed each other. Selena had a backpack she'd picked up in the hotel gift shop, one with *Suwan, Berzhaan* embroidered in flowing stylistic script beneath a silhouette of the generic rocky ruins so endemic to the area. The pack held extra magazines for her Beretta, heavy cord, a military first-aid kit—she hadn't forgotten about that blood, oh, no—duct tape, and snack food rifled from the hotel room's pricey little collection. The rest of it she'd packed away in her shapeless coat—the monofilament, the tiny flashlight, her knives…even the leftover bottle of fizzy water. She wore a navy hijab over her shoulders, ready should it become appropriate to cover her hair.

Dobry had his metal case. Big, shiny and conspicuous. Selena opened her mouth to tell him to leave it…and changed her mind. Yes, they needed to move quickly and quietly. But once they reached Cole and Aymal, it might well be best to change everyone's appearance. So she gave him a short nod, and he did the same in return.

Then they went outside and contemplated the ever-present issue of transportation. To buy, rent or steal?

"Stealing leaves a trail for anyone who knows to look," Dobry said as they stood near the entrance of the compact parking garage affiliated with the hotel.

True. But— "I don't think we're going to find any dealerships open at this hour." Though small motorbikes would be perfect, and Selena eyed a pair of them in the special parking corral just inside the garage.

"Rent, then," Dobry said, his voice assertive enough so Selena quit eyeing the bikes long enough to follow his gaze to a stout white car sitting in a No Parking zone. "Put that scarf on."

"You think it's a taxi?" She did as he suggested, although she wasn't as convinced as he. Berzhaani taxis came in two standard colors—yellow and white—and the white ones often had nothing to identify themselves other than their color and size. "This time of night?"

"Probably just dropped off some drunken Western businessman, and hasn't given up on paying customers yet," Dobry said. "And there's only one way to find out. Besides, if it's not a taxi…maybe it's someone willing to sell what they've got."

Nothing to lose. Selena pulled the scarf up and tied it beneath her chin, the conservative look. She gave her coat of many weapons a mental inventory and followed Dobry across the street to the potential taxi.

The driver saw them coming and put aside a magazine he'd been reading by the light of a rare streetlight. His window was cracked, and Dobry leaned over and said in his poorly accented Berzhaani, "Taxi?"

The man grunted and jabbed a thumb at the back door. As Selena settled into the lightly padded back seat next to Dobry and absently shoved the stinky console ashtray closed, the man said, "Airport?"

A reasonable assumption, even sans luggage.

"Ashaga," Selena told him, and waited for the inevitable query about the distance and the cost. But the man was evidently quite willing to let the crazy tourists spend their money however they pleased, and in the middle of the night at that. She could see the faintly puzzled gathering of Dobry's brow; he'd thought they were going to Oguzka.

And so they were. But better to have an actual reason for their quirky tourist whims. Selena patted his arm in a proprietary way. "I've been looking forward to the sunrise over the temple since we got here. And Oguzka is such a quaint little village."

Ugh. She made a good tourist.

But not so much of a tourist that she didn't figure the cab driver for having some English. He glanced at them in the tilted rearview mirror and she instantly looked aside—not quite the behavior of an American woman, but she didn't want to attract anything but a cursory curiosity, and the modest behavior would turn her from exotic to boring same-old, same-old. Dobry looked at her in surprise, as if he hadn't expected such subtlety of her.

Get real. As if managing recalcitrant governments, local informants and building cooperative counterterrorism efforts didn't take people skills.

Or, say...navigation skills. "This isn't the way to

Oguzka," she murmured to Dobry, leaving it up to him to raise the question.

Dobry cleared his throat. "Pardon my interruption," he said, a stock nicety in Berzhaan, "but I notice we're not headed for Ashaga."

"Ashaga?" the man said, looking at them in the rearview mirror with his forehead wrinkled like an old hound's; he didn't slow down. "You said airport."

Okay, maybe there'd been another reason he hadn't questioned them. He just hadn't actually listened to Selena. She should have had Dobry give the directions. Not that she wasn't perfectly capable of bowling her way through such chauvinism when the circumstances were right…but these weren't the right circumstances.

And meanwhile they still headed for the airport.

"Pardon," Dobry said. "We'd like to go to Ashaga."

"Or as close as we can get," Selena murmured, since the temple wasn't actually directly accessible by vehicle.

Dobry turned on a little Western charm. "The ride to Oguzka is long enough—we're not paying for the extra miles!"

"Yes, yes," the driver said, and slowed to take the next turn.

Except that it was a little too soon and a little too slow, and even as Selena caught Dobry's gaze to let him know she thought so, the car door flung open into the darkness, a space filled by the man who leaped in beside her, half on top of her. Braced against Dobry, she tried to shove him right back out—but her big, loose coat caught under the intruder and hampered her.

Dobry went for his pistol, fumbling to reach under his jacket—and then froze, right about the time Selena felt cold metal against her cheek. "All right," she said. "We'll pay for the extra miles. No problem. Really."

And at the same time she was thinking of the effort that had gone into this moment—posting a car outside the hotel, having someone in position—or close enough to it—to join them at this prearranged spot. She wondered...if she and Dobry hadn't walked right up to the taxi, would the driver have brought himself to their attention? Or simply followed them, waiting for the right moment to strike?

She had the feeling these men hadn't left anything to chance. For all she knew they had someone posted inside the hotel, watching the room. Or surveillance outside the room, making Dobry's debugging sweep a moot point.

No, they hadn't left anything to chance...and they weren't about to leave Selena or Dobry any easy openings. Who the hell were they?

"I heard you had an immodest mouth," the newcomer said, prodding her painfully with the muzzle of his gun.

"It's better than a dumb ass," Selena muttered in English.

Dobry overrode her words, a little too loudly. "Take my wallet," he said, gesturing with the hand that had been reaching inside his coat, and his Goff voice held convincing fear. "Take whatever you want."

The newcomer wasn't that easily fooled. "I have no interest in your wallet. Keep your hands where I can see them, if you want your partner to live."

"Really, we're just friends." Selena tried to take in everything at once—their route, the man's weak spots, and any details that might indicate their motives—but she'd lost her sense of direction and her heart had taken up its warp-speed beating, making her fingers tingle and her ears pound.

But Dobry's mouth was right beside her head, and she had no trouble hearing him over her internal distractions. "If this isn't a robbery, what do you want from us?"

"See if you can figure it out," the driver said. "It's not like you haven't been warned, even if you did kill the messenger."

Selena cleared her throat, trying to ignore the gun in her face. "We weren't, actually. Warned. If you're talking about the Kemeni—" been at anyone else's death recently, Selena? "—he never had a chance to say anything."

Her backpack sat at her feet and she fought the impulse to grab it, to lay into him with the first weapon that came to hand. Her words seem to throw the man off his stride, so she ventured, "So it would be only fair that we get a warning, right?" But she figured she was just stalling the inevitable.

When the man gave her a sneer of a grin, she was sure of it. "You should have stayed in your United States. So arrogant, to think you were in Betzer's league."

Crammed into the corner of the narrow back seat, Dobry stiffened; his hand tightened on her arm. "If you've got something going with Betzer, that's not our problem."

And Selena saw a glimmer of opportunity. Grabbed it. "I told you he was trouble," she snapped at Dobry. "We should never have gone to that bar in the first place!" Never mind that it had been her suggestion, making the unfairness of her words reflect in Dobry's astonishment. She didn't give him time to think it through, but roughly shook off his hand. "Now look where you've gotten us!"

One of the oldest tricks in the book, but she hoped their cultural conditioning meant her behavior would take them aback—her volume, her assertiveness, her disrespect…

To drive the last bit home, she twisted as much as she could within her confining coat and slapped Dobry with the hand that had been trapped between herself and their intruder. *Left hand, now free…* Dobry's astonishment turned to shock. *C'mon, c'mon, what do you* think *I'm doing? Get with it!*

And maybe he did, for as the driver slowed to look back at them, driving erratically enough to take up the road, and as the backseat invader shouted an annoyed curse over stupid American women, Dobry grabbed Selena for a quick shake. "You bitch!" he roared, and that gravelly voice filled the car, completing the satisfying chaos. The gun slid down, over her ear—*ow!*—and jammed to a stop in her shoulder just off her neck. Selena let Dobry's rough hands shove her away, gaining just a little room to move.

Enough room to turn, snatching the ashtray from its precarious perch to fling the ashes in the man's eyes. *Taz, on the loose.*

And then she dropped down, crouching in the limited space to reach her backpack, clearing the room for Dobry to wrestle with the gun as the man bellowed in incoherent fury, clawing at his eyes. She dipped a hand into the backpack, closed it around the familiar knife hilt within, and thumbed off the clip sheath. But she withdrew the knife only enough to clear the sheath before driving up right through the backpack, into the man's soft belly all the way to the hilt. Dammit, you should have left us alone.

He was so mad he didn't realize what she'd done, not until the jostling of the car hitting the curb twisted the knife within him. By then the shock of it had weakened his fingers and Dobry had the gun...by then Selena had jerked the knife free and twisted to lay it alongside the driver's neck even as he fought to control the car while he fumbled in the magazines piled beside him.

His own movement drove the blade into his skin; he abruptly stopped hunting for the gun now visible beneath the skewed magazines. And when the man in the backseat—she was almost sitting in his lap by now—snarled his fury and grabbed her from behind, Dobry shoved the gun in his face as Selena snapped to the driver, "Tell your buddy you'll end up dead if this knife slips."

"Stop!" the driver instantly cried, and in that moment the car hit the curb again, hard enough to jar them to a stop—for him to feel the cut of the knife again. "No, no, don't—!"

"Calm down," she told him crossly. "It's only a scratch. And it'll stay that way if you get out of the car. Get your buddy, too."

The driver fumbled for his seat belt, excruciatingly careful to keep his neck still. *"Parvaiz?"* he asked, his voice pitched high.

His partner muttered something angry and unintelligible, clutching his belly. "Wait," Dobry said as the driver reached for the door handle. "Here's your chance to deliver your little warning. Who sent you?"

Silence. Both men froze.

"Look," Dobry said. "I don't care who you're afraid of. If you'd done your homework you would have known this woman was left-handed, and paid more attention. Now you're screwed." He said the last word in English, then looked to Selena.

"Sikim," she offered.

"Sikim," the driver repeated under his breath, in full agreement.

"Your problem," she told him. "Because all we have to do is stall, and your pal probably won't make it." The part of her that hadn't meant to twist the knife winced in guilt. And the rest of her knew she'd been fighting for her life, and had only turned the tables. "You comfortable, Goff? Because I could stay like this for a while." Not at all the truth, not with a cramp already starting in her thigh and her arm about to get unsteady from the awkward angle at which she held the knife.

But it didn't matter, not as long as they believed her.

And the man with blood seeping out of his belly believed her. "Arachne," he said hoarsely, and then cleared his throat to try again. "Arachne."

"Who the hell is Arachne?" Dobry asked, perceiving that the name should have meaning.

As it did to Selena. And it made a certain twisted sense... *Be alert for any references to the code name "A"—now definitely confirmed to stand for Arachne...* And the contractor, Scott Hafford, had been listed in the Spider files. And that first attack in the deserted Suwan street, when she'd barely started the search for Cole.

But there'd been time for someone to observe her meeting with Scott Hafford. To single her out. Single her out, *why*, she wasn't sure. It didn't make sense to react so aggressively after one chance meeting in a public place. Unless her presence had been misconstrued...

"The Kemeni who came after me near Agabaji's," she said, and turned it into a demand with a little more pressure of the knife; she leaned closer to the driver's ear. "Was that about Arachne, too?"

"I don't know," the man mumbled. Selena knocked off his turban to thread her fingers in his hair, pulling his head back and exposing the arch of his neck. Panic fairly radiated from the man. Rock...hard place. She had no sympathy. He cried, "I don't know! Yes! Maybe!"

"...wasting time," said his bleeding partner. "Too many Kemeni with no cause...Arachne probably uses them as she uses us."

"Who," Dobry repeated with annoyance, "is Arachne?"

"Worry about that later." Selena shoved the driver away. He tumbled out the door he'd unlatched and scrambled to his feet even as she rolled over the headrest into the front seat, slamming the front door closed again.

Dobry pushed the man's bleeding companion out onto the sidewalk. Selena didn't wait for him to close the door before she backed the car away from the curb and threw it into gear, making a wild guess at the shift slot for First gear and ending up with Second. She nursed the car through a near-stall and did better with her guess at Third. By then Dobry had managed the very awkward process of climbing into the front seat, haphazardly dumping magazines into the back.

"Here." She handed him the knife. "Mind cleaning that?"

Dobry took it, wiping it against the car seat. "Nice move," he told her.

He might not have said it if he knew how hard her heart pounded, or how badly she needed to take the urge to act out on something. A punching bag, a hard run, a bike sprint from here to there. All her coping mechanisms, out of reach.

But out loud she offered patently false brightness. "And hey, look at this. We needed a car...we've got a car. One trip to Oguzka, coming up."

Hang on, Cole...we're coming.

And as for the school with the target painted on the playground...she could only hope they weren't already too late.

Cole took longer returning to Oguzka than he had leaving it. He chose a circuitous route, hauling his satchel into alleys and doubling back and at times simply sitting and waiting out the moment. The moon slowly passed its zenith and headed west, and he finally hitched a ride on a horse-drawn wagon headed to Oguzka. The driver had his own secrets beneath a heavily tarped load, and Cole didn't pry—not that the language barrier allowed it. He did manage to fumble a few Berzhaani words to indicate he'd like to make a casual visit to a doctor, and that got him a sharper look than he'd previously drawn, one he could just barely see as the moon headed down over the horizon with dawn still several hours away.

But the man gave him a name.

Good.

The darkness suited Cole. Once the sun came up, his true ethnicity would no doubt be obvious enough. He'd given up on the colored contacts somewhere between there and here, and the nose and mustache had both already taken a dive. And while his ethnicity wouldn't be an insurmountable problem, the obvious evidence that he'd tried to hide it…

That was gonna raise some eyebrows.

The man cleared his throat and offered, in a mix of Russian and Berzhaani, that Cole could trust the doctor.

Cole, woozy and exhausted, almost let slip the snort of disbelief.

He'd trusted Betzer to help him out. He'd trusted Aymal to do more than splash alcohol in the general direction of his *It's just a flesh wound, ma'am.* He'd trusted the local station to be secure and reliable. He sure didn't feel like trusting a man he didn't even know.

Not that he had the choice.

Besides, he'd chosen Oguzka for a reason. Not only could he drop Selena's name if the opportunity presented, but the reason they'd been targeted by the Kemeni eight months earlier—aside from the convenient location as a diversion—was specifically because of the village's reputation as pro-Razidae and antiterrorist. They wouldn't quail at the notion of helping two men on the run, not two men who were fighting for freedom in their own way.

Well. As long as they didn't figure out that Aymal was a geek terrorist turncoat.

A mile out from Oguzka, Cole bailed from the wagon,

offering heartfelt thanks as the man sent the horse into a trot and away. Cole jogged down the road in the dusty wake of the wagon, feeling every leaden step in his throbbing side. *Bleed, sucker*, he thought at it. That would at least help clean it out.

At the marketplace he went back into stealth mode. A few tricky moves meant to flush out anyone following him—or somehow waiting for him—and he made his winding way back to Aymal, desperately wishing the farmers had come early to set out their fall produce, that the butcher had his live chickens hanging around and eggs to sell. Even a raw egg—

Right. Salmonella on top of everything else. Good thinking, Jones.

He slipped into the hidey-hole where he'd left Aymal, his first priority to pinpoint the exact location of his Browning and get it out of Aymal's hands. The hint of dawn was all but shadowed out of existence in the stone alcove, but the stench from the public toilets was still very much alive.

Just like Aymal. He must have been sitting there with his eyes popped open in fear all night, for he leaped up to greet Cole with enthusiasm, *loud* enthusiasm. "Where were you?" he demanded, in a tone that would have gone better with *I'm so ecstatically relieved to see you! I must kiss your cheek!* But he limited himself to grabbing Cole by the shoulders and giving him an unfortunately emphatic shake.

Cole growled a warning, a mere grumble of noise in his throat. Aymal froze and backed up a polite step.

"Where," Cole asked, his voice still a growl, "is my gun?"

Aymal's expression in the growing light turned surprised, then abashed. "It's here..." he said, turning this way and that to spot it.

Could be worse. Could be a hastily hidden body secured back here, victim of accidental discharge.

Cole spotted the pistol before Aymal, on the ground in the dirt. His growl returned, and he bent to snatch it up—a strategic mistake he instantly regretted. Instead of straightening he just went down in a crouch, quietly reciting, "Shitshitshitshit," through clenched teeth. But he still managed to pull the gun out of Aymal's reaching grasp, and from there he lowered his knees to the ground until he could get his breath back.

Come to think of it, there was no particular reason to get up right away.

Aymal gave him a moment and then said, "You were gone too long."

"Yeah, tell me about." Cole finally straightened a little. He took a deep breath, let it out slowly. "Good news and bad news." He didn't give Aymal a choice of which he'd like first. "Good news—I made it back here to continue covering your butt. Bad news—the cavalry's not coming right away, Kemo Sabe."

"The cavalry," Aymal repeated blankly.

"The good guys. The white hats. The ones we'd like to haul our asses out of here ASAP." Another deep breath, and he felt some compassion for the dawning comprehension on Aymal's face. "You had to have suspected we were compromised from within the system."

At that, Aymal gave a reluctant nod. "I had wondered. But then what—"

Cole mustered up some devil-may-care. "We're not at a dead end yet. We're in a good place—a place I chose because it *is* a good place—and I think I can arrange for us to hang out here a couple of days with some like-minded people." *If anyone here speaks Russian.*

Hey, it could happen. The Russian occupation of this country had left deep marks, from naming conventions to architecture to language.

"I think we need more than a place to hide," Aymal noted.

"Once you're settled, I'll see about food. That's one damn thing that went right." Not much cash in his pocket, but enough. Berzhaan was a cash-based economy, and Cole hadn't hit the streets without it.

"Not what I was thinking of." Aymal nodded at Cole's side, now fully visible in what had turned into morning. Soon enough there'd be others out and about, ready to spring at the day.

"Yeah, that." Cole looked down, half-expecting to find some exterior sign of the wound he'd never actually seen—something oozing, or bleeding, or maybe just an arrow labeling the spot *ouch*. "Got the name of a doctor. He's right up there on the list of things to do, too." He gave the Browning a quick check, verifying that all the cartridges were still where he'd left them, making sure the magazine was pushed home, and wiping off the dew that remained when he'd done so. He tucked it away inside his abaya and dug his fingers into the crevices of the nearest wall to pull himself to his feet and then to steady himself there. "A-hunting we will go," he said, oozing false cheer. And then he held out his hand, palm up. "But not until I have that paper."

"Paper?"

Definitely not an accomplished liar, his geek terrorist. Cole held his hand steady, waiting. Eventually Aymal fished the folded paper out of his pocket, handing it over with much suspicion, as if he expected Cole to shoot him then and there and make off with the paper. "I left out details."

"Of course you did," Cole said in vast weariness.

"If your people go looking for those details, they'll only alert certain key individuals."

"Of course they will." And when Aymal gave him a look of patent skepticism, Cole shoved the paper deep into his own pocket and said, "I'm not going to dump you, Aymal. That's not what this is about. This is just covering all the bases."

Aymal said, "Of course it is."

"Good one," Cole said. "Smart, snazzy...building on the theme. Now how about we go hunt up a place to hang out for a few days."

And Aymal, after a few more moments of suspicion, nodded. With equal parts wariness and intent, they went out to make themselves at home in Oguzka.

Chapter 14

Selena drove as fast as she could on the long dirt road to Oguzka. It was a decent road and the appropriated car held the ground well enough to allow her some speed. Dawn tinted the sky, illuminating the jagged range of mountains ahead. Oguzka was tucked away between the first collection of ridges.

"Do we have a plan here?" Dobry asked, his first comment in so long that she'd thought him asleep…or perhaps pondering what had happened in Suwan. They'd worked together; they'd actually done well together. They'd survived, hadn't they?

Selena only hoped the stabbed man survived as well. Oh, definitely a hired thug who pretty much deserved what he got…but she wasn't sure it'd had to go down that way. That she couldn't have found another way, but that maybe she'd given in to the shrill edge of panic, going overboard.

Overkill.

But those weren't thoughts she wanted to share with Dobry. Ever. "We do have a plan," she finally answered. "A proposed plan, in any event. I'd like to ditch the car at the edge of town if not a little sooner—I don't think we want to draw the kind of attention this thing will bring us."

He grunted approvingly.

"I've got to go in as me," she said. "Same old, same old—that's how they know me, and that's what I'm trading on." She didn't mention that only two women and a little boy had even seen her, and for all she knew they'd moved elsewhere in the recent months. Even if it had happened, she hoped they'd spoken of her…described her. "I don't see any reason you shouldn't go in as Goff."

"No reason," he agreed. "And if you're right? If we find him here?"

"I'm not sure," she admitted. "The obvious answer is that we call TRAMMEL. But if I'm right that Cole thinks the station is compromised—and Cole's right that it *is*—then that's the last thing we should do."

"I noticed you didn't tell TRAMMEL we were headed this way." But Dobry didn't sound like he disagreed.

"I think we should just wait until we find Cole." Until, not *if*. "Get his perspective before we make any exfiltration decisions. He may have made connections we can use."

"If he can offer anything thoughtful at this point," Dobry shifted in the hard, thinly padded seat beside her. "I hope you haven't forgotten—"

"It wasn't that much blood," Selena said, all quiet determination. "And he set up that test meeting last night, so he's still plenty active." Besides, maybe Aymal *had* been driving. Cole certainly would have preferred to drive, but he might well have been otherwise occupied.

"If there's a problem with the station, then the best thing to do is simply show up there with our packages. Whoever's causing the trouble won't have time to act."

"That's an option," Selena agreed, keeping her voice noncommittal in a way that meant she didn't plan to make any decisions without Cole's participation in the conversation. "We'd still have to stay secure until transportation could be arranged." No doubt another chartered private cargo plane, right through the Suwan airport.

"Sounds like you want to cut the station out of the loop entirely. I'm not sure that's realistic." The habitual disapproval slid back into Dobry's voice, and Selena sighed inwardly. Well, that was Dobry through and through…but he'd handled things well enough so far in spite of the dourness.

"What I want," she said with some asperity, her hands gripping the steering wheel just a little too tightly, "is to talk to Cole about it."

Dobry didn't respond. In fact, he settled back into silence, leaving Selena free to concentrate on the driving. Now that she could see the road better, she'd upped their speed. In some ways the landscape reminded her of the area around Athena. No saguaro cactus, but just as stark. This particular stretch of land looked successful at producing nothing but rocks, but Selena knew how misleading that could be. And once they hit the foothills of the Dyek Mountains, the vegetation would creep up on them. Enough vegetation to farm goats and thinly spread cows, and enough water for subsistence farming.

But still. There were also plenty of rocks, including the substantial formations endemic to this whole region—slabby, chunky sandstones, rounded by age. Some of them loomed close to the road, looking like oversize hitchhikers; others scattered across the flat land as though they'd been crumbled by a giant hand from far above. And slowly, far too slowly, Selena drove past them, bumping over the washboard dirt without heeding it, dodging the occasional pothole that came up on her ever faster as she increased speed in what was now true daylight.

They flashed toward the final rock formation before Oguzka, having rounded the end of one ridge to drive along the base of it before reaching the next. It crossed her mind that this would be a good place to stash the car, only a mile or so away from the village and—if behind the rocks—out of sight of the local travelers. As they reached the rocks, she opened her mouth to say as much to Dobry and never had the chance. A donkey bolted out from behind the sandstone formation, directly into her path.

Selena's query turned to a wordless cry of surprise. Dobry shouted, "*Watch out!*" She hit the clutch and the brake at the same time, wrenching the wheel to the side and knowing the donkey would do as much damage to them as they to it.

The brakes locked with horrifying ease; the car skidded sideways. Selena's stomach lurched as two wheels left the ground and she fought the steering wheel, already knowing it wouldn't be enough. The car teetered another moment, smashing into the donkey with the back quarter before it briefly rode air. Chaos flashed in Selena's field of view, her vision a smear of movement and her ears full of a terrible smash and grind overlaid with the screech of painted metal over sparse, natural gravel right next to her ear. The driver's-side window shattered, peppering her with glass; the seat belt dug into her shoulder and hips and magazines from the back seat scattered throughout the car. And when the world finally spun to a stop, all Selena could think of was the look on that donkey's face. The terror.

But not at them.

Something had scared it onto the road.

Right *then.*

"Dobry!" She fumbled at her seat belt, found it jammed. "Dobry!"

He hung suspended above her in his own seat belt, not moving with any particular urgency but deliberately enough so she knew he wasn't badly hurt. She twisted, hunting her backpack—hunting her knives. Didn't matter which knife, so long as it had an edge. But she couldn't twist wildly enough to see the pack in the litter of the back seat. "We've got to get out of here. This was no accident."

"What do you mean, no—" But apparently he decided not to question her at this exact moment, and realized that her frantic movement had some purpose. He, too, looked in the back—and he stretched an arm far behind her to pull up her pack.

"Excellent," she breathed. "Can you get to your gun?"

"Not while I'm belted." He didn't waste time getting to work on it. "Not an accident because—?"

"That donkey...was timed...and aimed." Her words came in bursts as she came up with a knife and fought for enough seat belt slack to slip the knife beneath.

Dobry hesitated just long enough to be doing a mental replay of what he'd seen before he muttered an explosive, "Fuck!"

Selena finally cut herself free, falling against the door; she thrust the knife up toward Dobry and knew she didn't want to be anywhere near his landing zone—time to scoot. She disentangled her legs from beneath the steering wheel with every intent of ramming her feet against the spider-web windshield, simultaneously twisting to look out the back window. Intact but grimy, it nonetheless showed their two attackers clearly enough. Dressed in Kemeni colors and running crouched, they emerged from behind the rock formation and headed for the car, guns in hand.

She could almost swear she saw the distinctive outline of the faux Lugers that Jonas White had pawned off on the Kemenis as the real deal. And she hoped she was right, for if so their aim was likely to suck little green apples.

"Incoming," she warned Dobry, and flung her coat open to reach her own weapon, twisted and awkward and in no way steady. But she fired out the back windshield anyway, three rapid-fire shots that shattered it and sent the Kemeni skittering away.

But not back to the rock formation, and that meant…

An opening.

Selena scrambled over the headrest, dragging the backpack along—she had the feeling she'd be reloading in short order. The remains of the back window gave way before it; she battered away at the rest of it.

"Where are you…?" Dobry demanded, short of breath as he struggled to free himself.

"Getting a better vantage point," she told him. "They're coming up from the left side of the road, and they've got a perfect target in the gas tank. If I'm right, though, they've got bad Luger knockoffs, and they'll need to be pretty close before they take a shot at it." She shoved away a last section of glass. "I'll try to take care of them—but if I were you I'd knock that window out and take a blind shot now and then, at least until you can get out of here."

"Fuck," he muttered again, less explosively. "You're not leaving me here!"

"I'm not," she agreed, hearing in his stressed voice that he truly wasn't sure of her. "Don't forget, Dobry—I overreact, not run away."

Oddly enough, it seemed to reassure him. "Go overreact, then," he growled, and something tore as he applied her knife to tough fabric.

It's a plan, then. But before she speed-crawled her way out the back, she rolled the door's window down as far as it would go, crouching beneath it with her feet jammed against the transmission hump. A quick look, up and down again, netted her the information that the Kemenis were on their way back again, their body language more confident with the silence from the car. "Bogeys," she told Dobry shortly, and popped up to aim several more shots their way. Without pausing to see how effective she'd been, she dropped to the back window, sliding out to the ground with the back end of the car between her and the Kemenis, though only for a moment. She rose up over the fender and gave them something more to think about—and then had to give them credit. They knew well enough she was firing wildly; they'd done nothing more than increase the firing angle, heading toward the front of the car to put it between them.

Fine by her. In fact, perfect.

Selena sprinted for the base of the rock, slingshotting behind it. Once they realized her intent they took some shots at her, but nothing so much as plucked at her billowing coat and then Dobry's gun joined the fray, a sharper, thinner report.

The area behind the rock formation showed clearly enough that the men had been waiting, but not for any great length of time—only a single pile of donkey crap, not all that many cigarette butts, a shapeless canvas knapsack that looked like ancient military surplus. *They were expecting us...but didn't have a lot of extra time to get into place.* And on the heels of that thought, *If they knew we'd be here, they must suspect Cole is here, too.* Whoever "they" were this time. Arachne's people? Those who had been after Aymal all along? Independent Kemenis, out for revenge against Selena? But knowing could wait. What this moment demanded was an advantage.

Selena jabbed her arms through her backpack straps and eyed the rock formation, assessing it. Two stories tall, steep but not impossibly so. Especially not if she started with speed and never faltered…

She started with speed. She didn't falter. She sprinted upward, running with both hands and feet, leaving a constant trickle of falling stone behind her. She arrived at the top panting but with plenty of bottom left, and the first thing she saw was Dobry struggling to extricate himself from the car, not quite as suited to the gaping hole in the back window as she'd been. She squeezed off a shot to keep the Kemenis wary, and they froze, ducking down to the dirt in positions that only made them a bigger target from this angle.

They hadn't figured it out yet, then.

Good.

Her Cougar's slide had locked back on that last shot and she slipped off her pack to rummage for another magazine, digging her sneakered feet into the slight projections of stone that kept her from sliding right off the back of the pointed formation. Juggling pack and gun, magazine and balance, she swapped out the clip and settled herself in for some more deliberate shooting.

You should have run, she told them, carefully sighting in on the Kemeni whose position most exposed him to her, even as the man took a couple of quick shots at the undercarriage of the car. But the car failed to explode, and Dobry popped free from the other end, tumbling down to roll on the dirt and pick himself up in a crawl that kept the car fully between him and the Kemenis.

Selena aimed one last, resentful thought at the Kemenis. *I had never killed anyone until you stuck yourselves in my life*. Not until the hostage incident, when in the space of one savage day she'd killed enough men to have lost exact count. *Here we go again*. She squeezed the trigger.

Her target cried out in surprise and wobbled on his feet, dropping to his knees with blood blooming in the center of his torso. Not a heart shot—too hard at this distance, and there were plenty of major arteries to hit just below the breastbone.

The man's companion cried out in anger and lost his composure, risking a glance to confirm Selena's position before darting in closer, coming within range to bravely fire a volley of shots at the car. Dobry took the hint; he scrabbled away from the vehicle on all fours, climbing to his feet on the way but never fully straightening. Probably a good thing; it kept his profile low as the car finally exploded, the nearly empty gas tank going up in a ball of black-edged flame. Dobry hit the ground on one side of the car; the Kemeni hit the ground on the other, sprawled in a perfect target.

Selena made sure he wouldn't get up again.

To her astonishment, Dobry ran back toward the car, hesitating at the edge of heat-distorted air until Selena shouted down at him, "Get away from there!"

Even then he hesitated, and she suddenly realized why. She had her backpack, but his case of many disguises was still in the back seat of the car.

"Leave it!" she called to him, and gestured widely to indicate the other side of the car. "Check them out!"

She stayed put as he nodded, warily circling the burning car, a conflagration already waning. She could have come down from her perch…but she didn't. Not until she was certain these men had no lurking backup.

Within moments Dobry stood, holding two weapons up for her benefit. Selena took another few minutes to examine the road in both directions, finding nothing as the sun peeked fully over the eastern horizon, painting stark shadows across the harsh landscape and filling this valley with light.

In one direction, Suwan was no longer visible. They'd come around the point of the foremost ridge to enter the valley. In the other, Oguzka was clearly visible, a cluster of homes, a temple, a handful of merchants and the small, crowded daily marketplace. Ashaga watched over it, spare outlines of rock and shadow weighted by history and portent.

Just a short jog away.

Down below, Dobry waited. Flames still licked around the edges of the car windows, but the violent fire had quickly consumed the vehicle's combustibles and now sullen smoke smudged the sky above it. The donkey lay in a heap near the car, dead. Poor animal. Of the men Selena had shot, one also seemed dead—the first one. Dobry had his foot between the shoulder blades of the second, and he gestured at her impatiently.

She gave her descent a quick assessment and decided for a controlled backward slide on feet and hands, using the backpack to protect her hands as best she could. She ran to Dobry in a near sprint.

"He's got a thick dialect of some sort," Dobry said. He'd removed his foot from the man's back, apparently no longer deeming it necessary. "I can't understand him."

"What have you asked?"

"Who sent him. It would be nice if we could get to the bottom of that particular question. *Arachne* isn't an answer."

Not for you.

Selena crouched to assess the man, lifting the bloody fabric of his shirt to locate the bullet hole—lung shot, if nothing else. His struggle for air seemed to confirm it. He snarled something feeble and rude at her for presuming to touch him, and she ignored it to ask, "You have a phone in that gear of yours?"

After a hesitation, he said, "Radio."

Not something that would do them any more good than their cell phones. When they were ready to risk exposure, they already had a way to do it. She glanced at Dobry. "His gear is behind the rock. We might as well let him call his people once we're on our way."

"You must be kidding." He was definitely peeved at the loss of that case. Like Selena, he'd taken a myriad of scratches and bruises, and his reddened face made her think he'd gotten too close to that fire after all. And were those infamous Goff eyebrows just a tad shorter?

She rested her arms on her thighs, letting her hands dangle—letting the Kemeni see that she still had a gun. "I don't think there's any scenario under which he can get medical care in time. And you know if he's got back up, they're already waiting to hear—if they don't, they're going to come in anyway. There's nothing to lose by offering him a little humanity." She eyed the man, who'd rolled slightly away from her so he could eye her back. "Or at least in dangling it in front of him while we're asking our questions."

"I can get behind that," he agreed with a grumble, and dusted his tunic off as he turned away—an ineffective effort on behalf of the once-white garment.

Selena turned her attention back to their captive, noting the bloody froth at the man's lips, the bluish color of those lips. Not getting enough air, that was for sure. *You started it*, she thought fiercely at him, unable to avoid a pang of guilt.

She'd done what she had to, in the moment she'd had to do it. She made her voice hard as she asked, "Who sent you?"

He stiffened, drawing himself up with an obvious pride. "We sent ourselves."

She hesitated, sensing the truth of those words behind the thick regional accent Dobry had mentioned. *Then you asked the wrong question.* "All right," she said. "Why did you send yourselves?"

"Retribution." He probably would have stood to sing the Kemeni version of the Berzhaani national anthem, had he been able.

"Pretty full of yourself for someone who failed," she noted.

"Do you have a car any longer?" he asked. "Do you have anyone to turn to? Do you think this is the end of it?"

"For you, probably." She still tried to make her voice hard; it didn't quite work. It might have been the barely perceptible waver that actually convinced him. His eyes widened slightly and he wiped at his mouth, noticing the blood for the first time. Probably no time to waste, not with the shallow way he struggled to breathe. "Retribution for what?" But as his mouth opened, she instantly held up a hand. "Not the whole laundry list of the all the reasons I deserve it," she told him. "Just the most recent."

"Stupid bitch," he grunted, and his voice had gotten wet and gurgly. "For the killing in the street two nights ago."

"That's hardly fair." Selena stood, looking down on him. She glanced over to see Dobry on his way back. She wanted to wrap this up before he got here—before he heard enough to wonder about Arachne. "I didn't even kill him. Not that he didn't deserve it."

He tried to spit at her but ended up with bloody drool on his chin.

"If you can't breathe, you can't spit," she told him. "Did Arachne send you?"

He swiped ineffectively at his chin. "No. We work for no one. We uphold the goals of the Kemeni—you're wrong to think us scattered. We're as powerful as we've ever been, and soon you'll know that for truth."

"Posturing's just not effective when you lose *and* you're dying." She stepped back, angling her body to include Dobry in the conversation. "Here's my partner, and he's got your radio. The radio on which we'll let you call your buddies, and maybe you won't die after all. Either way, I'd say it's going to be a close thing, so if I were you I wouldn't waste any more time. Quit making me ask questions and put it together for us."

"We don't work with them," the Kemeni said, his voice even thicker. "But we know of them. You told the driver of the taxi that you wanted the car to go to Oguzka. He contacted me. And we came for you, of our own intent. Because you killed one of ours…and because you killed Ashuerbeyli."

She hadn't done that, either. She might have, given the chance—the intense, charismatic terrorist leader had certainly earned it—but she hadn't had that chance. She didn't bother to correct him; he wouldn't believe her. "Nothing worse than a sore loser," she muttered to herself, stepping back from the man so she could cover him while Dobry dug into the lumpy old pack and came up with a very spiffy new radio. Satellite radio at that. *Impressive, for a member of a dead organization.* There was indeed someone new behind them, she'd bet on it. *Delphi needs to know it…* To Dobry, she said, "I think this was a little revenge action for the Kemeni who died the other night. Just to confuse things."

"Did a hell of a job of that," Dobry grumbled. "The inside of that suitcase is probably slag. But I want it anyway. "

"Then go see if you can pull it out of there," she told him. "We won't be alone for long, and we've got another mile to go before we have any chance of hiding from this guy's pals."

"Might gain us a few minutes if we don't give him the radio." Dobry's short, harsh words came of concern more than anything else, she thought—and besides, he hadn't actually handed over the radio yet, even though the Kemeni lifted an unsteady hand for it.

"Yeah," she agreed. "But he won't get it until we're good to go." She wasn't even sure the man could complete the call. She checked the pack for weapons as Dobry headed for the car, dancing with the heat for a few long moments before he pulled off his coat, wrapped his hand and arm in it, and ducked his head away as he dove for the case.

He emerged with it, but Selena wouldn't call it any kind of triumph. Misshapen, melted...she couldn't imagine anything inside had actually survived. She gave the Kemeni his pack, including the radio but minus the extra faux Luger that had been stashed within. Then she shrugged her own backpack into place, walking briskly down the road to meet Dobry. Her knee ached in a way she hadn't noticed until now, and her face stung in a dozen pinpoints of ouch. Minor annoyances, unlike the dying man behind her. She looked back one more time, hesitating to leave any man to die alone.

But no. They had to get away from here...and they had to find Cole before someone else, drawn by their very presence, beat them to it.

Dobry hefted the case, his hand still wrapped. "Too much evidence of our affiliation," he said, and she had to admit to herself that she hadn't even thought of it. Too caught up in the conflict...in the results of the conflict.

But she just nodded at him, glancing back one last time—

this time at the car. "Well," she said, "we were going to ditch it right around here anyway."

To her surprise, Dobry snorted in amusement. And when she picked up a brisk jog, he matched her pace. Running to Oguzka.

Running, she hoped, to Cole.

And to the man who could save schoolchildren.

But not for long. Because they'd only gone a matter of paces when Selena heard that for which she'd been listening all along—the high-pitched whine of a jeep engine under stress. Too soon, too close to have been the results from a man who had probably died with his hand around the still-closed radio. Already on the way—probably since one of the dead failed to answer a crucial call.

Dammit, sometimes it's not good *to be right.* She exchanged a look with Dobry, saw from his expression that he'd heard, that he'd come to the same conclusion.

They ran.

Chapter 15

Cole jerked awake in complete disorientation. "*What*?"

Maybe someone answered; maybe not. Cole floundered, wrapped around the pain that radiated up his back and squeezed out a grunt of a curse. By the time he opened his watering eyes again, he pretty much had it. *Oguzka. Doctor's digs. Hard little bed. Stupid little wound. Aymal.*

And when he did open his eyes, Aymal said calmly, "We're at the doctor's home. He's out treating someone else. You fell asleep. And you look like dung, and should eat something."

"I'm fine," Cole said, because he didn't want to think about the consequences of not being fine.

Aymal glanced at him. "Good," he said, one eyebrow raised as if to say *how stupid do you think I am*. He scooped up a bite of a rice-and-meat dish in a piece of flatbread. "Then join me in this meal the doctor's wife has so graciously provided us."

Cole eased up from the bed and over to the small table at which Aymal sat, never quite straightening all the way. "She speak Russian?"

"She appears to understand some of it. She is a modest woman, and has not emerged from the next room. Her young son brought the food to this table."

Cole took in the room for the first time. It was barely big enough for the table and the bed and a few wicker storage drawers, though herbs hung from the ceiling and a shelf lined the walls above window level, crammed with jars of medicinal this and herbal that.

"It's a start," he said. "We just need to find someone who knows a good place to hunker down when we're done here."

"Eat," Aymal said, and pushed the plate to the middle of the table, passing Cole a piece of flatbread. Cole tore it in half and contemplated the food, gone beyond the simple pain to hot and queasy. The bread shook in his grip. He scowled at it and scooped up some of the rice and meat, and then could only bring himself to look at it for a moment.

"It's lamb," Aymal volunteered. "Very tasty indeed." He took a tiny spoon from the plate and dipped it into a sauce cup, letting the contents drip over his food. "If you aren't feeling so well, perhaps I should take custody of the—" and he gave a meaningful wag of his eyebrows and the faintest tip of his head to the next room where the woman of the house could overhear them.

Cole straightened, narrowing his eyes. "That's staying with me." That was the last thing they needed, Aymal with the gun inside some innocent family's house.

"Good. Then eat."

Cole made a snarly face at the man and took a bite of the laden flatbread. "You're right," he said. "This is excel-lent." In truth it was as leaden in his stomach as he'd imagined it would be, but he couldn't blame that on the cook...and she was listening.

After a few moments and several more forced bites, the boy came into the room. "My father is away," he said, slowly and distinctly and obviously operating under the assumption that they would understand more Berzhaani than they spoke. Not a bad assumption in this area, actually. "Until he comes back, my mother asks me to ease you. I have a tea."

And be dulled by whatever painkillers were in the thing? Herbs...just because they were natural didn't mean they weren't strong. Could be laudenum in that cup for all he knew. Cole shook his head, firmly—and then had to swallow hard when those bites of food tried to reappear. That would just make Aymal's meal complete, he was sure.

The boy was no fool...and not dealing with his first fugitive. Perhaps not even his first fugitive with tea-brown skin and bright blue eyes.

Then again, this area's penchant for resistance activity was the very reason he'd come.

"For the fever," the boy said. "You will stay awake."

Cole took a long look in those wise dark eyes and decided that if the boy was that good at lying and was working against them, they were sunk in any event. He took the tea with thanks.

He hoped it would stay down easier than the food.

"My mother, she also asks me to—" and here Cole's ability to understand broke down. He looked to Aymal, who shrugged. With infinite patience, the boy retrieved a jar from one of the wicker drawers, and showed it to Cole. It appeared to be bag balm. For cows. "This is most excellent for the wound gone bad. Only until my father returns with proper full treatment."

The wound gone bad. Even the kid knew it. Had he even looked? Cole twisted to peer at the spot—still couldn't see it—and to give a little sniff. Not quite that bad yet. The kid saw him, though, and grinned. "A little," he said, and gestured for Cole to move to the bed.

"Jeez, how old are you, kid?" This in English, just slipping out. "You sure you want to do this?"

"I can—" Aymal started, but Cole shot him a look that said *I probably wouldn't be in this fix if you'd done it right the first time* and eyed the distance between the table and the bed. Surely he could make that step or two without falling on his face.

He'd damned well better. If the infection got into his blood, then he'd be in trouble. Real trouble. Sepsis. Organ damage. No field kidney transplants here in Oguzka.

If. Very good at denial when he wanted to be, Cole was. Believing he could do the impossible sometimes allowed him to go out and damned well do it.

"Sir?"

The look on the boy's face told Cole this wasn't the first time he'd tried to get Cole's attention in the past moments. Dammit. "Okay, kid, I'm moving. The bed. Me. Moving."

Aymal snorted, and Cole figured he knew at least that much English.

In the adjoining room, conversation broke out; Cole figured someone had arrived and he didn't give it much thought until the voices—both female—rose in tension and emphasis. The kid, too, knew there was something wrong. He shoved the jar into Cole's hand and ran into the other room. In his wake, Aymal stood, gathering his things around him and tossing Cole his abaya.

Cole didn't move fast enough to catch the heavy robe;

it landed half on his shoulder and hung there. "You understand them?"

"No," Aymal said shortly. "But I know well enough to get ready to move when I hear voices in such discussion."

In spite of himself, Cole grinned. Not totally inept, his defector terrorist. In slow motion, Cole shrugged on the robe, finally standing to straighten it all out. Aymal ducked beneath the table and came up with Cole's satchel, handing it over with an expression that said *see, I had the gun anyway*. Just in time for the kid to turn around and run the few steps back into the room, speaking so quickly neither of the men had a chance to decipher his Berzhaani words.

"Whoa," Cole told him, in Russian this time. He put a hand on the kid's shoulder, gave it a little squeeze. "Slowly, yes?"

"Big *something* on the road," the kid said, and seeing the incomprehension on both men's faces, flung his arms out wide and said, "Boom!"

"An explosion?" Cole exchanged a glance with Aymal. "No kidding."

It might have nothing to do with their presence at all.

And then again, it might.

Either way, this family was smart to make sure Cole and his defector were well away from their house before whoever had caused that explosion, whyever they'd caused that explosion, got anywhere near.

"Hide!" the kid exhorted them, gesturing emphatically. *Follow me* and *hurry up!* all in one. He scooped up the salve Cole had placed on the table and thrust it back into Cole's hand, then gave his arm a tug that had no concern whatsoever for the way it pulled on Cole's back.

Well. Priorities, he supposed. Couldn't say as he faulted the kid's. With effort, Cole got the jar into his courier bag and courier bag over his shoulder—and then was surprised to find Aymal there, ready to prop him up. He got cranky fast. "I'm fine," he said, in English, then repeated it in Russian. "Just go."

Aymal looked as convinced as he ever did, but gestured for the kid to move on, following him out of the room and taking a sharp turn to a back door, never impinging on the family's personal space. Cole lurched after them, but after a couple of steps got his stride and by the time he emerged into daylight, felt steady enough. Sleep, food, tea…see? All is well.

As long as they didn't slow down and check the momentum he'd built up. That could be bad.

He needn't have worried about it. The boy chivied them along as fast as they could go, and for Cole that was a stumbling jog that took them behind and between blurry houses and blurry, surprised people and over to the other edge of town. Before he knew it he looked up the rock-strewn path of a steep hill, and only then did he realize, his thinking muffled, that they were headed for the old temple.

Not so abandoned after all?

The boy looked back at them—it seemed he was halfway up the hill already, spry and ready to sprint to the top. "Hurry!" he shouted. "Boom!"

Right. Boom.

Of course, if the guys who'd made the *boom* had cars, the kid was right. Hurry it was.

Then again, maybe the *boom* was good. Selena was here; she'd have her ear to the ground. The *boom* would tell her *look at me* and she wouldn't miss the significance of the location.

Yeah. Except for this hill, the *boom* was good.

His own breath sounded harsh in his ears, and he'd lost track of his feet. When he stumbled on a rock—since his eyes weren't doing him too much good either—Aymal caught his arm and hauled him back up, tucking his shoulder beneath. "I'm fine," Cole said. "Really."

Aymal acted as though he hadn't heard, and then somehow they were at the crest of the hill—or as far up as they'd have to go, for they'd come upon a shallow bench in the side of the mountain, and upon the temple—rocks and walls and nooks and crannies and the stone enclosure for the eternal flame that no doubt deserved more respect and reverence than Cole had to give it just now.

The boy ran on, looking over his shoulder, his feet too nimble to falter despite the uneven ground. "Over here!" he said. "You can hide—" But he seemed to realize that the shouting was counterproductive to the hiding, and cut himself off, waving at them emphatically.

At that moment, Cole was quite certain that the image of this child endlessly urging them onward would become a staple of his nightmares. "Coming," he muttered to himself, wasting precious breath. Past the imposing remains of the temple they went, past the oval, exposed interior lined with tiny underground pilgrim cells, past square pillars that weren't holding anything up and maybe never had. Past the temple itself completely, and around a small point of rock to what could only be called the other side.

"Here!" the boy said proudly, stopping before yet another pile of rock. Cole stopped when Aymal stopped, regaining his own balance well enough to move away and stand on his own, not certain what it was that had made the boy so triumphant. He exchanged a wary glance with Aymal, who returned it in kind, and finally gave the kid an "eh?" expression.

Pride turned to frustration. "Here!" And he disappeared.

Cole blinked, and straightened in offense. "I'm not that bad off," he said, and meant to say it in English so Aymal wouldn't understand, but the words were out of his mouth in Russian before he knew it.

And Aymal just gave him one of those looks and said, "There must be a cave."

Of course. A cave. Aymal would know about those, what with the whole terrorist hideout thing. The kid popped back into view, and this time they needed no urging. As they rounded the final few feet, the slash of the cave opening became obvious.

As did its regular use. It had all the basics—pallets, a stash of pilfered MREs, a few tattered paperback books, a kerosene lantern and fuel can…home sweet home. Even a bucket off to the side.

Way off to the side.

And Aymal was talking to the kid, a voice that seemed farther away than it ought to. Exhortations to keep quiet about their presence here should anyone come looking—

Not counting Selena!

And beyond that, quick words about Aymal's worth, how he could help the Berzhaani people—

Say again? The Berzhaani people? What was that about?

How he had information that was important to them, could keep the Kemeni from making one last final, violent statement—

The Kemeni? The Kemeni were dissolved, broken by Selena's defiance at the capitol. A defiance Cole wished he could muster now, with the cave going fuzzy around him and Aymal's words lingering in his ear. His heart hadn't settled from the dash up the hill; his breathing still came hard. Maybe some more sleep was in order after all. Yeah, that would do it.

Aymal's voice rose. "Tell your people I can save the capitol!"

What? The *capitol? Again*?

But they were Cole's last thoughts before the world went gray to black with only the faintest awareness that the hard rocky floor of the cave had come up to slap him hard.

Chapter 16

For once, Dobry's dour voice perfectly suited the occasion. "This certainly turned out well."

Selena kept her hands away from her pockets, not quite reaching *raise 'em high* altitude. The generous number of gun muzzles pointed their direction trapped her gaze and didn't quite let her look to the people beyond. She risked a glance over her shoulder, slowing her ragged breathing by sheer force of will. Inside she raged for freedom, wanting to strike and fight and even lose rather than stand here unresisting.

The tiny jeep-thing that had chased them the last quarter mile to the village had turned around, leaving a dust trail behind.

She cleared her throat, resisting the urge to spit out the crud at the back of her throat, dust and thick saliva left over from the chain of events. *Car crash, explosion, gunfight...*

and the unexpected foot chase at the end of it all, with the jeep-thing coming up behind them fast and mean, the village within reach…

The men in the jeep-thing had known better than to encroach upon the village so directly.

And the village had known better than to let two strangers under pursuit enter unchallenged.

"There's a good side to this," she said, back to back with Dobry, her backpack taking up the space in between. "The village is still strong. Reports of its role in squashing the Kemeni during that distraction attack before the Kemeni took the capitol last year—"

"I read it." Dobry cut her off, his voice as close to snappish as she'd heard it. "I'm not seeing how it does us any good at this particular moment."

To Selena it couldn't have been any clearer. "It means if I'm right and Cole did come here, they didn't just hand him over to whoever might've come along looking for him." Was it her imagination, or had those guns moved in closer, hemming them in like two wild animals, a crowd of faces and loose clothing and robes blending together beyond?

Dobry stiffened, alerting her. A man's voice rose above the general chatter of the well-armed welcoming committee. The arrival of someone new, someone commanding. "Who are they?"

"Who knows?" a man responded. "They speak English. And they haven't shut up since they got here."

"They also speak Berzhaani," Selena said, her voice calm in spite of her inner turmoil.

The new arrival pushed to the front, fully visible. "There," he said, as dry as this harsh land around them. Most definitely someone in charge. Probably the village magistrate. "They also speak Berzhaani. Blessed are we to have such enlightened visitors, bringing their violence to our homes."

A leader with a dark sense of humor. Great. Selena offered, as humbly as possible, "That was an...unexpected development."

"Does the man not speak our language as well?"

A leader steeped in his testosterone-centric culture with a dark sense of humor. Even better.

Dobry shocked her then. "Not with skill," he said, meaning, as far as Selena knew, barely at all. "And this woman is the one who knows your people. Who has saved your homes in the past."

The pause was excruciating, long enough for the people surrounding them to drop back slightly, guns now pointing at the ground, and for the magistrate to walk deliberately around Dobry to examine Selena. An older man with a full, gray-shot beard, his hair hidden under a turban, flowing white-and-blue-striped clothing worn with as much dignity as the most formal dress. He looked her up and down, and Selena winced inwardly. Her hair was exposed, the hajib slanted across her shoulders. Her long coat was battered, her face stiff with a dozen cuts, the blood dried and crusted. Just as well he couldn't see how many weapons she carried, or that the Cougar was well within reach, inside her coat pocket.

When he finished his examination, the man let the moment stand a little longer. Then he said, so mildly, "Is that so?"

Selena suddenly realized that this man would not hesitate to order their deaths if he truly thought they were a threat. Their own intentions wouldn't matter, only the potential dangers from their presence. Ruthless in the defense of his people...and probably a lesson hard learned. She bit her lip—not so much from nerves as from the effort to hold back her words until she thought she had the right ones. She kept her gaze carefully just south of center from his own, not challenging him, and waited for the slight nod he eventually gave her. "I was here this past winter," she said. "I was visiting the temple. I called for help when the Kemeni attacked."

"There was a woman here," he agreed. "We are quite grateful to her. We would look amiss at anyone trying to gain favors with her name."

"You don't even *know* her name," Selena grumbled.

That made him narrow his eyes, ever so slightly. "We do. We know she is Selena Jones—"

"Selena *Shaw* Jones." Selena let her cranky tone come through, not sure they had much to lose. Dobry nudged her. He stood beside her now, facing this man who held the key to their next moments.

The man didn't bother to acknowledge either of them. Selena knew his type—strong, decisive, the very glue holding his small village together. She'd dealt with many of just that nature in her legate work. Unfortunately, he hadn't been one of them. He said, "We know she was of the American FBI. We know she worked here against terrorism." Then he smiled. "What we *don't* know," he said, "is who *you* are."

She opened her mouth.

Closed it again.

Eyed Dobry and found him eyeing her back.

Because of course they didn't have papers on them. Dobry might well be able to prove he was Kenneth Goff, but not Steven Dobry, CIA, working against the terrorists thank you very much. And Selena…

She'd simply not gotten used to a mind-set where, while in a country she'd worked officially as a legate, she'd have to prove her true identity to anyone. She'd rushed out of that hotel room thinking only of finding Cole, certain they were closing in. She had only the most cursory of ID. Nothing that would convince this man. Damn, didn't they have television here?

Out of the corner of his mouth, Dobry said, "Don't tell me—"

"No," she said. "I don't." After a moment of silence all around, she said to him, "Just shut up, okay?"

"No problem," he told her, all his dourness set to *full*. "Words fail me."

Had he been even a whit less dignified, the man before them might have rolled his eyes. He pointed to a big rock at the edge of the village, looking no more significant than any other rock in this landscape where they were so generous. "There is the bus stop. There should be a bus here around midday." He glanced over his shoulder at the crowd. "Today is bus day, yes? Or is it tomorrow?"

A dozen murmurs came in return, assuring him this was the day.

"But your village has a reputation for resisting those troublemakers—for providing sanctuary to those hiding from such men." Selena mustered patience, trying to wrap her brain around the magistrate's unexpected response. Oguzka hadn't been known for its refusal to offer sanctuary.

Then again, Selena had changed in the intervening months. Maybe the village had, too.

The man seemed to think so. As their magistrate, he probably had a lot more schooling and wordly experience than he was letting on. His demeanor had turned almost offhand by the time he said, "We've filled our quota for the day. You may wait for the bus there, or you may start walking."

With the Kemeni gathering to have their revenge? It would

be a short, hard walk. Those Kemeni...they were a development she hadn't counted on. Her presence seemed to have galvanized them right out of retirement and into action.

Dobry nudged her. "Your hijab has fallen," he reminded her, and it was his way of reestablishing his dominance in the eyes of these people—and of restoring the respect she showed for their culture when she wore it. She hastily regathered her hair into a ponytail, snatching up the rebellious stray locks from the side of her face. By the time she'd settled the featherweight cotton scarf into place, the magistrate had turned to a quiet, serious conversation with several of the men—grim men, handling their SKS rifles with easy familiarity, who split up and headed out of the village with obvious intent to make sure the Kemeni in his little mini-jeep didn't return.

The others from the crowd were drifting away, throwing the occasional frown back toward Selena and Dobry. Two men remained behind, pointedly waiting for the interlopers to move to the bus "station." They didn't appear to be armed, but Selena wasn't making any assumptions.

Besides, they didn't need to be armed. Neither Selena nor Dobry had any welcome to wear out in this place. She watched a boy darting between the stone buildings of the town's edge and sighed. All those months ago, she had saved an Oguzka boy not that much older than he.

Dobry sat cross-legged by the stones and set the aluminum suitcase before him, examining the warped latches and then, with effort, getting them open. Selena didn't ask what he'd do if they didn't close again. Beg of her some duct tape, no doubt. She let her pack thump to the ground with a puff of gritty dust.

"Any ideas?" Dobry said, and his voice was studiously neutral. He'd pulled his cell phone out and set it by the briefcase, as though it might inspire him. It drew his attention often as he examined the melted, hardened contents of the case. The rubbery face-molding material, especially, had been first activated by the heat and then set by it, forever cast in amorphous nonsense globs.

"Thanks for that," Selena said, meaning the lack of blame in his tone. Dammit, this whole Agency thing was supposed to be about staying undercover, not providing her own identity; she just hadn't thought—

He seemed to understand what she meant; he only shrugged slightly in acknowledgment before scowling at a cake of useless skin dye. She sighed and added, "And no, not at the moment. They're antsy about something, which makes me think there's been activity in the area before we got here. What it has to do with us, I don't know."

"Maybe they've had their quota of *activity*, too." Dobry pushed aside a jumbled mass of melted synthetic hair with one thick finger. "It's still early morning—sounds like we've got time before the bus gets here." He left the ruined supplies for a moment, to contemplate his cell phone.

Making a decision, Selena would have said. About calling the station for a ride? They already knew communications might not be secure...best to take the bus, or to call Allori's office and have Bonita send someone out. Otherwise, the way the Suwan buses ran, they'd have plenty of time to wait. Time enough to get thirsty, with all their water boiled off back in the car. She felt in her coat, and her hands found the familiar shape of the fizzy-water bottle. Not enough to last them...but something she could ask to have refilled, even if with kvass.

Time enough for the day to get warm, too, a beautiful clear fall day that made her long for a drive in the North American country in the Adirondacks, changing leaves on all sides. She slipped the coat off, aware that her cargos and fatigue-style shirt weren't nearly loose enough to suit the Oguzka sensibility.

And then Dobry's words struck her, the sense of them hitting home—the way he'd been playing on the magistrate's pronouncement—*we've filled our quota for the day.*

The unwitting implication that there had been others.

Cole.

"It's Cole!" she said to Dobry, startling him with her sudden vehemence.

He looked up with an expression that was already skeptical. "*What's* Cole?"

"Cole and Aymal—their quota! I said they were antsy—maybe they *do* have good reason. Cole and Aymal are here—*now*."

"You know," Dobry mentioned, so casually she knew it was going to be a hit, "your belief that he was here in the first place was based on nothing more than gut feeling. You're just piling gut feeling on top of gut feeling. I have to say it...I'm getting indigestion."

Yeah, a hit. "And just when we were working so well together," Selena said, and sighed dramatically. "Then again, that's why they sent me, isn't it? Because I'm the one most likely to track him down on a *gut feeling?*"

Dour turned to sour. "And look where it's gotten us."

"We're not done yet," she told him grimly. She looked over the town—small stone houses set close together in the oldest parts of the town and straggling near the edges; the marketplace, just within view at the other end of this short main street. People pretending to be busy between here and there, but still casting surreptitious looks at the rejected visitors. People who might listen, if they had a chance. Might believe her, if they were even allowed to hear her.

With a few long strides, she defied gravity right up the side of the bus stop rock formation. Only four feet up, this one…but enough to make her impossible to miss. She stood a long, defiant moment—long enough for Dobry to scramble to his feet and back slightly away, probably desperately wishing for a shirt that said *I'm* so *not with Stupid.*

Tough luck for him. Cole and Aymal were here, and Selena wasn't going fail them. Maybe Dobry was right; maybe her nerves were too permanently stirred up for her to work in the field. Didn't matter…she hadn't expected to. But she'd been given this one chance…this one crucial, important job. And if she failed, it wouldn't be because she had meekly walked away.

"My name is Selena Shaw Jones!" she shouted. "I'm looking for Cole Jones!"

And oh, she was getting attention, all right. A small group of women off to the side, a gaggle of pointing and giggling children, and there, down the main street, two men coming toward her with much purpose in their strides. "He's my husband! We're working for the same thing—a world safe from terrorists! Go ask him yourself!" Damn, those men were moving fast. Salwar kameeze and turbans, dignity and flowing cloth—very much beyond intimidating. "My name is Selena Shaw Jones—" still loud, but not quite the need to shout "—and I'm looking for Cole Jones! I'm his wife! Go ask him! Ask him if he wants to talk to me—"

"Good God, Selena." Dobry backed another step. "They'll never let us just walk away after this."

She turned on him, her balance absolute at the top of the rock. "I don't *want* to walk away, Dobry. He's *here*, and we gain nothing by leaving!"

"The chance to try again," he said pointedly.

"You think TRAMMEL will give us that opportunity?"

She glared down at him. "Well, a hearty *go team* for you—because I sure as hell don't." The men were closing in, annoyed and already gesturing at her to get down from the rock. "My name is Selena Shaw Jones—tell him that! Tell him *Shaw* Jones!" He'd know it was no ruse, not with that emphasis.

The men were there, right *there*—they could have yanked her feet out from under her if they wanted—but they weren't quite ready to do that yet. Not a cruel people, these Oguzkans…just stubborn. They'd had to be, to keep so much independence.

Selena was stubborn, too. She'd had to be, to survive at Tafiq Ashurbeyli's hands. The look she gave the two men was a dare—*I dare you to believe me. I dare you to do ask him.*

"I know he's here somewhere," she told them, her voice quiet and a little harsh after the shouting.

"Come down," one of them said, and gestured at her peremptorily.

"I'm right where I was told to be." She crossed her arms. "And if you don't make ultimatums, you won't be embarrassed when they don't work. An early lesson in diplomacy. I share it with you freely."

"Selena…" Dobry had gone beyond annoyed and into distinctly uneasy.

She lifted her head, looking out on the women who gathered around the edges of the buildings. "My name is Selena Shaw Jones! Cole Jones is my husband! He's hurt, and my place is at his side!"

One of the men reached for her ankle; she sidestepped him, but not by much. She could have stomped his hand…didn't. This would only work so long as she didn't draw blood. "My name is Selena Shaw Jones! Last winter

I shot two Kemenis here—I fought the Kemenis at the capitol! I'm *on your side*, and *I want to see my husband*!"

At that they did grab her. One man wrapped his arms around her calves and pulled her off balance; another yank toppled her. And of all the things she could have done in response—*a kick in the throat, a jab to the eye, a fist to the nose with all her falling weight behind it, a twist to freedom*—she did none of them.

The second man caught her—like Cole, not a big man, but wiry and strong. He had no trouble taking her weight, or in bouncing her to a more secure position. "You," he said, "will wait for the bus in a quieter place."

But she wasn't there yet, was she? "My name is Selena Shaw Jones!" She ignored the man's wince as she shouted into his ear. "I'm looking for my husband. He's here and he's hurt—my place is by his side!"

The man gave her a shake. She contrived to wiggle at just the right moment and tipped right out of his arms, barely putting enough spin into her movement to roll upon landing. *Oof.* She needed more padding on her ass if she was going to be landing on it.

Though the men reached for her, she scrambled to her feet and right back up on the rock, right past Dobry's muttered dismay. She had perhaps a few seconds—less to judge by the men's thunderous expressions. "My name is Selena Shaw Jones! I'm looking for my husband—"

That was it, and they wouldn't be as careful this time—hands closed on her ankles—

"I know her!"

A child's voice. A young boy. Eight months older than he'd been when she'd sent him to hide at the ruins of Ashaga—when she'd stormed their house and saved his mother and aunt—but no less the recognizable for it. And behind him, a woman in a chador, her hands on those young shoulders, gripping a little more tightly than was probably comfortable. Her voice was low and melodious, and she said, "I know this woman. She tells the truth. She saved my family."

Hands released her ankles. Selena grinned down at Dobry, who didn't grin back, and then she turned back to the woman, nodding respectfully, gratefully. To the man, she said, "Now…take me to my husband."

Take me to Cole.

Chapter 17

This can't be good. Body sluggish, joints aching, side on fire and no doubt in Cole's mind that he'd had his little nap now and it was time to get up and assess things because…

Okay, there was a problem of some sort. Danger. He was sure of it. And more than that, the urgency to…

Well, to do…

Something.

Just what seemed worth some thought.

Deep thought, in spite of outward things that might otherwise catch his attention. Voices. The smell of food. Of smoke. A personal scent so beguiling, so familiar, that Cole took a deep, sudden breath in spite of himself. Enough to trigger a sharp spike of *dammit that hurts* and jar him right out of that profoundly deep thought of his.

When he opened bleary eyes to diffuse daylight, he found Selena. Face smudged with dried blood, rich, dark hair straggling from its ponytail and the lightweight hijab all but slipped off the back of her head, expression...

Expression fiercely worried.

He didn't stop to consider the improbability of her presence here, or to ponder the depth of his reaction—the surge of utter relief, the physical ripple of it through his body. He reached out, cupping his hands behind her head to pull her down to his mouth. And though he saw her startled expression on the way down, she met his kiss with one equally hard, her mouth settling right into his and saying all the same things—physical words of relief and possession and promise.

"Now I know how to wake you up," Aymal's darkly amused voice said. "But don't count on it happening."

Selena grinned, her lips still against Cole's. She gave him a final kiss that made him want to follow when she pulled away—but it turned out his body was as heavy as it had ever been, and he went nowhere. Selena straightened, and he realized that she knelt next to him on hard rock.

We're in a cave. He remembered finding it, then. And the impossible run from the doctor's, the need to hide, and the need to do...

Something.

Just not what it was.

The news of the *boom,* he also remembered. "Boom?" he said. "That was you?"

"In a manner of speaking." She glanced at Aymal, and he knew she wouldn't yet speak freely, not certain just how much English he had. Nor was Cole, if it came to that. She nodded toward the cave entrance. "Steven Dobry is here, too. I'm sorry it took so long for us to find you...we've run into some resistance."

"Tell me about it," Cole mumbled. He closed his eyes,

thinking of all the betrayed trusts…the station that should have been a safe haven but wasn't; the friends who should have given help but who had put him here, flat on his back, laid low by a damned flesh wound. Aymal, who had every interest in keeping Cole alive but who hadn't been able to bring himself to deal with the blood and pain that might have averted this infection. Armchair terrorist. He said, "I've got a written record of Aymal's intel. Do whatever you have to so it reaches the right eyes, if it comes to that."

"Okay," Selena said evenly. "We'll take care of it. But first, you."

"And a plan," said a deep, rumbly voice from the cave entrance—speaking Russian, as had they all once Selena introduced Dobry. "If we can't trust the station, and we can't be sure our phones are secure—"

"The border." Aymal's voice came firm and decisive. "We were going to head for the border, and the embassy there. Out of the reach of Suwan."

"Not a bad idea, if we can get there."

The border…something about that…

"Pardon my bluntness, but we don't *all* have to get there." Aymal hesitated, and when no one spoke against him, added, "Once I am separate of any of you, your danger in this ends."

"Oh, I wouldn't take that for granted," Selena muttered.

It wasn't enough of an interruption to stop Aymal—not words from a woman. "*I* need to get to the border. I need one of you with me. And no offense, my fine spy," he said to Cole, "But I don't think you're the one to take me. And I don't think she's going anywhere without you."

Beside Cole, Selena grew particularly still. She didn't like where this was going, no doubt about that; she'd gone to her lawyer face, the inscrutable one.

But she'd do what she had to. She'd proved that. And when she said, quite pointedly, "Dr. Aymal, I advise you not to make assumptions about what I will and won't do," he knew she meant it.

"That's right," Aymal said, reluctance and cultural conditioning showing through. "I've heard about you. Selena Jones—"

"Selena *Shaw* Jones," she corrected him.

"As if anyone here is ever going to forget that," Dobry grumbled.

Okay, *that* was something to ask about.

But first, there was the need to…

Damn. He couldn't dredge it up. But it brought a scowl, and it brought Selena's attention back to him. "First," she said, "you." She rummaged in her backpack.

"Unless you brought—" He stopped short at the sight of the military-issue first-aid kit she pulled out. "Oh."

"I knew you were hurt," she said. "You left blood in the vehicle you stole." She caught his eye. "Driver's seat."

She'd known it was him, then, and not just guessing. He winced, knowing what it was like to live with such knowledge. Seeing again that moment when she'd appeared on international television at the top of the steps to the Berzhaani capitol, and he'd known at a glance that she was hurt. Just the way she held herself…

It had torn at him unlike anything he'd felt before. So now, keeping her gaze, he said, "I'm sorry."

She glared back and said, "You should be." But her expression softened, big blue-green eyes he could never resist when there was that slight wrinkle of worry between them. "It couldn't be more obvious that you've got an infection. But let it not be said I come unprepared." To Aymal, she asked, "Got any water around here? Kvass? Anything to drink? For Cole, of course." She'd noticed his earlier reaction, then.

"I'll get some." He moved farther into the cave, and when he came back he had an MRE along with a bottle of water. "For later," he said, and left it next to Selena.

She murmured thanks and helped Cole half out of the abaya, rolling him over with strong hands when his own body didn't quite cooperate, exposing his flank. "Let's see," she said, half to him, half to herself. But when she pulled the tunic up—stiff, stained tunic, he could tell just from the way it moved over his too-sensitive skin—she made a noise of dismay. "How the hell did you get into this mess?"

He could have told her exactly how. He could have recited those reasons he knew too well—that he felt to his bones. All betrayals of trust.

Instead he told her what he suddenly, deeply knew—that which had struck him with such acute clarity upon seeing her dirty, worried face—those strong features highlighted by the hijab, revealing the depth of expression she showed only to him. "It doesn't matter how I got into this mess," he said. "We'll get out of it together."

Don't think about it. Just take care of it. "You don't want to know how ugly this is," she told him, gently pushing the tunic up his back until it stayed. Aymal returned from the inner depths of the cave and offered her a bottled water before returning to his chosen station by the mouth of the cave. Their escorts had left them here, unwilling to expose themselves by hanging around. Just as well; by hanging around, they might expose the fugitives.

Cole looked over his shoulder at her, his face as pale as ever, big bruises of fatigue under his eyes. "It's just a through-and-through."

Okay. Technically, maybe so. "I'm thinking," she said, and couldn't help the wince, "that the bullet was tumbling before it reached you. It doesn't make sense, but—"

He shifted straight to *oops*, and admitted, "It was a ricochet, I think."

"You think?" she murmured. Both entrance and exit were ragged and visibly infected even through the partial coating of stringent salve; the surrounding skin was hardened and red and spreading. And didn't smell so fresh, either. "This is gonna take more than some New-Skin."

Cole might have cursed; he might have sighed. She wasn't sure which. She rubbed the spot between her eyebrows and allowed herself one short moment to recognize how very badly she didn't want to do this. To hurt him, not even in helping him…and she knew damned sure she was going to hurt him.

"Here," she said, rummaging in the first-aid kit. "Made sure there were antibiotics in here. And pain meds, but you shouldn't take them on an empty stomach. So you can eat, take the things, and we'll give it a little while to work—"

"No," Cole said, with surprising clarity. He twisted back long enough for a quick look…an apologetic look. "Those things make me queasy. Best-case scenario, I'm losing it while you're at work. It's halfway likely to happen anyway, the way I feel."

Selena closed her eyes, just briefly. A deep breath's worth of time. "Okay," she said. "Later. And meanwhile we've got other…choices."

"We could wait for the doctor," Aymal suggested, from the safety of the cave opening, looking as gaunt and bruised by the last days as Cole.

"There's a doctor? He's coming?"

Aymal looked away. "At some point. He might."

Cole laughed, short and dark and muffled by the rock beneath his pallet. "Just think of us as a Keystone Cops spin-off," he said. "Really."

Didn't that just figure. "Ohh-kay. No doctor." Just choices. It had to be cleaned, no doubt about that. And then… "So we can either stick a drain in it and keep things flowing, or open it up and cauterize it."

"Ouch," Cole muttered.

Dobry moved into the cave, squinting over her shoulder. "Too late for cauterizing. You'll just trap some of that infection inside." And then he leaned closer to her. "What we *should* be talking about is where to go from here—and then we should do it. Fast. We didn't exactly get here without making waves."

Selena's voice was sharper than she intended. "Those Kemenis are after me, not Cole." All because she'd been seen with one of Arachne's subjects, dammit. "We have no reason to believe they even know about him."

"They *will*. They probably *do*. If you wanted time to play nurse, then we needed to get here without dumping two bleeding thugs off at the curb, stealing their car, and letting it get blown up just outside our objective."

Selena couldn't decipher the particular noise Cole made, but his low voice was clear enough. "Oh, yeah," he said. "That's my girl."

"Don't think I won't swat you," she warned him. And to Dobry, "Get this straight. We're hidden. We're as safe as we'll be until we get out of this country. We've got Dr. Aymal and we've got a hard copy of his information. There's nothing to be gained by being hasty. If we can find that doctor, we may well decide the best option is to wait out the scavengers—a week, two weeks…it can be done."

Though privately, she thought she'd find a working landline phone and call on Allori. He was the one she knew; he was the one she trusted.

Dobry held up both hands in surrender. "There's certainly no reason to start doing things my way now." But then he nodded at Cole, curled around to expose his wound, and his face held more understanding than she'd expected. "I can do this if you'd like."

Cole startled them both, and his voice was, for a short-lived moment, strong again. "That's not gonna happen." He didn't open his eyes as he shook his head, a slight movement that looked as though it nonetheless took his remaining effort. "No offense, Dobry. But we both know this is coming down to the short hairs, and I'm..." He stopped to gather another breath, and Selena doubted very much he knew he wore that dry little smile, one she could recognize even from this barely visible angle but not one she'd ever seen with such meaning. "I need someone I can trust." Another pause, but this one more thoughtful. "Also, I'm feeling inclined to kiss the hell out of whoever gets me through this. I think we'd both rather avoid that."

"That would be my choice," Dobry said, his voice as dry as Cole's smile.

Selena looked up at him, her hands busy pulling out surgical scrub, gauze, scissors. "I won't be long. And keep Aymal out of the light, will you?"

"I'm watching for intruders," Aymal protested, giving away at least some understanding of English.

Cole said, breathy and faint, "He doesn't have my gun, does he? Make sure he doesn't have my gun. Seriously."

Dobry shrugged, as baffled as Selena. "Will do."

And Aymal, sulking, said, "It's in his bag."

"Promi—" Cole said, and broke off with a hiss as Selena swiped his reddened skin with antiseptic-soaked gauze.

"I'm sorry," she whispered.

But she didn't stop.

She worked as fast as she could, while Cole shuddered and stiffened and sometimes forgot to breathe.

Sometimes, so did Selena.

The cleaning was bad enough—scrubbing out the obvious dirt of the wound and then going deeper. Then the trimming, doing away with curling, tightening edges of dead skin and flesh. Cole's back twitched involuntarily. He swallowed convulsively so many times that Selena understood why he'd refused the painkillers, how close he was to that edge. And then came the drain, a piece of gauze soaked in Betadine and threaded through the wound with a pair of hemostats.

By then his breath came short and panting, his control ragged. "I'm sorry," she whispered again, taping a loose bandage over the area, and he gave the slightest of nods, some whisper of reassurance she didn't catch. His hands shook on the bottled water she handed him along with half a pain pill and the antibiotic. She put her fingers over his to steady it and, when water escaped to run down his chin, wiped it off with her thumb.

She glanced at the front of the cave, glad for the jut of rock that hid the other men from direct line of sight. Then she shoved aside the first-aid kit and stole time Dobry would have resented. She eased down behind Cole, spooning against his shoulders, careful to avoid contact with his lower side even as she curled her hips and legs around his butt. She touched her lips to the back of his neck and left them there, let the contact soak into them both…an exchange of warmth and touch and skin as she automatically regulated her body to his, smoothing out the ragged, irregular edge to his breathing. Soothing him.

Spooning. Could there be anything more out of place than this, here in this cave under these circumstances? Probably not. But she took it with greed, and she waited until the faint tremors playing along his spine relaxed, until the tension along his arms and whitened knuckles eased.

And that's all they had. Stolen moments over. She kissed his neck again, the unnaturally dark strands of his hair tickling her nose, and as she pulled his filthy abaya up like a blanket, she told him, "Rest a few moments. You've got time."

Maybe, maybe not. Time enough, at least, to heat up a meal for him, and one for herself and Dobry. Then she'd get more meds into his system, and then…

Then they'd do whatever they'd settled on doing. Whichever equally unlikely thing seemed best.

Aymal saw her first, and stood from the crouch he'd assumed at the lip of the cave. "He is fine?"

She snorted, slipping into her long coat and wishing they'd managed to draw this op in summer. "He's a long way from fine. What the hell happened? I can't believe he went without cleaning that wound."

Aymal froze, offended—offended and a little something else. Regret? He glanced at Dobry. Selena tried again, this time in Berzhaani for privacy, her words snapping out with command. "What happened?"

He stood, smoothing the front of his tunic, and replied in kind. "I am not a doctor. I have never pretended to be a doctor." But his dusky complexion had gone darker with displeasure at this conversation. "I thought it was clean enough."

She saw from his face that there was more to it…that

he'd in some way more willfully failed to do what was necessary. "He's here to save your life!"

"And I'm not a doctor!" He glared at her, a look that should have put her in her place.

If she'd bothered to acknowledge any such place. "You'd damned well better be a good defector, then. You'd better save some lives before all is said and done—you'd better *save those school kids*."

"Hey," Dobry said. "Can anyone get in on this conversation, or is it invitation-only?"

Aymal switched back to Russian without faltering. "I told your man about that. The first of you."

"The school threat," Selena clarified for Dobry, also in Russian. "And no, you didn't. All we know is that there *is* a threat. There are way too many schools in the States for that to get us anywhere."

Aymal frowned. "But I told him…"

"He was badly hurt," Selena said, moving back from him slightly to take the conversation down a notch. She wouldn't devalue herself for his comfort, but she couldn't afford to drive an irrevocable wedge between them. "He didn't remember."

Aymal's face looked pinched with the effort of this blunt conversation with her. "Then you'll have to keep me safe, won't you? You can't call your people—even I know that much. You'll have to get me to safety. Just don't choose that paper over me—it has less to offer than I."

"That's a given," Dobry said, looking no more surprised than Selena felt. Of course Aymal had kept back details in order to make himself more valuable. She'd have done the same. Except… "Write down the school details," she said. "Keep them on you if you want. We can't risk—"

"*I* can't risk," he snapped at her, drawing himself up. His gaze wasn't even close to level with hers, a fact he gave every impression of failing to notice. "You give me back the other paper. Then I'll write the information about the school."

Selena opened her mouth to argue with him, to tell him they wouldn't leave him just because they had both papers. But Dobry cut her off, leaving her there with her mouth forming words as he said, "Agreed. Selena will get the other paper from Cole."

She closed her mouth with a snap that felt audible. But she somehow kept it closed, understanding what Dobry had done—that he'd done, in fact, exactly what he was here for. Dealing with men whose life experience made them reluctant to interact with a woman, especially a woman as uncovered as she.

So she turned around and went to search Cole's clothing, not the least bit sorry to take advantage of the moment to check on him. It hadn't been long enough for the painkiller to kick in, but she could at least see how he was weathering the aftermath of her poking and prodding.

He rolled slowly onto his back to greet her, holding a battered, folded piece of butcher's paper up between two fingers and murmuring. "Isn't he just a hoot?"

She closed her fingers on the paper, but he didn't release it. Not quite yet. It gave her time to frown, crouching beside him. "Tell me you don't feel as bad as you look."

He shook his head, only a hint of movement. "Lena," he said, and it meant *don't go there, because neither of us will like it.*

She made a face, wrinkled nose and squinchy eyes. "Sorry," she said. "Look, give the pill a few more moments to kick in…eavesdrop from here if you can. The last thing I want to do is get my whole story about this mess from your defector."

"*Our* defector now," Cole said, and grinned in a way that would have been too damned beguiling if his hair wasn't sticking to his damp forehead and his eyes weren't still watering at the corners. "Us. Together."

"Us, then. Together," Selena said, lowering her voice even more. She made a wry little face at him. "All four of us. One big happy family."

Cole made a face back at her. "A twisted Brady Bunch. Very twisted. But I wouldn't worry too much about Aymal. He's not a good liar."

"I noticed."

"He worked a desk, you know. Mathematician turned accountant. Because someone has to do it."

Selena covered her mouth to keep the laugh from escaping; the others would never understand it. "Ah. That explains some things."

"And seriously. Keep him away from the Browning. Although if you put the safety on, we're probably okay. He'll eject the magazine and hit the slide release before he ever finds the safety."

"I can see you've had an interesting couple of days." She plucked the paper from his fingers, finally, and closed her hand around his when it lingered there in midair. "Get ready for some food. Dobry and I already ate, and Aymal's been eyeing the basket the kid brought up with us. I expect the food in it is probably halal, though his observance of his spiritual needs has probably taken a hit in the last couple days."

"Remember that," Cole said, his gaze not quite focusing on hers. "Give Dobry the face-to-face time with Aymal."

Right.

She released his hand after a final squeeze, and returned to the shallow portion of the cave, offering the paper to Aymal.

"You were there long enough to copy it," he said, inspecting it as though he could tell.

"Just checking on Cole," Selena said, keeping her voice low and level, avoiding Aymal's gaze. It rankled, but right now that tiny bit of lost dignity and presence were the least of her worries. She breathed deeply of the fresh air so close to the cave entrance, letting the hint of cool air brush her face. Outside, the rugged, twisting mountains of Berzhaan, with them right in the middle. The terrain was similar enough to Athena's White Tank Mountains for her to well understand the sparsity of cover they'd have out there, and the equal scarcity of survival resources. They might well go make an offering to Ashaga tonight, if they wanted every advantage in getting out of this place.

Dobry gave Aymal the chance to tuck the paper away, and to produce another scrap of paper with Cole's no-nonsense block handwriting on one side. On the other, he used a nubbin of a pencil to make a few quick notations in Arabic script, which he then handed over to Dobry.

Dobry gave them to Selena. She hesitated, surprised, knowing this gesture wasn't nearly so simple as it might seem. He had nothing to gain from it. Unless…

Unless he meant to push for that which Aymal had suggested, breaking up the group to make their separate ways to safety.

He didn't leave her wondering for long. "I'm liking the idea of heading for the border," he said. "And I'm thinking there's no way in hell that Cole will make it."

"Depends on when we leave," she said, her voice remarkably even.

Dobry shook his head, hard and short. "I'd like to go tonight."

"Because you know this area so well that you can find

your way in darkness? Because Aymal knows it so well?" She didn't miss Aymal's sharp look; it didn't matter that they'd slipped into English. He could certainly read sarcasm without understanding all the words. "Look," she said, taking a deep breath to get some of her moderation back. "Take tomorrow to see about finding a guide. By then we'll know better about Cole. And then…"

It was probably the look on her face that alerted Dobry. The reluctance, mixed with conviction.

"What?" he said. "You think you should be the one to go?"

Selena shifted back to Russian, angling her body slightly to be more inclusive of Aymal. "I think," she said carefully, "that anyone looking for Aymal will be looking for two men, not a man and a woman. And I think—" she took a deep breath for this one "—that staying here—trying to work through Suwan—is a poor choice for me. As you've noted, we weren't quiet about being here. We *deliberately* weren't quiet about being here, and that was before the boom and the stolen car and the stabbed thug."

Aymal looked at Dobry in surprise, eyebrows climbing up toward his kufi cap. "You stole a taxi? You stabbed someone?"

Dobry almost looked as though he wished he had. "Actually," he said, "that was Selena. My job is to get us out of here without attracting attention. And dammit…Selena could be right. They won't be looking for a man and a woman."

Aymal eyed her with some trepidation, and said anyway, "I suspect she *is* right. But it would mean leaving her husband here to fend for himself."

"To fend with Dobry," Selena corrected, and couldn't believe the words coming from her own mouth. She had to work to get the next ones past a jaw gone stiff. "I said I'd do what had to be done. I meant it."

"And you're right," said Cole, his voice echoing slightly as he moved forward in the cave. Not strong, not of its normal timbre. But when they turned as one to look at him, he shrugged. "The conversation was getting too interesting. Besides, I understand that I'm supposed to eat." He looked at the MRE packet in his hand, making no immediate move to do anything about it.

"Are you sure—" Selena started, but finished the sentence with a narrow-eyed expression that Cole would interpret well enough.

Dobry jumped into the conversational opening. "Are you okay?"

"I'm fine," Cole said, so casually he might have been practicing the line for days. But then, that's what he was known for, wasn't it? Casual. Confident. Come-what-may—in spite of flushed cheeks, blue eyes stark behind stained skin and dyed hair, his kufi gone missing along the way. He probably hoped no one noticed that he propped his shoulder against the rough, angled cave wall. And that's when he caught Selena's eye and she found something lurking…something that kept her from stating the obvious, that he wasn't fine at all. Something that let her know he needed to at least pretend. It didn't matter if they all knew otherwise, as long as no one *said* otherwise.

Aymal looked at Cole with a different kind of surprise. "You want the woman to go with me?"

"I think she makes a good point." Cole blinked, a vision-clearing effort. Slowly, he slid down the cave wall, the whole time wearing an expression that indicated this was how he always chose to sit. He gave the MRE packet a puzzled look and set it aside. "Seriously," he said. "She's right. The border is my idea, and I still think it was a good one. But the whole world is alert for two men. And

Selena..." He looked at her, went a little distant, and closed his eyes to give an infinitesimal shake of his head. It seemed to bring him back, and his eyes were clear when he looked at them again. "Selena seems to have attracted some attention. So...Selena and Aymal head for the border. Dobry and I can head any direction we want. Perfect solution." He waved his hand in a vague gesture of *voilà!* And then, as they regarded him in silence, he added, "Except not tonight. Tonight Dobry should go down there and hunt up a guide. Unless you brought a compass?"

No. No, of course they hadn't brought a compass. First-aid kit and a zillion little useful tools, but no compass. Still, Selena said, "It might be better if Dobry came back with a compass instead of a guide."

"The only thing I really like about *this* plan," Dobry grumbled, finding his Goff voice again, "is that it delays departure until at least morning, if not tomorrow evening. We'll have more time to rethink things." And reconsider his original plan, no doubt. He bent down for Cole's MRE and pulled out the main meal, dumping what remained of a bottled water into the flameless heater before stuffing it back with the food pouch into the box. "I'm going to catch some sleep before I go hunting this evening." He handed the box back to Cole, who set it aside to finish heating. "Any objections?"

"I'm thinking it sounds good for all of us," Selena said. Plenty of pallets and blankets farther back in the cave...it had clearly seen extensive use.

"Sleep," Aymal said approvingly, "would be welcome." He picked up the food basket, hesitated just long enough to see that no one else would make a claim on it, and walked past Selena to head for the darker part of the narrow, zigzaggy cave—past the food stores, past the little jumble of belongings left by previous occupants.

Dobry watched him go and said, "Well…at least one of these infamous caves is being used for the good guys." He glanced back at Selena. "I'm going to grab a meal, and then I'm out of it. We've got the whole afternoon to use up, and I'm not in the mood for small talk." Except then he belied his own words by hesitating, looking between Cole and Selena. "You're sure about this? Splitting up again?"

Instead of responding, Selena looked at Cole. He lifted one shoulder in a shrug, sitting more or less cross-legged against the cave, here where the strong light still reached indirectly. Not so much as a peek of blue sky from here, just pale limestone with calcite flowstone and curtains hugging sections of rock, the worn sections attesting to generations of touch by human hand.

Or weary human body. And when she looked at Cole, Selena couldn't help but think of the look on his face only…what, was it no more than an hour earlier?—when he'd realized who she was. When he'd grabbed her and kissed her, revealing a hungry desperation she'd never seen in him before. And then moments later when he'd refused Dobry's help, a flicker of wariness crossing his expression.

When he'd put his trust in her and her alone.

"If I go…" she started.

He shook his head, cutting off her words. "It's okay," he said. "*I'm* okay."

Through sheer strength of will, she suppressed the entirely disbelieving snort that worked hard to find its way out. She saw the faintest hint of a smile at the corners of Cole's eyes, as if he well knew it.

Well, he couldn't fool her, either.

Cole looked away from her long enough to tell Dobry, "It's not about us. It's about getting the job done."

"Well," Dobry said, awkwardly enough so Selena suspected he'd detected the currents of emotion swirling between herself and Cole. "We've got through the night to think about it, anyway. I might find something in Oguzka that changes our minds."

"There's that," Cole agreed, and then offered up a hazy frown. "And there's something…something I should be doing…or remembering…or stopping…I just can't get a handle on it."

"Maybe by tomorrow," Dobry offered.

"Maybe." Cole gave up on it, his expression clearing. He nodded at Dobry as the man moved on, back toward the area where chiseling and tool marks indicated that this particular cave, like many in this area, had had some homo sapiens help.

And that left Cole and Selena alone together, watching each other. Just watching, with Cole's focus visibly wavering but his fortitude holding fast. Selena moved closer—a few steps was all it took in this limited neck of an opening—and crouched before him. "The thing is," she said evenly, "I don't *want* to leave you."

He grinned; it looked a little loopy. He'd always been susceptible to pain meds. She hadn't even given him the other half of the pill yet. "Well, that's something else again." He patted the ground between his knees, a little scoop of ground just big enough to sit in. Which she did, leaning back against the same cave wall that supported Cole's shoulder, her knees passing over his outside leg. A partial pretzel. "Dobry will do well enough by me."

"That's not the point." She raised an eyebrow at him to let him know she wasn't that stupid…not that distractible.

"No," he said, and pulled her in close enough for her head to rest on his shoulder, her hair scraping the rock behind her. "It's not." He kissed the top of her head. "And

I don't really want you to go, either. So just sit here a while and let me soak you up."

He smelled of barnyard; he smelled of sweat and pain and something herbal she couldn't identify. He smelled…

Wonderful.

So she sat with him, and they soaked each other up while they still could.

Chapter 18

While Dobry headed out in the early evening to hunt either a guide or a compass, Selena again cleaned Cole's wound. With the pain meds and food already in his system he had an easier time of it, and afterward, together they made what Selena quickly came to think of as the grossest decision she'd ever thought to contemplate.

"Hospitals use 'em," Cole said.

"Those are *sterile* maggots." Selena paused with her fingers dipping into the salve from the Oguzkan doctor's office and looked down at it. "What am I saying? Here I am about to put bag balm all over you. There's something totally surreal about this whole situation. Yes indeedy, maggots would be *perfect*."

Cole grinned, and if he still trembled tensely from her administrations, the grin was still more convincing than it had been earlier in the day. Sleep, and food—even with the infection still eating at his back and into his body—made a difference. "They didn't have sterile maggots in the Civil War," he said. "And it worked back then."

Selena sighed, rubbing one eyebrow with the heel of her hand. "I wouldn't have expected it this late in the season...but there have been a few flies hanging around the bucket." No need to say just which bucket. At this point in the day they all had a constant awareness of its presence.

"They say you can't even feel them," Cole added, far too cheerful about the prospect. She wrinkled her nose at him, but it was acquiescence. So she rubbed the salve on her fingers only around the thickening, reddened circumference of skin on his back, trying to be gentle with the sticky stuff, backing off when Cole swallowed too hard, too frequently. But she left the wound itself alone, and made no effort to cover it with gauze.

"God, you're good," Cole said when she was done.

"Not the conditions under which I really want to hear those words." She gave him a little shove—but gently. Carefully.

"Seriously," he said. "The thought of Dobry doing this job...? No. No, thanks." He rolled to his back—not quite flat, just far enough to sit up—and made sure his tunic was still pulled up. "Come and get it, little blowflies." And, adopting a professorial tone that Selena confidently labeled as drug-inspired, he said, "A day for the eggs to hatch. And three days of liquifying and munching the bad stuff before we need to pull them."

"There's plenty of liquid in there already." She scowled at him. "And you'd damned well better be in friendly hands by then."

"I could be in friendly hands right now," he suggested.

And from the interior of the cave, Aymal said loudly, "Do you two never *stop*?"

No, Selena decided. Not if she could help it. And she realized if it weren't for Cole's injury, she'd actually be enjoying this time with him. Stuck in a narrow cave, stuck with a cranky defector, stuck waiting out their fate. Enjoying his cutting humor...enjoying their partnership, a newly discovered facet of their relationship. She'd always done her work apart from his though they shared the same goals, sometimes the same risks. He'd always done his in silence, sworn not to reveal details. And now here they were in the same place at the same time, and no explanations were necessary.

"If you're serious about getting some fly buddies, you'll have to move closer to that bucket," she told him.

"I'm thinking not." He returned to his side on the pallet and beckoned to her, and she lay down in front of him, letting him be the outside spoon, his lower back still carefully exposed. He tucked his arm around her, snuggling up under her breasts. His breath came softly across the side of her neck. And if his body was still hot, his breathing still ragged, still catching on pain, she was nonetheless content for the moment.

Sleeping, eating...saving their energy.

Because soon enough, they were going to need every personal resource they could muster.

Dobry returned after dark, slipping into the cave with a sigh of tired relief.

"Guide or compass?" Selena murmured, not moving from Cole's sleeping grasp except to straighten the leg that was cramping.

"Compass," he said. "Though it's amazing how much more willing they were to talk to me without you there."

Selena pondered whether she should awake enough to determine just how much sarcasm had been present in those words, and decided against it. Typical Dobry, either way you looked at it. "Any trouble?"

"All quiet." He paused, hesitating on words so close to being said that Selena could practically feel them. Words other than what he actually said next. "We'll talk in the morning, then?"

She woke a little more at that. "I don't think any of us are ready to move tonight. Did you see anything that made us think we should reconsider?"

"No," he said, quickly enough. She woke a little more at that, and then decided the man was merely tired…relieved, as they all were, at the prospect of stocking up on food and energy. She herself was replete…she'd easily caught up on what little sleep she'd lost by getting up in the middle of the previous night, and the nonstop nature of their day until they'd hit the early afternoon cave nap had been nothing compared to the hostage incident.

Right. Because that's the sort of thing everyone should have in their lives as a benchmark.

Her body, on the other hand, was waking more fully with every passing moment—offering her all the signs of its hyperawareness of the dangers their situation posed. That superfluous adrenaline rush, sly in the way it sneaked up on her, leaving her caught unaware when she could barely stop herself from leaping to her feet and going for a midnight run.

Yeah, that would be the safe thing to do at this moment. Wouldn't attract any attention at all.

Better to try to sleep through it—to give Aymal the chance to rest, to give Cole the chance to heal—and hope he didn't simply sink further into the infection, into sepsis and organ failure and death. It was already beyond a simple local infection, or he wouldn't have the fever with which he so clearly burned.

She suddenly realized that Dobry still waited. "There's room back by Aymal." She slipped her hand in the pocket of the bulky coat that now acted as a blanket, and pulled out the tiny, flat LED flashlight, angling it to light his way.

"Thanks," he said, in a gruff voice that sounded like the Goff voice but..somehow wasn't quite.

When he'd found his way, he murmured his thanks again, and she snuggled her arm back under the coat, resting her hand on top of Cole's. Of course he'd slept right through it. Just as well.

The next day was likely to be a big one.

Selena ran her tongue around her teeth and decided that the MREs should come with those little finger tooth swipes. Fresh breath on the run.

Second thought of the day…surprise that she'd gone back to sleep, after an hour or so of deep breathing and ineffective visualizations of calm. Surprise that she'd slept through Cole's departure from their shared pallets.

She sat, scrubbing her hands across her face and through her hair, then turning to hunt her hair band out of the pallet bedding. "Don't give up on me now," she muttered at it upon finding it, discovering that it had lost some of its stretch. She finger-combed her hair back and bound it in a low ponytail, and then covered herself with the hijab. From the front half of the cave she heard low conversation, including a high voice she didn't recognize. So after she straightened her shirt, she shook out the long, proper coat—somewhat the worse for wear—and slipped it on. It not only served as an excellent tentlike shelter for her good-morning encounter with the bucket, but the morning was still chill, and the locals would still be appalled by her formfitting clothing.

A few moments later at the cave entrance and sitting just within the sharp morning sunlight slanting into the cave, she found an interesting little men's club. Comfortably hunkered down next to Cole, the boy she'd saved eight months earlier spoke with some animation, relating a tale in such a swift stream of Berzhaani words that she doubted anyone else could follow it. His four-year-old's lisp didn't help things; she couldn't help but wonder if his family knew he'd come up here.

Boys. The same the world over.

Cole looked little better than the day before—still bleary-eyed, still drained by fever. But he'd had food and he'd had sleep, and though he favored his back considerably as he shifted in the half cross-legged position that seemed easiest for him, he no longer looked as though he might possibly fall on his face at any moment.

Not quite.

Dobry noticed her first, and nodded a greeting, one that Aymal echoed. The boy leaped to his feet. "Selena Shaw Jones!"

"Hey," Selena greeted them all, figuring English would do for a word that didn't really mean anything anyway. The fresh breeze from outside the cave reached in to brush her face, and she breathed it in. The cave itself, it had to be said, was already getting a little ripe.

Cole turned to look at her—carefully, so carefully—but did it with a grin on his face. *"My name is Inigo Montoya. You killed my father. Prepare to die."*

Selena couldn't hold back the healthy snort of amusement at the infamous quote from *The Princess Bride*—one repeated endlessly during the movie in much the same manner as her bus-stop performance. "I gather our little friend has been telling stories."

"As near as I can tell, he thinks you were magnificent. He says even when the strongest men of the village removed you from the rocks, you defied them."

"That's one way to put it." Dobry plied a toothpick between his front teeth.

"Hey," Selena said, not at all the same tone as when she'd said that word moments earlier. "It worked, didn't it?"

"Oh, you got attention all right."

"Point made," she told him tightly. "Point made last night. Now let me make a point—you were going to give up. You didn't offer any alternatives. You might as well have not been there."

"Whoa," Cole said, but the bulk of his attention landed on Dobry. "Let's just look to the future on this one."

"The choices we make about the future are affected by those moments in the village." Dobry, never one to let go of a matter.

"Fine." Cole's voice got grittier, and Selena watched Dobry take notice. "Now let's figure out the best way to move ahead. You got the compass, and we've had some rest. Our friend here—" the boy who watched them, suddenly silent, and very much recognizing the tension running between them "—says there haven't been any more new visitors. But that doesn't mean there's not someone lurking outside the village."

Selena turned to the boy. "Do your people watch the area around the village? Out beyond it?"

The boy nodded. "Since the big fight…sometimes."

The exchange had been too quick for any of the others, so Selena translated into Russian, adding, "So we might have advance warning, and we might not."

That put one of Dobry's sour looks in place; Aymal just looked disgruntled. He said, "Then we will have to be careful when we leave. Perhaps early this evening, just as night is falling."

Selena winced at the thought of leaving Cole with Dobry, but forced herself to add, "We could at least slip past the town perimeter, make it out far enough to hole up and start fresh at dawn. It's two days to the border, if we keep a good pace."

Dobry opened his mouth, closed it…and then finally spoke up. "If you wait until this evening, we might discover more options."

"You have a stealth chopper coming in that we don't know about?" Cole asked.

Dobry offered a more or less obligatory grin. "Yeah, don't I wish." He rubbed his upper lip, and said, "I suppose there's no rush on heading to Suwan on this end."

Cole looked startled; Selena didn't wait for Dobry to think through what he'd said. "The sooner Cole gets medical help," she said tightly, "the better. All we've got is maggots and bag balm." And broad-spectrum antibiotics, but if things went septic he'd need IV meds and support to have a chance.

"Won't do either of us any good if they're waiting out there for Aymal. You think they won't take us as a consolation prize?"

"Then don't get caught," she snapped at him. "You're the disguise mogul—think of something."

Dobry spoke distinctly, carefully. Looking from Cole to Selena, watching them for reaction. "I only meant…we, too, might wait until this evening. It seems best. Then no pair of us is left here alone in the cave."

Selena exchanged a look with Cole, her attention lingering on the unnatural flush of fever over skin tones she couldn't even assess because of the dye. He was strong… he had medicine now, even if it wasn't enough. The wound had been cleaned and though she hadn't seen it today, the afternoon before it had drained nicely. Still, she hated to think of any delay.

But Dobry had something of a point.

"Look," he said. "I can go back down there now and try to make arrangements, but that puts me in plain sight in daylight. But if we go down after dark, I can appropriate some transportation much more easily."

"There's that," Cole said.

"But we leave tonight for sure," Aymal said. "For the border. I want to get out of this accursed country."

Cole shifted uncomfortably. "It's either the border or…" But he trailed off oddly, looking at Aymal with a puzzled frown. "Son of a…" he said, still not quite certain, and then shook his head, abruptly more assertive. "Son of a *bitch.* You were going to do it, weren't you?"

Selena wanted to ask *what*, wanted to demand it. But when she saw the same on Dobry's face, she shook her head. This was between Cole and Aymal for the moment, and they'd know soon enough.

Whatever it was got Cole to his feet quicker than she would have thought, if no more steady. Aymal jumped up to meet him, his trepidation speaking clearly of his complete understanding. No fool, the boy ran into the cave to Selena, and hesitated between doing the manly thing and putting himself in front of her or hiding behind her. But he was, after all, a very young boy, and he ended up behind her.

Cole stalked Aymal like prey, his abaya hiding the stains from his wound but the movement of it highlighting every unsteady moment he had. Not that he seemed to notice. All his attention was focused on Aymal. "You would have let Selena take you away without even mentioning the capitol. You would have let us head for Suwan with no warning of what's about to go down there."

"Saving the day," Aymal said tightly, his lips tense and thin and trying to peel back from his teeth, "is *your* job. I'm here to save *me*. And I have plenty of other valuable information to trade for that privilege."

Okay, now. Now was a good time to ask. Before Cole actually reached Aymal.

"What—"

It was as far as she got before Cole whirled around to stab out the words. "The morning we got here. It's fuzzy, but not so fuzzy it didn't eventually come back to me." Back to Aymal, and another stalking step closer to contact. "*Tell them I can save the capitol.* What the hell was that supposed to mean, Aymal? And did you really think I wouldn't eventually remember it?"

"I *hoped*," Aymal snapped, though he'd flushed at Cole's words. "I thought you'd already fainted!"

"I don't *faint*," Cole snapped back, but Selena barely heard him. Suwan? Or the actual capitol building? *Again?*

Selena tossed aside the demure facade she'd been wearing and stepped up next to Cole, effectively cornering Aymal. "What about the capitol?" she demanded. "What's going to happen there? And when?"

Dobry had gotten to his feet. "Selena—"

"I didn't go through hell last winter just so some new idiot could come along and bring that building tumbling down!"

"Voices, voices!" The boy gave a tentative tug on her coat sleeve from behind. "Voices!"

"Even a child gets the point." Dobry stepped firmly

between Cole and Aymal. "Whatever there is to say, *do it quietly*."

Silent glares filled the communication gap well enough. At least until Aymal, his voice much lower, grudgingly said, "Soon. It will happen very soon."

"Define *soon*." Selena nudged Dobry aside and filled the space directly in front of Aymal. His eyes widened slightly. "That's right, it's me. The woman. And this is exactly where I'm going to stand, right here in your personal space. And guess what—I've even got my *period*."

And that did what she wanted it to do—aside from horrifying Aymal, it made Cole snort in dark amusement. She felt more than saw him relax, and something within her relaxed, too. She'd seen him upset, she'd seen him intense…she hadn't ever seen that look in his eye, that deadly tone in his voice. Fevered or not, wobbly or not, Aymal had been the one in danger there.

And amazingly, Aymal seemed to realize it. As disgusted as he looked, as much as he tried to draw away from her, he said, "It's too late. It's this evening. Eight o'clock this evening."

"Why the *hell* didn't you say anything?" Cole demanded, just as Dobry said, "*What's* this evening?"

"Because!" Aymal blurted, a reply so ridiculous that Selena drew back to give him some thinking space. "First your people promise me safety, and then leave me open to attack. I lived for weeks in that miserable city, hiding out in the worst of it, smelling as if the streets were my home! Weeks! And finally, this man finds me there. I get a bath. I trim my beard. I have new clothes. And then I'm beset *again!* And now I've been running and hiding and riding the damn bus for *days*, and I am no closer to that promised safety than I ever was." He glared, spreading the blame thickly and indiscriminately. "Why didn't I say anything? Because it was your job to take care of me, not those in Suwan. Because you were hurt and couldn't do both. Because I knew you *would* try to do both. And you would die and I would be caught."

There was a moment of silence. Dobry looked at Selena, his expression as clearly asking *What have I gotten myself into with you people* as it ever had been. And Cole looked at Selena with anger glinting in his eye, and she instantly knew Aymal's diatribe hadn't nearly gotten him off the hook. But his voice remained low, his tone harsh…and if it cracked on the edges from the sickness he fought, he was no less imposing because of it. "You came to us with information to trade," he said. "That's part of the deal. Prove you're not good for the information, and we'll have no interest in you."

"I *am*—"

"No," Cole said, and he relaxed slightly, letting go of the energy he'd kept coiled up and ready to move. Suddenly he looked sick and bleary again. "Not if you wait until it's too late. Not if you pick and choose, denying us the ability to set our own priorities. That's not the way this works."

Strong words. But they could walk away from Aymal and live…he couldn't say the same of them. And they all knew it.

Including Aymal.

He managed to gather his dignity about him as Cole turned away, finding a narrow rock shelf to perch against. "As I said, the attack is this evening. This is the last thing I learned before leaving my home. Gossip only, you understand? Not part of my people's doing, only that they… advised." A deep breath. "The prime minister plans a special private open house for the capitol staff. The repairs to the building have been completed, and Razidae has decided to install all his people in their offices before the public opening next week. There will be no special security, to avoid drawing attention."

"But the place has state-of-the-art security as a matter of course," Selena said. "Dobry and I met the contractor ourselves." Scott Hafford.

A man who had been stressed and tense and whose name had been on the Spider File list. Arachne's list.

Selena felt an undeniable tingle of foreboding. She struggled to hide her suddenly fast breathing and racing pulse, the trembles that came with it all. *Don't be stupid,* she told it. *This isn't about you.*

But she had the feeling it would be.

Selena didn't look right.

Cole could tell it at a glance, could see her demons coming to roost. And in the background, Aymal's resigned voice droned on, words that painted a picture Cole couldn't ignore.

"The contractor has been…influenced. I don't know details. The safeguards will not be fully activated this evening, and the leftover Kemenis are willing to martyr themselves to this cause." Aymal shrugged; it was there in his voice, even as Cole watched Selena fall into her deep-breathing routine, the one that had lulled him back to sleep early this morning when she'd woken him with her sudden start into awareness. "You have to understand. If they so much as break through the first line of defense into the building, then their symbolic success will be irrefutable. They expect to die in the process, but this is as nothing to a Kemeni who seeks glory after failure. And then those who have spoken against Razidae's ability to lead will take it as their proof that the man cannot. They will turn to his deputy. And you must know that Davud Garibli is a conservative man who very much disagrees with Razidae's course for this country."

"Garibli is behind this?" Dobry demanded. "The new deputy prime minister?" There was an eager note to his voice that Cole couldn't remember hearing before. And he still found himself bemused by Dobry's new looks—his padded torso, the intense eyebrows, the glasses...this was a man who knew how to hold a cover.

Another shrug from Aymal. "Speculation. It hardly matters. The Kemenis are poised to act, no matter who drives them."

"And if we call in..." Cole heard his own voice, hoarse and tired. He shouldn't have blown up at Aymal as he had; he should have marshaled his so very limited resources.

"If we call in, we reveal our location," Selena finished, and the full realization of their predicament came through in her expression. "We might even trigger the attack early." She looked at Dobry, fresh realization widening her eyes slightly. She might well have forgotten the young boy, had she not had a quiet hand on his head. "This is why we had so much trouble in the village. They weren't just letting Cole and Aymal hide up here. They had an interest in keeping them safe."

Cole sent Aymal a sharp scowl. "What exactly did you tell them?"

"What does it matter?" Aymal responded, and he looked as weary as Cole felt. "It gave them reason to protect us."

"A little too well," Cole grumbled, but ceded the point. It didn't really matter at that.

But Selena knew these people better than he did. "It

matters if they've gone off on their own to do something about it."

Aymal responded with a withering scorn. "Do you think I told them it was tonight? I didn't know how long we'd need to hide here. I told them it was in the near future, and that if they sheltered us until Cole recovered, I would tell them what I know."

"Risky," Dobry said. "They might have decided to convince you to tell them sooner."

Dobry merely received a shrug. Aymal reached a finger under his kufi to scratch at hair that had to be every bit as dirty as Cole's felt. "I gave them no reason to think it was urgent. And frankly it is still not *my* urgency. I still intend that I should leave here this evening. I want to go to the border. I want to find *safety*."

Selena returned the scorn he'd directed her way only moments before. "Funny," she said, "that's how most people feel. They just want to be safe. From, say, terrorism."

Dobry plunged into the middle of it with the clear intent of driving the conversation forward. "I don't see any reason we can't continue more or less as planned. Selena and Aymal leave tonight—but instead of waiting, Cole and I will head straight for Suwan. We've got time to warn them before this evening."

"You're kidding," Selena said, her voice flat.

And Cole heard himself say in the tired new voice that seemed to be a permanent fixture, "Let's get real. I'm not in any shape to pull my weight. It might be better if I waited here." Not better for him, of course. Selena had already said it—he needed to get some serious medical care, and he needed to do it as quickly as possible.

But Dobry nodded, his mouth opening—except Selena cut him off. "You're kidding," she said again. "Is that because you're so fluent with the language, or because you know this area so well—?"

"Give me some credit," Dobry said, though his face had taken on the same flushed hue he'd worn for a week after his ambush of Selena in Virginia had gone wrong. Cole felt a sudden foreboding, and Dobry's next words did nothing to forestall it. "I've arranged for help."

Selena, Cole and Aymal responded in startled unison. "You *what?*" Even the boy understood enough Russian to blink in surprise.

Into the long silence that followed, Dobry finally muttered, "That's not exactly how I'd planned to tell you."

"No," Cole said. "I imagine not." And he would have been able to dismiss the tension that tightened the skin down his back, triggering pains both dull and sharp, if he hadn't seen it in Selena's posture as well. She had a remarkable instinct, his Selena. It had gotten her through the hostage crisis, and if they listened to it, it would help get them through this.

"I didn't see any reason to stay out in the cold alone." Dobry crossed his hands over his padded chest, awkward over the padding. "When I went down to the village last night, I asked to use a phone. It might not have been scrambled, but it wasn't tapped, either. And I didn't call the station—we still don't know where the compromise it. I called Betzer."

"Fuck." The word was out of Cole's mouth before he even knew it, damn that fever. The utter, stunned shock didn't help any either. "You didn't."

Aymal understood. Aymal had gone as pale as a man could be and still be breathing. He pressed himself back against the cave wall as though he hoped to disappear. He whispered a few words that no doubt amounted to a pleading prayer.

And Selena's eyes, as blue-green as they ever got in the early-morning light near the cave mouth, riveted on Cole. "What?" she said, and it might as well have been a private conversation between them. "What about Betzer?"

Cole all but snarled the words. "Sonofabitch shot me, that's what."

Selena's breath hissed out. "I knew there was a reason I didn't like him. I *knew* it." She glared at Dobry, who seemed to be in shock. "I *told* you I didn't trust him!"

"I—" Dobry said, and went nowhere with it.

"Do you still think it's coincidence that he killed that Kemeni? He knew damned well I had things under control. The man either knew something we weren't supposed to hear or Betzer did it deliberately just to gain my trust. To gain *our* trust. And it damned well worked on you, didn't it?"

"Don't hurt him too badly, Lena," Cole muttered, swamped by the implications of what he'd heard. "We're going to need all the help we can get to make it out of this one."

Chapter 19

Fury combined with imminent danger to build up in Selena, demanding action. She couldn't go for a run, she couldn't hit the shooting range...she couldn't hit Dobry.

She really wanted to hit Dobry.

Instead she let the energy explode into motion, harmlessly slapping the cave wall. Slapping it hard enough to make her palm sting reproachfully...hard enough so Aymal's eyes widened.

Dobry's might have done the same had he not been stuck in his stuttering shock of reaction.

"Fine," Selena said, her voice so low and controlled she surprised even herself. She was peripherally aware of the boy now hiding behind her, but...first things first. "Tell us everything. What do they know?"

Dobry cleared his throat. It seemed to take some effort. Good. She couldn't believe—couldn't *believe*—that he'd done this. Been so eager for his success, been so eager to take the credit for it, that he'd gone behind her back. He'd assured her he'd put his all into this operation for his own sake, and then he'd been so blinded by his goals as to sabotage them all.

But to his credit, he didn't hold back now. "They know enough. That we're here, hiding in the ridge above Oguzka. That we won't move out until tonight. By then I'd hoped to change your mind about going with you. I figured Cole might well be better by then."

"I told you he needed a hospital," Selena said, incredulous—but just as quickly as she'd said it, she shook her head. "No, never mind. Of course you hoped I was wrong." So many things made sense now—Dobry's hesitation the night before, almost telling her what he'd done…his preoccupation with various phones…and before that, his willingness to strike out for the Plush and meet Betzer.

Well, she'd asked him to take more initiative. She'd just underestimated his desire to earn the credit for this op.

Badly underestimated.

"They won't expect it if we move out now," Cole said, and he looked terrible—haggard and far too aware of what they faced. "They won't expect us to be together."

"You can't—"

"I'm fine," he said abruptly, and she knew how to translate that: *I'll get through it because I refuse to believe I can't.* "Listen. I set up a meet with the exfiltration team—it was just a test, when I suspected the local station was compromised. Betzer showed up. I overheard some conversation…enough to confirm everything Aymal said. For so many reasons, we need to get out of here now."

"We can try the phone in the village," Dobry said.

From inside the cave, a small voice repeated, "Phone?"

in Russian, and then added in Berzhaani, "No phone. The *damned rebels* did something because of the woman." The words were startling from that child's voice, even if they were obviously parroted. "Maybe fixed later today." Clearly a conversation overheard…and all the detail they needed. Although the boy added, in a much more natural voice, "I think they meant you."

The woman. No doubt.

"We can't wait," Dobry said, and he scrubbed both hands over his face, momentarily distorting his features. "We need to move. And we need to do it together. If we can find a vehicle in the village—even if we grab someone's wagon—we can still make it to Suwan in time to stop the attack. And if we make it that far, we can get protection at the embassy."

Assuming Berzhaan didn't find a reason to detain them. Selena's hero status wouldn't buy her any favors if Razidae became convinced she'd been covertly manipulating events on Berzhaani soil.

More like events have been manipulating me.

"Let's pull it together, then," she said. "Our little visitor needs to get out of here ASAP, just for starters."

Dobry and Aymal looked into the dimmer recesses of the cave with surprise, having clearly forgotten the boy's welfare. Only Cole reacted immediately. "Hell, yes." He beckoned to the kid, who responded immediately, and rested his hands on the boy's shoulders to ask, "Lutfi, do you understand what's happening?"

The boy looked at Selena, worried. He'd almost certainly understood some of their conversation, although the anger in the cave was enough to send any kid into hiding. She spoke to him in Berzhaani instead of the slow Russian Cole had used, glad to finally have his name. "Lutfi, we just found out that some people will try to hurt us. We've decided to leave right away. It would help if you let your family know, so they can let your magistrate know. Tell them we intend to stop the Kemenis."

"That's a lot," Cole murmured in English.

"If he gets half of it, it'll send them thinking in the right direction," she responded, keeping it light in utter contrast to the heavy feel of her stomach. "We'll be there soon enough, hunting a car. At least he'll think he's off to do something important."

Lutfi's gaze switched back and forth between them, waiting for the side conversation to end so he could tell Selena, "I can go right to the magistrate!"

"That's good, too." Whatever. He just didn't need to be here, with them. Or anywhere near them when they first emerged into the morning sunlight, blinking and getting their bearings and providing Betzer and his men the first opportunity to cause trouble.

Busy fellow, Betzer. Selena would do her best to make sure his social calendar became much more restricted. Berzhaan would hardly be kind to foreign terrorist criminals on its own soil—and that's all Betzer had become. Selena drew the boy from Cole's gentle grasp and turned him around, facing him toward the cave entrance. "See how fast you can do it," she suggested to him. "I bet you're a lot faster than last time, when I asked you to run up here."

Lutfi scoffed. "I was just a kid then."

"Exactly. Now show me!" Just the slightest of nudges and he was off, running with much surer steps than the last time.

Little boys in terrorist country. They grow up too fast.

But Selena didn't linger over such thoughts. She barely spared a glance for Dobry as she headed into the cave to gather her things—the backpack o' stuff, a few precious bottles of water, whatever else she could scavenge from the supplies here. "Let's go," she said, keeping her voice tightly controlled. "I need to tape up your side, too."

"Time to close the impending baby maggots into place," Cole said, the false cheer not enough to hide his understanding of just what they faced.

As he stood, a scream slashed the air. A high, shrill, terrified child's scream. Selena froze in mid-step, her horrified eyes meeting the grimmer reflection in Cole's as Dobry cursed repeatedly under his breath.

Lutfi. Betzer was here, and he had Lutfi.

And then, loud and garbled and mixed with shrieks that made it sound as if he was being tossed from one person to another, Lutfi cried, "In the back! Go…the back!"

Selena translated for Cole without hesitation, then asked, "Does Betzer speak Berzhaani?"

Cole shook his head, came to his feet to stand with one hand against the cave wall. "As far as I know, he does what most of the guys do—gets by on Russian."

"Go…the back?" Dobry said, also on his feet. "What's that supposed to mean?"

Betzer hailed them from outside. "Hey, Dobry—the party's come to you. Let's go!"

As if they were just that stupid.

Except one of them had been. Selena glanced at Dobry, kept those particular thoughts to herself for now. "Stall him," she said. "You're the only one who can do that. Make him think Cole is out of it, that we don't know Betzer's true colors." And then to Cole, "That kid knows more about hiding and surviving than we do. If he says go to the back, we damned well ought to check out the back end of this place."

Dobry cupped his hands to his mouth and leaned toward

the mouth of the cave. "Glad to hear your voice! Jones is out cold, we're making a stretcher!"

"Need help?" That was closer, and accompanied by the muffled sounds of a child's struggle. Selena hesitated, already turning toward the back of the cave.

Cole caught her gaze and held it, complete understanding in his torn expression. He knew how she felt about children caught up in the center of adult conflicts; he knew how she felt about protecting them. He shook his head, looking as miserable as she felt. They couldn't help by rushing into the middle of it. Not without thinking things through.

She didn't know as she'd be much use at all, with the stutter-beat of her heart hammering away. But she straightened, and tore her attention away from the front of the cave. "Just stall them," she muttered again, and ran for the back, fumbling for her flat, tiny LED flashlight along the way.

Because Lutfi wouldn't send her here without a reason. And he wasn't old enough, wasn't possibly altruistic enough, to think of it unless it might help him. *Let there be a back way out...* "C'mon, c'mon," she muttered, barely aware of Dobry's voice in the background, still hearty and relieved as he declined help. She swept the light along the walls of the cave as she entered total darkness, several twisty turns away from the cave entrance. The harsh, narrow beam played over the flowstone and popcorn calcifications, creating harsh shadows and twice, deep pockets of darkness that fooled her into stopping, running her hands over rock only to discover nothing more than a depression behind those formations.

Third time's a charm...

And it was.

"Gotcha," she breathed.

Or so she hoped. It was a narrow opening, not inviting.

She peered within, hunting clues, and stumbled over rocks at her feet. She caught herself with one hand, bringing the light back to illuminate the ground.

Spray-painted rocks. *Can't get much clearer than that.* She reversed course, running through the cave with long strides and duck-and-dodge moves. She found Cole at their pallet, finishing a hasty gauze-and-tape job on his own back. He let his tunic drop as she drew to a stop, and didn't hesitate in his next chore—stuffing things back into her pack, pulling his own courier bag closed with the other hand. Dobry's damaged Case o' Many Faces sat open and within reach, and Dobry himself came jogging from the front of the cave. "I convinced them it's cramped in here, but I've got no good reason to put them off. I think maybe I should go out there."

"And I think we should avoid that for now," Selena said. "There's a back tunnel. I don't think Lutfi would even have thought of it if it wouldn't help him, so I'm assuming I'll end up nearby." She glanced at Cole, at Dobry—saw identical words about to spill out. "No," she said, forestalling them both. "Cole has to save himself for whatever comes after this. And even without the vest, there's no way Dobry will fit. Besides, Dobry's got to be available to talk to Betzer. Did you ask him why he grabbed Lutfi?" Not that there was any real question, but a Dobry who still thought Betzer was on their side would certainly ask.

"Just said he didn't want the kid stirring things up—quiet in, quiet out."

Yeah, didn't Betzer just wish. "Okay," Selena said, but had no doubt Betzer would use the kid for leverage if it came to that. "You got anything in that case that might help?"

Dobry flipped it open and gestured that she should see for herself. And she did, right off the bat. A woman's wig, long black hair—half of it singed away, but that wouldn't matter. She grabbed it, and held up a misshapen plastic jar of red liquid. "Fake blood?"

"For fake deaths." Dobry stirred the chaotic contents and came up with melted plastic squibs. "Always pays to be prepared."

Hmm. She kept the hair and the jar, stuffing them into the so-convenient pockets of her coat. Dobry stood, aiming himself at the front of the cave. "You'd damn well better hurry. I assume the plan is to come in from the side, take them out as you can?"

"As I can," Selena said.

And Aymal said, querulous and demanding, "I don't suppose I have a say in this? Why don't we all use that exit, and leave this place?"

As one, Cole, Dobry and Selena snarled at him. "*No!*"

Cole stood, an understanding but restraining hand on Selena's arm as she took a step toward Aymal. She stopped, restricting herself to words. "I would tell you to go to hell, but if you can even think of abandoning that child, you're clearly already there."

From outside, clear tones of impatience. "C'mon, Dobry—what the hell are you doing, knitting the thing?"

"We may need to mock up a stretcher and patient," Dobry said, hustling back toward the entrance.

Cole didn't release Selena's arm; instead, he gave it a gentle squeeze. "Go make it happen, babe."

And Selena put her hand over his, knowing he could feel the tension along her arm. "I feel like I know too much this time around."

He gave her a crooked, weary grin. "You know what it can really come down to," he said. "You know the reality of the consequences."

"Yes." But it came out as a whisper.

He touched her cheek, his hand grimy, his own blood still on his fingers. His voice matched hers. "Then use it. Take what it does to you and use it."

Just exactly what she'd decided on the top of a desert mountain in Arizona. Except…

That had been lip service.

This was the real thing.

Not Taz, not any cartoon character.

Just Selena, and what she could dig down deep and find in herself.

She nodded at Cole, short and sweet.

And of course he knocked the weight of the moment to its knees with that cocky grin and his next words. "And hey, babe…if you can't do it, then fake it till you make it. That's what I do."

"Gah," she said. "You're…*you're*—"

"I am," he agreed cheerfully, though he'd gone back to leaning on the wall. "Now *go*."

And she did.

She'd barely reached the tunnel when she heard Dobry's annoyed shout. "You in some kind of hurry, Betzer? This is my operation, and I'll make sure you get paid. But I'm giving the orders, and if I want Jones secure for travel before we go, then we'll damn well make sure he's secure for travel!"

Good, she thought. It was about time to take that tone with Betzer, who'd gone far over the bounds of any contract employee. She hesitated at the tunnel entrance long enough to strip her coat off, going on the assumption that it was going to get tight in there. *Not too tight*, she hoped. The men who used this route no doubt had never considered the logistics of doing so with breasts, and even a good solid B cup was enough to get any woman in trouble in a place like this. Otherwise…

She was abruptly coming to appreciate the body she normally thought of as too angular, and the ass that could have used a little J-Lo mojo. A little twist here, a turn there…she scraped by a tight spot, the tiny flashlight in her leading hand, the coat trailing behind her and laden with her gun, her disguise goodies, and a few fun items from her backpack. Quickly enough, she lost her sense of direction; she gave thanks that she didn't come to any forks in the road—and then gave thanks again when she realized sections of tunnel had been widened by hand. But the roof of it suddenly brushed her hair, and within short order she was crouching, working her way forward until the roof pushed her down to all fours.

She stopped, then. Took a deep breath, trying to assess the time it had taken her to get this far…convincing herself that she wouldn't get stuck. She tucked the collar of the coat through the back of her belt so it followed her in the manner of a bizarre wedding-gown train. The gun she pulled out and stuck into her back pocket.

It wasn't until she prepared to move forward that she recognized the faint wash of daylight across the rocks. She flicked the LED off and waited. By the time she'd stuffed it into her pocket, her eyes had adjusted; she eased forward into a space that grew even tighter.

But she'd fit. She could see that she'd fit, and she scrambled for the opening.

What she saw there made no sense. She looked out into the bottom half of a pit lined with tightly fit stone—a pit just big enough for someone to curl up in, with a narrow opening at the upper edge. She could barely hear conversation in the background, argumentative enough to fire her with urgency. She crawled out into the pit and eased up to the narrow opening—and quite suddenly knew where she was.

The temple.

The pilgrim cells, built along the bottom edge of the half-circle wall inside what was left of the courtyard. From here she could just barely see the freestanding structure that housed the eternal flame, off to her left. Unless they had a guard stationed right here, she was good to go—plenty of cover on hand, between the naturally occurring rocks, the fallen walls, the old pillars…

She shoved the coat out before her and pulled herself up through the opening. There she hesitated, her hips balanced on the edge of the pit wall, her elbows locked to support her weight—and she saw movement.

Sonofabitch. Of course they'd left someone in this general area. From the eternal flame you could see the entire village and the stretch of road coming in from Suwan, not to mention the ridge that ran parallel behind the village.

But he wasn't watching the temple itself.

Without taking her eyes off him, Selena went inward. She hunted the surge of awareness, of intensity. The impulse to strike out, to run a punishing series of six-minute miles.

She remembered what it was like to kill a man, and she weighed it against the stakes. *Cole. Aymal. Two countries once more at risk.*

Then she silently emerged from the pit, moving slowly but steadily, kneeling right there with her feet still trailing off over open air so she could remove her belt.

Because this wouldn't do any of them any good if she alerted Betzer to trouble from the start. This first one…he'd have to come down quietly.

* * *

Hurry, Selena. Cole lay on the hard ground, tangled in the stretcher they'd quickly rigged from two blankets. More like a sling, except that at the moment it wasn't slung between anything. Aymal and Dobry had set him down just outside the cave, where the sunshine warmed his body in a decadently pleasant fashion that seemed totally at odds with the situation.

And there was only so much longer Dobry could hold this little farce together. They hadn't planned to take it even this far, all of them exposed, all of them playing precarious roles—still armed, because there was no reason in their false scenario not to be, but the guns weren't close at hand.

Except for Cole, who had his hand wrapped comfortably around the grip of the Browning and hidden beneath a carefully arranged flap of blanket.

"You still got the kid?" Dobry said, and managed convincing surprise with the Goff voice he'd identified for Cole and now still used simply because it was how Betzer knew him. "Forget him. Tell me you have good solid transport."

"It's not a Hummer," Betzer said, "but it'll do." The very sound of his voice so nearby triggered Cole's temper, his memory of being under fire from this man. Retribution lured him, the urge to leap up and—

But no. Even if he was capable of such mayhem, his job for the moment was to be still and look sick and unconscious. Not a huge stretch, if it came to it.

Fly-egg incubator, that's me.

"Great," Dobry said. "How about you drop the kid and get serious here, then?"

C'mon, Selena...

"I think we'll keep the kid until we're on our way out."

Betzer wasn't trying quite so hard to sound amiable anymore. Lufti made a series of small grunting noises that sounded like an unsuccessful attempt to break free. "Where's Jones's wife? Selena?"

Dobry's irritation might well be real. "Taking a last trip to the bucket. You know how women are. She's probably waiting for the flies to move off—like that's gonna happen."

"I'll get her," a man said, making a satisfied noise in his throat. "I owe her."

Betzer's voice turned to a low grumble. "Not now, Buzz."

Cole noticed he didn't say *not ever.*

C'mon, c'mon, *Selena*. But there was no telling how far she'd have to go in the tunnel, or how far to return here. They had nothing more than Selena's belief the boy wouldn't have mentioned the tunnel if it wouldn't help him. And meanwhile the pebbles beneath Cole's hip and shoulder made themselves apparent, and the role of unconscious man became harder to play.

"Funny," Betzer said in Russian, and Cole figured he must have turned his attention to Aymal. "I was sure you'd recognize me once you got out here."

Oh, God. Aymal, the geek terrorist defector. Not so good at these situations. *Just keep your mouth shut.*

As if. "I do," Aymal said. "I saw you at both of the failed attempts to reach safe transport. I assume there is some good reason for that."

Betzer laughed out loud. "Oh, yeah," he said, and there wasn't anything amiable about that voice at all, not any longer. "There's a reason for it, all right."

Damn well better hurry, Selena.

Hurry. The little voice in her mind made it hard to stay steady, to think clearly. She only knew it had taken too long to get this far. Their one hope lay in Betzer's willingness to play the friendly role—and that Dobry could make it seem expedient to do so.

Selena checked her gun, her knives…hung the belt around her neck. She left the coat draped at the edge of the pilgrim cell and crept out across the inlaid stone of the temple ruins. No grass dared to grow between the stones, no persistent local plants. Just grit laid over stone, making the footing less secure than it might have been. She kept her focus on the back of the man she'd targeted. He stood slouched, bored…a Westerner's heavy build that stood out in this land of wiry men. By all rights his back should be twitching from the intensity of her gaze on him, but he remained oblivious, watching that which lay beyond her line of sight.

Selena moved laterally until she put a stone pillar between the two of them, and then she ran up to the pillar on silent feet, halting there to breathe deeply and listen for any sign of movement from the other side.

He was either as quiet as she, or still engrossed in the scene beyond. She didn't think he could see the cave entrance, but he could probably watch Betzer and his crew. *How many?* How many would she have to go through before they gave up or ran out of mercs? At what point would Dobry dive in? Would Cole even be able to help?

Just assume you're on your own.

She'd done it before, after all.

With no sign of awareness from the other side of the pillar, Selena dared to peek around it.

Oblivious.

Idiot. No wonder he was back here out of the action.

Selena tested the stones of the pillar, reaching up to dig her fingers into the insecure handholds. One careful step at a time, she climbed the thing—nearly seven feet up to the uneven top, which she peeked over just enough to see that the faint noises of her progress had finally caught the man's attention. Not enough to make him wary, just enough to bring him toward her at an angle, his gun ready at his shoulder.

Selena silently pulled the belt free from around her neck, taking a wrap at either end. She lurked, waiting as the man drew closer, nothing exposed but the very top of her head over the pillar—and he'd have to look up to see it.

He didn't look up.

One final step drew him close enough to the pillar that she couldn't see him, and she leaped into action, shoving her hands against the top of the pillar and surmounting it, coming to a stop on her knees at its very edge, three square feet of landing pad. *Gotcha.*

There he was, just on the other side; his head jerked up and he tried to bring the gun to bear—but as he turned, she flung the belt over his head; her foot lashed out to kick the gun away. Leverage did the rest for her, slamming him back against stone with the belt tight against his throat and his feet getting light on the ground.

"How many of you?" she asked him, breathless rather than demanding. A quick deep breath, a jerk on the belt as he scrabbled blindly at her, and she had a more commanding voice at hand. *"How many?"*

"Fuuughuu," he rasped, and his hand dipped below her field of view. Her warning jerk wasn't enough and when the hand reappeared it held a gun.

For a split second, the muzzle of the gun loomed large, closer to Selena's eyes than she'd ever imagined, a sight she knew right then and there would remain etched in her memory, acid and astonishing.

She threw herself back off the pillar.

She couldn't have released the belt if she'd wanted to. Her arms stretched in a painful, awkward hold, one elbow nearly bent unto breaking before she managed to jerk herself into a better angle. By the time she got her breath back, by the time she could pay attention to the wild activity on the other end of the belt, it came with the beat of heels against stone…and then it stopped altogether.

Sigh.

Selena finally extricated her hands from the tight wrap of the belt, twisting and turning until she dropped the short distance to the ground. A quick look revealed them reddened and bruised but essentially whole. She gingerly rubbed the scraped webbing between finger and thumb, and then did what inevitably came next. She checked the other side of the pillar.

Yep, there he was, sprawled awkwardly against the stone with the second gun still in his hand and a spreading stain at his crotch. Dammit. She hadn't meant to—

"Idiot," she told him, and plucked the gun from his hand. "You really thought that through, didn't you?"

One down. Who knows how many left.

Here we go again.

Chapter 20

Now, Cole thought loudly at Selena. *Seriously. Now.*

Too bad he didn't know if she'd even emerged from that tunnel yet.

He did know that they were running out of time. *Had* run out of time. Betzer's impatience was out in the open, his feigned *you're the boss* attitude slipping fast. "Look," he told Dobry. "I've got other things going on. Places to go, people to kill. You know how it is."

"I'll go get her," Aymal offered—probably the worst thing he could have done, because Betzer knew well enough that no Muslim man would offer to fetch a female stranger—an infidel female stranger at that—off the john. Especially when the john was an unsanitary bucket without so much as a privacy sheet hanging around it.

And Betzer knew. There was a snap to his voice as he said, "No. You'll stay out here. All of you. One of my men will go."

"This is my op," Dobry said, hardening his voice. "I'll make those decisions."

And Betzer just laughed. "Goff, you have been a true fucking joy to work with. But it's time to stop pretending. Jones's wife didn't want you to call me, did she? She's got better instincts. You should have listened to them."

Right damn now, *Selena.*

"This is no good," Selena told the dead man. Anyone walking between the cave on the village could easily spot him along the way. She looped the belt around her neck and applied herself to moving the body. Not far—because *God is he heavy*—but out of sight. Behind the pillar, behind the crumble of rocks just beyond it. She recovered both his guns, including the Glock she'd kicked into a pilgrim cell, and doubled her firepower on the spot.

Not that it mattered, when she was still in quiet mode—still trying to work her way back to help Cole and—

She shouldn't have thought of it; she faltered, her steady focus turning into a bout of *what if I can't…*

Screw that. None of them had the time for it. Fake it till you make it, Cole had said. She'd feel better if she knew just which of those roles she'd taken. *Faking…or making…*

And meanwhile she'd crept up to the point of rock where she could look beyond, to find Betzer in the small level oval of ground in front of the cave and, to her surprise, Dobry just outside the cave opening itself. And Cole—she suddenly realized that lump of blankets on the ground was her husband, looking feeble and limp enough to make her wonder if he even breathed.

He's playing the role, you idiot.

She'd believe that…because she had to.

Betzer had Lufti pulled up against his leg, his hand

dwarfing the boy's mouth and jaw and plenty of leverage to both silence and entrap the boy. Aymal hung near the cave entrance, ready to bolt.

Whatever Dobry and Betzer talked about, it grew less amiable by the moment.

Too bad there was a sentry between here and there. And he was loaded down with a Colt AR-15, an assault rifle he held with easy familiarity.

She pulled back slightly, enough so she wouldn't be seen as she took the belt from her neck and unbuckled it. There were four men facing off at the cave; they thought themselves still six total. She figured she could make them four, perhaps three, and then…free-for-all, with Lufti in the middle and Cole vulnerable on the ground.

Great plan.

Without taking her gaze off the man's far-too-sturdy back, Selena bent down and felt around for a pebble. Not hard to find in this terrain. *Take two, they're small…*

And hesitated. *What if I can't…what if I lose myself in overreactions…*

Selena found herself moving without thought—because it was the only way she could move at all. *Just do it.* She dropped a pebble on the point of rock and it trickled downhill with a murmur of sound. The belt ready in one hand, she waited…but not long. She dropped the second pebble. Finally he shifted, looking over his shoulder.

Selena struck. She snapped the belt like a wet towel and the buckle cracked into the outer edge of the man's eye even as he brought the rifle to bear. He screamed—damn straight he screamed, with that eye ruined and the bone of the socket giving way—and Selena kicked the rifle away, a high, long-legged move she'd turned into second nature with recent endless hours of gym work. By then he'd bent over his eye;

by then they'd gotten Betzer's attention. No time to play games; she dropped the belt and grabbed the man's arm, pivoting him around and slamming him into the rock.

And still he scrabbled for the knife stuck through his belt, the blood streaming down his face, his eye socket a gory mess. She pulled her gun, shoving it right up against one nostril even as his hand closed firmly around the grip of his knife. "No," she told him, and quite firmly at that.

His one good eye stared at her; she saw in it the moment he gave up, even before his hand eased away from the knife. As quick as that, she brought the gun back and slammed it against his temple. That eye rolled back in his head and he slid bonelessly down the slope of rock. She winced at the sight of his face, but at least he was still alive.

And that's when she turned and found the muzzle of Betzer's AR-15 headed her way.

Eyes still closed, ears on full alert…Cole heard the scuffle in the distance. Betzer cursed, Aymal made a choking noise, Dobry grunted satisfaction…

Yeah. Selena.

Cole opened his eyes, found the nearest target and pulled his pistol free of the blankets—rolling over in that same motion, bringing the gun to bear in spite of the lead in his limbs and the tight stretch of pain along his back, a smoldering fire branding the wound itself. In that instant he found their four targets, recognized the bulk of flak vests, discovered Betzer sighting in on Selena…discovered Dobry standing in his line of fire. Betzer had the only assault rifle and should go down first, but Cole did the next best thing, sighting the man who'd targeted Dobry.

Aymal ran, but it was only to be expected. They'd never given him a gun.

The action came in fast sequence, shots overlapping. Dobry twitched and stumbled even as Cole drilled a neat hole through the forehead of the man who'd shot him, at the same time that Dobry fired a shot that went just wild enough to smack into Betzer's arm, not even enough impact to stagger a big man in a balanced stance.

Lufti bit down hard on Betzer's hand and squirmed away as Betzer bellowed a curse, and then damned if Cole didn't lose his precarious balance, just enough to waste the next bullet at the feet of the man beside Betzer. He rolled, came up to his knees…ignored the pain of such movement and took bead on his target. A squeeze and the man gave an astonished grunt, far too confident in his flack vest when he should have considered wearing a gorget instead. Blood frothed at his throat and Cole left him to choke it out—and, feeling his own strength drain, aimed at the kneecap of the fourth man and rode the trigger, letting the recoil take the aim all the way up the man's leg.

And then there was Selena, facing off with Betzer, walking forward in those long, confident strides, the big Cougar in a double-handed grip as she took her shot and fired, took the next shot and fired, getting her shots in steady and solid as Betzer fired a wild burst near her feet. Squeezing that last shot off as the rising breeze lifted the loosened hijab from her hair and freed it, her face a study in focused calm and her feet not missing a beat as the gun's slide racked back and stayed there. She dropped it, reaching into her belt for a Glock she'd acquired along the way.

An entirely unnecessary Glock. Betzer's rifle never made it all the way up to become a serious threat and now it drooped back down again. Selena waited, legs braced in a classic Weaver stance, as Betzer swayed on his feet, spit blood, and gurgled, "I should have let Buzz have you in the Plush."

"You could have tried," she said, and watched him fall.

Yeah. That's my girl.

Gun still covering the fallen men, Selena ran from one to the other, kicking aside their weapons in the first pass, then going through them again to check for concealed weapons...and finally, for pulses. None. "Weebles wobble and they *do* fall down," she told them, glad enough to hear Cole's incredulous choke of laughter by the cave entrance.

She patted them down one last time, starting with Betzer—hunting for something entirely different this time. *Keys.* They had to have their own transportation—something with wheels and an engine. Just too damn many pockets among them, and no one with an obvious bulge of keys. Could be on the man at the temple or the only survivor from Betzer's little group.

Remorse washed over her for those lost lives; she closed her eyes at the unexpected strength of it, and then at the surge of anger that the dead men had put her in this position in the first place. *One survivor.* "Didn't have to be that way," she muttered, purely to herself.

She glanced at the man, found him on his hands and knees and crawling away with unsteady determination. But she wasn't ready to run after him, not just yet. "Cole?" For the first time she gave him more than a glance, and discovered that he'd made his way to Dobry to fuss over what seemed a bloodless wound.

"We're good. Aymal's in the cave somewhere. Lufti got away. And we need to gather up and get the hell out of here. Betzer's got a vehicle somewhere, and there's no telling if someone's waiting with it."

Someone who'll come looking for him. She heard the unspoken words loudly enough. "Grab what you can," she said. "I'm going to find out about those keys."

"Go," he told her, and staggered away from Dobry to get their things from the cave.

Selena jogged up to the point, easily overtaking the wounded survivor and circling him to plant her black sneakered feet at his outstretched hand.

He didn't even try to look up at her. He didn't say anything, either. He just waited, dropping blood from temple and eye, waiting for either mercy or death.

There was no question in Selena's voice, just expectation. "Where's the vehicle and where are the keys."

The man stiffened in expectation of some sort of blow, and Selena crouched, hands dangling over her knees, to bring herself up close and personal. "Vehicle," she said. "*Keys.* And while we're at it, might there be anyone waiting back at that vehicle?"

"No." That one he could answer simply and quickly, and did. The rest of it…not so easy. "Keys…under a rock. Near the truck. So we wouldn't have to retrieve them if the wrong person went down." He blew dripping blood off his upper lip, his head still bowed, his face pretty much wrecked.

"Under a rock," Selena said flatly, glancing around at the very many rocks available for such a role.

"Near the truck. That dead-end access road—"

She knew it. It never entered the village, but wound along the point and dead-ended well behind the temple and a little above the village. She'd used it the last time she'd been here, driving an embassy vehicle…before the Kemeni had first struck. "And while we're at it," she said softly, "what do you know about an attack on the capitol this evening?"

He shook his head, slow and numb. "Not our thing. Betzer said Arachne..." He made a pained noise and managed to continue. "That's all I know. Don't have a fucking clue what Arachne is." And then, incredibly quick, he made a swipe at her ankle, a grab and snatch to dump her on her ass and—

He never got the chance. Selena smacked his hand away with the Cougar, a bone-jarring crunch of impact. "Oh, stop it," she said. "I had planned to let you crawl away from here—" he might deserve justice, but he was no continuing threat; he was a merc with no payroll, not a man with a cause "—but you could still change my mind."

He froze. No doubt he'd been anticipating death as soon as he'd given her all she needed to know...no doubt it's how he would have handled the situation. Then he shifted away from her and went into high gear, even making it up to all fours.

"Good luck with that," she muttered. She added a little more loudly, "The villagers are not your friends, by the way."

At that he hesitated—he'd been heading toward the village, clearly visible even to a recently one-eyed man. "I want to come with you."

"Whatever." Selena stood, brushed her hands on her thighs, and shrugged even though he couldn't see it. Aymal, tentatively heading her way with her coat in hand and an abrasion or two on his face, opened his eyes wide at her response. "We're not waiting, though."

He rose to his feet for a few stumbling steps, heading for the truck, and fell, only to repeat the process.

"You can't mean it," Aymal said, holding out her coat.

"I'm sure the embassy marines will gladly handle him for us," she said. "And frankly, I see no reason we should foist him off on the good people here." She shook her head at the coat, in spite of the lingering chill of the morning. "You carry it. Go help Cole and Dobry—Dobry's hurt and I don't know how badly."

"And Cole," he said, and widened his eyes in realization. "There's just you and—"

"Yep. We're the able-bodied ones. Now go help them. I'm going to find that key before our friend does. It would be suicide to try to drive in that condition, but I don't doubt he'd try it."

Aymal's expression turned resistant, somewhat sullen... very much *you are not the boss of me*. And suddenly it didn't matter that Selena understood perfectly that his culture molded him to respond to her in this way. "Tell you what," she said, impatience coloring her tone as she watched Betzer's lone survivor stagger out of sight around the temple. "We'll have a much better chance of actually surviving the rest of this day if you just pretend I'm a man."

His eyes flicked up and down her form as if in spite of himself; his neck flushed dark and it spread into his face.

"I'm not kidding," she said. "Just do it. And then do as I said and go help Cole. I don't know how badly Dobry is hurt." And maybe she should have hesitated long enough to check it out, but unless she commandeered that vehicle, it would be moot point. "And do it because I have friends in high places, and how your life goes after this might very much depend on what I tell them."

That, he understood. He put some hustle into his steps as he trotted down toward the cave entrance...and Selena put some hustle into her own jog as she went after the wounded man. She had no trouble overtaking him, no trouble finding the battered old military transport, its canvas sides missing but the rest of it sturdy enough. The key wasn't far, he'd said...and she turned over rocks until the man came up behind her, chose the correct rock and dangled the key at her.

"Hand it over," she said. "Or do you really think you're going to overcome me and drive this thing out of here in your condition?"

"I might." The bleeding had stopped and begun to coagulate, creating an even more gruesome collection of gore on his face. But he'd recovered somewhat from the blow she'd dealt him.

Obviously not hard enough.

They stared at each other a long moment.

"Oh, fine," she said. "Whatever." And crouched beneath the wheel of the truck, plucking wires and pulling out her short tanto blade to strip them, never losing her awareness of the man. But he didn't move, and when she had the truck started and took a moment to assess her best off-road strategy for getting closer to the cave, he actually looked a little lost. She jerked her head at the back of the truck. "Get in."

He looked down at his useless leverage of a key and tossed it away, and then took so long to climb into the end of the cargo bed that she got out and shoved him up, leaving him sprawled in the back.

It took only a few moments to move the truck as far as it would go, and backing out around the rocks would be no joy. But every step she saved Cole and Dobry…

She pulled the wires apart and slammed the door, checking the truck bed on the way past. "Are you going to be good, or do I have to slap you around a couple of times before I go?"

He lay on his back, ungainly and bloody, with no apparent interest in moving.

"Because if you're going to be trouble, I can put a gun in Aymal's hands and set him to watching you. Word is, he can hardly tell the trigger from the safety—"

He cut her off with a grunt and a wave, not bothering to open his remaining eye.

Yeah, and I believe you, too. Poor wounded mercenary. She just didn't believe he could extract the ignition wires from where she'd stuffed them and get the right wires sparking, not with a quarter of his face missing.

At least, not before she got back.

She hopped off the back bumper and jogged for the cave—but she'd only just reached the temple when she ran into the exodus. Cole and Aymal both supported Dobry, whose pasty-white face declared his injury even if Selena couldn't see it, not beneath the wool blanket draped over his shoulders. Aymal came festooned with her backpack, her coat, and Cole's courier bag. Cole's steps were unsteady beneath his share of Dobry, and his face still had the flushed look of fever over the drained complexion of a more extended illness.

Selena took his place under Dobry's arm; he moved ahead to drop the transport's tailgate. "Ah," he said. "I see we already have company."

"We're leaving enough litter around the place already," Selena told him. Good God, Dobry was heavy—every bit as robust as he'd looked before he'd put his padded vest on. She helped him to turn around, to hoist himself up to a sitting position on the tailgate. She looked at him with a critical eye. "Are you good to go?"

"I won't feel better for the waiting," he said, and had a point at that. As long as the bleeding was under control—and it seemed to be—then getting him to Suwan as fast as possible was his best bet. Just the same as Cole. He met her gaze, straight on. "At least it was me."

She blinked in shock. "Say that again?"

"This." He gestured at the mercenary. "My fault."

Selena pressed her lips together, hard. It *was* his fault.

But… "Okay, yeah," she said. "Your fault. But I would prefer for you to come out of this whole so I can rag you about it as extensively as possible." She took her backpack and coat from Aymal; Dobry's gaze sharpened at the hair hanging out of one pocket. She shrugged. "Sometimes you use these things, sometimes you don't. Now get your ass into the truck so we can reach Suwan before this evening. I figure on driving straight to the capitol to warn them there." There was, in fact, probably a phone somewhere between here and there that would serve. But finding it would be a crapshoot, taking time they couldn't afford to lose. If she drove them straight there…plenty of time.

"Sounds good to me," Cole said. "And from there to the hospital, I'm guessing."

"We do things right, and you'll both ride to the hospital in style." Do them wrong, and they'd all four end up there…or worse. "You gentlemen get settled. We're outta here. And be nice to our guest…as long as he behaves himself."

"I'll wager my Browning that he behaves himself," Cole said, giving the merc a meaningful look. The man only waved him away from behind closed eye, lost in his own misery.

Selena gave the coat a second thought and tossed it Cole's way. "Have some padding. At least Dobry's got the blanket."

He wadded the coat up into something resembling a seat cushion, using his own abaya for warmth. "I left cash," he said. "Dollars. We owe them enough…and we used supplies."

"No argument from me." Selena assessed them, pinning Aymal with one last look. "Let me know if anything goes wrong back here."

"Yes, Mr. Jones." Aymal's response came as drolly as she expected.

"That's Mr. *Shaw* Jones, and don't you forget it." She caught Cole's mystified and amused look, and winked at him. She'd tell him later.

Because she was quite determined there would be a later.

Chapter 21

Selena only stalled the truck out once, backing it up off-road until she could find a place just big enough, just flat enough, to turn the ungainly vehicle. But as she made her way to the main road, she found the junction blocked. She didn't think there could possibly be any adrenaline left in her system, but her body proved her wrong. Even once she saw Lufti on the hood of the diminutive vehicle, her pulse raced on.

"Shut up," she muttered to herself, and plied the heavy brakes until the transport came to a stop. At second thought, her hands sought the hijab still loosely draped over her shoulders; she settled it into place over her head. Her hair escaped and the scarf was more a loose cloak hood than a concealing hijab, but it was better than nothing.

At that signal, the magistrate unpeeled himself from the side of the little produce-crate-stacked flatbed vehicle and came to the driver's door, waiting as Selena cranked the resistant window down. "You got what you came for?" he said, his sardonic tone a clear reference to her rebelliously persistent behavior in town.

She chose not to notice. "Yes, thank you." More than what she'd been looking for, to be honest. Much more. Betzer's treachery revealed, Aymal's manipulative ways exposed...all leaving them no choice but to head back to Suwan instead of getting Aymal over the border and Cole directly to medical care. And Dobry had indeed paid for his ambition, so determined to turn this operation into a personal success that he'd withheld crucial information until Betzer was nearly upon them.

She just had to make sure that Prime Minister Razidae and his people didn't pay for any of it.

"Miss?" the man said politely. "Or should I say, Miss *Selena Shaw Jones*?"

Selena winced. "How lucky for me that once I leave this place, I can leave that little incident behind."

Don't be so sure. You didn't exactly leave the hostage incident behind when you left Berzhaan the first time, did you?

"It would perhaps seem best if you didn't return," he agreed. "Considering that young Lufti seems to find himself in dire trouble whenever you arrive...for his sake alone."

She didn't answer that one directly, either. "We just learned about the strike against the capitol. We're going to stop it."

"At some expense, it would seem." He nodded at her passengers.

"Yes." She spoke tightly, resisting the urge to turn and check on Cole and Dobry. "I'm sorry to say we left something of a mess. If you care to contact the embassy, I'm certain the MPs will come for those we left behind. We're grateful for your protection, and we hope the gift we left will make it seem worthwhile."

"It will be worthwhile," he said, very much the disapproving magistrate, "if you protect the capitol. A stable government is the only chance my people have, and if your people would cease to meddle, Razidae might even accomplish that."

So many responses sprang to mind—a number of them right on the tip of her tongue. But she stopped them there. She had no business arguing with this man, not when they had yet to stop the final Kemeni assault on the capitol. She had no business arguing with a man who had done more than most to make his village a place where insurgency was not tolerated, and where the vulnerable could come for sanctuary. What he thought of her…

Let him think it.

But as she shifted the truck back into gear, the magistrate's signal to step back, she couldn't help but look at the lone vehicle blocking her path, and at the boy now standing on the hood. "What would you have done if it hadn't been us? If the other men had come back down this road?"

At that the man only grinned, the first real humor she'd seen on his face. He lifted his hand, and the rocks sprouted turban-covered heads, manifestations that grew into men with rifles. At that, Selena grinned back at him, fully appreciating the savvy that had kept this village separate from the terrorist underground for so long. She nursed the truck past the shift-point and into movement, and in the side view mirror saw the men behind them lift their rifles in salute. *Okay, cool. Maybe they don't think you're a complete ass after all.*

Now for Suwan, and the end to the last of the Kemeni rebellion.

* * *

If only they'd made it that far. With a matter of miles to go after a grinding journey during which Dobry, Cole, and the wounded mercenary endured, the transport rumbled quietly to a stop. Selena barely had time to crank it to the side of the road, glancing at both her watch—nearly six, with the sun heading toward the horizon directly before her—and the gas gauge. It read half-full.

Broken gauge…broken truck. Who knew? They didn't have the time to mess with it. They didn't have the wherewithal to go out on foot.

At least, some of them didn't.

Selena rubbed her hands over her face, taking a moment—one sweet short moment—to remember those hours before the day had started, when she'd been warm next to Cole in a cave so quiet they might have been the only ones there.

Okay. Moment over. Time to get moving. She climbed from the truck, hauling her backpack along.

Aymal leaned over the sideboards of the truck bed. "Why have you stopped?"

For a moment, she had no idea how to respond to such a question. In the end she decided against responding at all. She climbed up on the wheel to look into the truck, realizing that Cole had somehow found a way to bandage the mercenary's face even as they traveled the uneven dirt road. To judge from the man's relaxed mouth, he'd popped some morphine into the guy, too.

But Dobry looked terrible, in spite of the lack of blood. She traded a look with Cole, sharing his concern. Cole needed a hospital damn toot sweet to survive in the long run, but Dobry needed that help if he was going to make it through even the next hour.

And she was about to leave them.

"I've got to go," she said, speaking to all of them, looking only at Cole. Cole with his dark hair and his stained skin and his amazingly bright blue eyes. Understanding what she was about to do…and what it would cost her.

What it might cost him and Dobry.

"I'll send someone as soon as I can. I've even got my damned cell phone—but I don't dare—"

"Betzer might not be the only one at the end of that leak," Cole agreed. "You go, Lena."

"Na Baba!" The words burst from Aymal. "You cannot be serious! You cannot leave us here unprotected!"

"Ahem," Cole said, and gestured with his pistol. "Not entirely."

"You! Who knows when you'll faint again!"

"I don't—" Cole started, but Aymal interrupted.

"I'm coming with you," he said, most decisively.

"Sure," Selena agreed, suddenly glad to be in her sneakers. "How's your six-minute mile?"

This stymied the man for a moment. A short moment. "Then at least leave me with a—"

Selena and Cole reacted in unison. "No!"

They wasted a moment trading glares, and were interrupted by a car tootling on out of the city, zipping along here where the road was still paved. Selena and Aymal tried to wave it down and failed; they resumed glaring. Then, with brusque, economical movement, she pulled a small semiautomatic from her backpack, one of the guns she'd taken from the first sentry. She released the magazine, ejected the chamber from the cartridge, and shoved the magazine back home without racking the slide. "Here," she said, and handed the gun to him. "Just don't touch anything but the trigger." And she caught Cole's eye, checking for awareness there. If they truly got into trouble, Aymal would have to rack a cartridge into the chamber before he could add to the firepower.

Cole gave her the slightest of nods, and shifted to remove her coat from beneath himself. "Here, you'll need this."

She snorted. "I can't run with that thing."

Aymal caught her meaning and his jaw dropped slightly. "You cannot run in those clothes out in public!"

"Mr. Shaw Jones can do a lot of things in these clothes out in public," Selena told him. She lifted her head, spotting another vehicle on the way out of Suwan.

A vehicle of sorts, anyway. One with real horsepower. One that would bring Cole and the others right along with her. This time, she didn't wait to see if the driver would stop at her waving. She hopped off the transport wheel and into the road, waving her arms, backpack and all.

Clearly, she'd encountered a horse who'd seen everything. The animal didn't so much as flick an ear, but the driver pulled back on the reins with alacrity, eyeing Selena and the truck with such wariness that she knew he was on the verge of making a break for it. "Peace to you," she told him in Berzhaani, pretending she wasn't wearing other people's blood and that her face wasn't still smeared with her own. She eyed his wagon, a square box with high sides and a bench seat up front. Built on a car axle, from the looks of the tires. When she thought he'd backed off to a lower personal DefCon, she cut straight to the chase. "Can I interest you in a trade?"

"You aren't serious!"

She was inspiring a lot of that particular reaction this day. "I am." And losing time, to boot. If she ended up running after all of this…

Just a couple of miles. She could do it. Even after a day like this. And if this worked, she wouldn't have to leave the others behind.

The man spent his time looking at the transport. "I will talk to your men," he said grandly, resting his forearms across his thighs to let the reins dangle.

"Only if you speak Russian." Selena rested her hand on the horse's nose; it nuzzled her. *Sorry, no treats...only various dried body fluids*. "Or English. But I assure you, I only convey the wishes of my husband, who is in that truck."

"He lets you go out like—"

Selena shrugged an interruption. "I'm an infidel. What can you expect?" And then she got down to business. "We want to trade this truck for your horse and wagon."

"If the truck worked, you wouldn't be sitting here." He'd dropped into haggle mode, which was all for the good. He might even forget she was inappropriately clothed and that he was indignant about it.

"Very true," she said, which startled him. The horse sighed and shifted its weight to one back leg, the sun low enough to shine between its ears and make a mule of its shadow. "But I believe it to be out of gas."

"And how will I get more gas from here?" He shook his head. "It is an old truck, and ugly. And it might not even work at all."

"Come into the city with us," she said promptly. "You can pick up gas and find a ride back out. And you risk nothing but time. The horse and wagon will be yours again, if you pick them up at the capitol."

"What business have you at the capitol?" He might as well have said *the likes of* you; it came through in his voice.

"Oh," Selena said, most cheerfully. "Just a tourist."

He just looked at her.

"You risk nothing," she repeated. "You get your horse back, and you can sell the transport for parts."

"And you get..?" Too good to be true, that's what he was telling himself.

"Where I want to go, when I want to be there." She gestured at the transport. "Which obviously won't happen in this."

He could hardly deny that. His eyes roamed over the vehicle another long moment, while Selena petted the horse, her hand not so coincidentally close to the reins. She was preparing to reach into her back waistband for the Cougar, tense and ready, when he finally nodded. "You are, of course, insane," he added. "Or in a great deal of trouble, or perhaps about to get into a great deal of trouble."

"Or perhaps both," she muttered.

Definitely both.

Back in Suwan with a defector who's desperately been trying to leave, carting along her injured mercenary, a wounded fellow CIA officer, and a husband well into a systemic infection that would kill him as surely as a bullet. And was she headed for safety?

Of course not.

If only she could call Allori at the embassy. He'd get the word to Razidae's people. But as often as she found herself tempted to do it, she stopped herself. Phones were not a given in Suwan. If she wasted time looking for one—in one of the already closed establishments she passed, in a private home—and didn't find one, then she'd never make it to the capitol in time to give her warning in person. Not to mention that Allori himself was most likely at the endangered open house. She glanced at her watch again, unable to stop herself.

"We'll make it," Cole said.

"Of course," she said. "How could we not, when we've

got Seabiscuit here on our side?" The truth was, they did have time. They could do it. The horse trotted along, oblivious, nicely responsive to her hand and offering enough energy that it had probably only traveled those few miles out of Suwan before they'd intercepted the wagon. At least she'd had those miles of open road to get reacquainted with the heavy feel of the lines…not much like holding a contact on the short rein of a horse under saddle.

And, most unexpectedly, the ride was actually smoother than that of the jarring truck.

Cole sat beside her, having climbed into the seat the wagon owner had vacated when they dropped him at the edge of the city. She'd taken the back roads from there… horses and donkeys were common enough on the edges of the city, but rarely seen in the majestic central area that held the rebuilt capitol, the government buildings, a few exclusive apartments and hotels. It was an area overlaid with the stone remains of old walls and fortifications, ancient vines and carefully tended trees. As they drew closer to the capitol, the streets narrowed. She learned from experience that the horse tended to slip on cobbles, and kept it to asphalt.

She again wore the bulky coat, and she could still feel the heat off Cole's body.

"I'm fine," he'd said—again—when she'd once taken her eyes from the road to convey her concern with a look—just before the sun went down, and the light of it shone clearly off his face to reveal how not-fine he was, his blue eyes shining so eerily that Selena couldn't decide if it was the sharp sunlight, his dyed skin or the hollows the fever had already carved in his face. *Right. Just fine.*

Now the light was fast fading and the old-fashioned streetlights struggled to fill the void. They trotted on through back streets and alleys almost too narrow to take them, until at last the familiar outline of the square, stolid capitol building filled the marginally lighter sky before them. Selena pulled the horse in beneath a streetlight…and a rare public phone. She checked her watch. "We've got a few minutes. Time enough to do this carefully." She looped the harness lines over the stout U-bolt on the front of the wagon meant for just that, and stood, digging into her pockets as she looked back at Aymal. "You," she said, "are going to make a phone call."

His brows drew together in vast doubt. "You're going to leave me here?"

"Damned right," she told him. "You're too valuable to risk. And those schoolchildren are too valuable to risk, too."

Startled, he said nothing.

"You're going to call a woman named Bonita at her personal cell phone. She'll know how to get a message to Dante Allori, the American ambassador—be sure to mention the rumors about Davud Garibli. And then you're going to lurk around this building until one of us comes for you. It's full of government offices—there won't be anyone around to bother you."

"And what if you don't come back?" His voice rose slightly, and Selena figured this was one defector who'd been pushed to his limits.

"Then forget the CIA. Head straight to the embassy. Tell them you have a special appointment with Dante Allori and Selena Shaw Jones. Tell them it's regarding pest control."

Cole unsuccessfully muffled his snort. "And I thought the Agency got corny sometimes."

Selena cleared her throat, a little more loudly than necessary. "That'll get you in the door. You'll probably have to wait for Allori, maybe all night. But don't tell anyone but Allori who you are. Let him know the local station has been compromised. Got it?"

Aymal muttered a few quick phrases to himself and nodded. "Give me the number." And then he sent her a sour look. "If you think I believe this will work, after all I've been through…"

"You don't have to believe it," she told him. "Just do it." She finally found the change she'd been hunting, and dropped the coins in his waiting hand as she gave him the number, made him recite it three times, and then gestured him out of the wagon.

And then she turned to Dobry. He sat propped in the corner, opposite his mercenary counterpart, and he looked purely terrible. His face took on a grayish-green cast under the streetlight; his breathing came in short, shallow efforts. "I don't get it," she told Cole, climbing over the back of the driver's seat to crouch by Dobry, who seemed barely aware of it. "I didn't think he'd been hit that badly."

Cole followed her, much more slowly. He crouched beside her in increments, and then gave up and dropped to his knees. "It's got to be internal bleeding—I just can't figure what. It's not all that different than mine. I've decided to call it George, by the way."

"Call what?" Selena opened Dobry's jacket and then his shirt, pulling the Velcro on the torso padding.

"My war wound. The infection. George."

She hesitated with what she was doing long enough to look over at him. "Just so long as we don't start naming other body parts."

"Hey, some men do," Cole protested. And then, his eyes widened and his face was grim. "Holy shit."

That's when Selena realized her hands were warm and wet, and she jerked her attention back to Dobry. The torso padding was sodden, heavy with blood. "Dobry, you fool." He had to have known. He'd been bleeding into the vest all this time, showing no sign of it from the outside. "We should have checked him—" But when she looked at the thick wad of bandages Cole had wrapped in place, the top layer was still dry. The bandage had come loose from around Dobry's abdomen, and the lower layer of the bandage had wicked off to the padding.

"I *did* check him," Cole said, and shook his head. "Damn. If he'd said something—"

Dobry's eyes dragged open. "Then you just would have had to make another hard decision. I made it for you. I…I got us into that mess. I've got nothing to complain about—"

Selena said fiercely, "You *want* to be a black star on the Wall of Honor?"

"Not…particularly."

"Then shut up." She yanked her Buck 110 from her thigh pocket and held it by the blade, flipping it open to a locked position. The stout working blade cut through the bottom of Cole's abaya with only a whisper of noise. Cole might have made a surprised noise, but he didn't; he merely turned to make the work easier. And when she was done, he took the strip of material and worked it under Dobry as Selena supported Dobry's heavy weight, lifting him slightly. Together they tied it off, making a pressure bandage out of the whole thing.

Not that it would really matter, if he kept bleeding internally. Dobry groaned a sigh as Selena released him. She said, "Look. We've made it to the capitol—it's just down the block. We've got a capitol security cop to get past—"

"Didn't see him," Cole noted.

"Trust me. There's at least one on this end of the street, even with the building officially closed. If I get past him, I've got a good shot at the stairs."

"We," Cole muttered.

"The point is, we're almost there. We're almost to help, for both of you. Dobry, just...*hang on*."

"Give it...a try," Dobry breathed.

Selena cursed under her breath and almost took the coat off to put it over him...she'd be warm enough, soon enough. But she still had to get past the local law, and she might well keep covered until she did. She twisted, looking down the street, pondering options. One cop between them and the building, others scattered around the grounds, unless Aymal was wrong about the low-key security for the event.

They'd find out soon enough. First they had to tackle that one cop. She said, "I could just go ask for help, but..."

"But it won't get you anywhere if he takes so much convincing that the action starts around us," Cole finished.

Selena stood, jammed her hands into her coat pockets and encountered a day's worth of gatherings. The wig, the blood, the first sentry's gun...

She looked down at her pocket. Cole looked at her pocket. And then they looked at each other, the same idea finding fruition at the same time. "Decoy," they said in chorus.

"Decoy and tangle," Cole added. "Get him out of your way."

"It's a plan." Selena set the wagon brake and jumped out, snagging her backpack along the way. Cole followed more slowly. By the time he reached the street corner, she'd laid out the coat, rumpling it so the stiff material held a vague body shape. The wig sat atop the collar, the singed side toward the ground, serving as a head. And the blood...she spilled it out in the corner streetlamp, hoping that the poor light would obscure the odd clumping caused by the heat damage. "You ready?" she murmured, and Cole faded back into the shadow of the low, decorative wall on the corner.

Selena checked her scarf, took the abaya Cole handed her and deliberately let herself slide into the fear that drove all her overreactions, all her barely controlled fight-or-flight. She hyperventilated a quick couple of breaths, and then she ran for the capitol building. She ran with clumsy steps, arms in an excess of motion—and when she saw the uniformed patrolman, she came to a flailing stop fifty feet away. "Help me!" she cried to him in her perfect Berzhaani. "My sister! A man has attacked her! Help us—!" And she reversed course, staying just out of the light—just far enough away so he wouldn't see what she wore under the open-front abaya. "He hit her hard!"

The man hesitated, but he followed her. His steps quickened as he saw the faked body, and it was an easy matter to shove him stumbling toward Cole. Cole loomed out of the darkness and spun the man right into and over the decorative wall—and by then Selena had shed the abaya and could pounce.

In moments they'd secured the man with his own cuffs, a strip of duct tape from Selena's bag over his mouth and around his ankles. They tucked him away in the inside corner of the decorative wall. "It won't last," Cole said, not quite able to stand up straight.

"It doesn't have to." Selena bent to look in the man's eyes, furious and glittering even in this poor light. "I beg pardon," she said, "but we don't have the time to convince you. I promise, we're here to save Razidae." *Again.* And they were empty words to a humiliated guard now worried about the security of the capitol.

No time for anything more than regrets. Selena snatched up the coat and ran it down the street to cover Dobry, then started to work on the horse's harness. When Cole caught up, his own eyes glittering from fever and his ragged breath betraying his pain, his expression nonetheless lit up. "You're planning a grand entrance, I take it?"

"I need something they can't ignore." She yanked a trace strap free of the wagon's trace hook while Cole more slowly did the same on the other side, and left him to coil up the leather while she freed the breaching straps and the belly band of the harness saddle just behind the horse's withers. The shafts drooped. She caught her side and waited for Cole to get the other, and they backed the wagon away from the horse, out of the light of the streetlamp.

"Don't tell me," Cole said, voice strained with the effort. "You drove horses at that school of yours."

"A time or two," Selena said, hating the sudden wobble in her voice. She returned to the horse and pulled the lines through the terrets on the harness collar and saddle, then slashed them short with her knife to make reins.

The wobble knew the consequences of failure. The wobble knew the consequences of success sometimes weren't much better.

"Hey," Cole said, and caught her hand as she tied a knot in the reins, resting it behind the bearing hook on the saddle piece. "Until you came along, this op was totally FUBAR. I've seen in you action and there's no one I'd rather trust to pull this off."

Whoa. She hadn't expected that.

Then again, she hadn't expected to fall into such seamless teamwork with him. He was the one with the experience, the one with all the moves. The one who took life so casually on the surface that she'd had to learn to look hard to see beneath, to the man who needed her as much as she needed him.

"It's not the same as it was," she told him, thinking of who and how she'd been before the hostage incident.

"No," he said. "It's never the same. It'll be a little bit different after this one, too. For any of us."

The truth of his words struck her, there at the side of the street, their hands connecting over the withers of a restless horse. At Athena, she'd learned confidence. She'd learned skills. As a legate, she'd honed those skills, and she'd had to use them. But nothing could have prepared her for facing off against the Kemenis, the only chance for a dozen young hostages and another dozen innocent adults.

She couldn't ever be that young Selena Shaw again. But that part of her was still there. Changed, recast, but still there. The basic Selena. And the basic Selena could still use those qualities, building on to them with everything that had happened to her since.

The good and the bad.

Slowly, she nodded. "Okay," she said. "Time to go do this thing."

Chapter 22

I can't believe I'm going to do this.

Mr. Secret Agent Man, about to watch his Secret Agent Wife head off into the middle of it. Alone.

But Cole assessed himself, painfully honest…and just plain painful. Fire branded his back. He couldn't pretend any longer that the chills he'd so far hidden from Selena were from the cool night air, or that the racing pattern of his heart came from anything he'd actually been doing.

Doesn't matter. We're almost done. And Dobry…Dobry was dying fast. If he didn't get help soon, it would be too late.

"He might not be used to this," Selena said, making some final adjustment to what remained of the horse's harness, glancing at her watch. "Hang on to his head, will you?"

Cole reached for the reins directly beneath the half-cheek driving bit and giving a reflexive glance at his own watch face. They still had time. She could do this her way.

Selena vaulted onto the horse's back with the athletic fluidity of practiced skill. The animal was typical of those Cole had seen in the area—wiry, capable, not terribly big. Selena's legs dangled along its sides. She gathered the reins and shifted around to a secure place behind the harness saddle, ignoring the horse's jigging as it adjusted to the new situation. "I'll send someone out as soon as—"

Staccato gunfire cut into her words.

Cole lip-read her succinct curse well enough. The party had started early, and that changed everything.

Everything.

When the horse surged forward, Cole kept a hand on the reins, stopping it suddenly enough to evoke a little rear. "I'm coming with you."

"You can't—"

"I'm *fine*—" he started and, at her patent disbelief looking down at him, shook his head. Regretted it, fighting a surge of dizziness, but persisting. "Okay, I suck. But I'll take care of myself."

"Let go of the reins!" She fought him for them, unsuccessful only because she took care not to hurt the horse's mouth.

"Lena!" He leaned into the animal's shoulder, risking those shod hooves and the potential impact of the hard, bony knee. The horse snorted loudly and wetly and Cole raised his voice over the gunplay. "You're not going in there without me! You think I can't stop this horse? You think I'm not perfectly capable of letting this thing play out without us? You've done this alone once already...*but not this time.*"

"Cole—"

"Let me cover your back, dammit! Don't you dare leave me behind to hate myself the rest of my life if—"

"And what about me?" She glared. "I'm supposed to just live with it if—"

"*Trust me.*" Cole released the horse and held out his hand, the one she'd need to take to help him up behind her.

"*Dammit*," she snarled, and grabbed his forearm, sticking out her foot to act as an erstwhile stirrup.

Cole swung up behind her. Not graceful; not even remotely impressive. Little Joe Cartwright, he wasn't. He reached around Selena's tight waist to latch onto the harness saddle—and when he clamped his legs around the horse's flanks, it gave a startled grunt and flung its butt in the air. Cole's nose hit the back of Selena's head and she said, "Lighten up!" before she used her own heels more appropriately, sending the horse forward. A few strides of jarring trot were enough to shoot sparks all the way up Cole's back. Then the horse broke into a lurching canter, not at all the gait of an experienced saddle horse. Cole clutched the hard leather of the harness saddle, working so hard to stay on that narrow back that he barely realized they'd arrived at the base of the capitol, gunfire everywhere, bodies everywhere, and *damned if my Browning's not stuck between the two of us and then damned if we're not going right up the fucking stairs—*

With only one hand on the reins. He realized it as Selena took aim to the side and ahead, a carefully considered shot that must have found its mark—the horse made an ungainly leap over the body that rolled into its path. Cole had a flash of black and khaki—*Kemeni*—and the horse floundered to find its footing on the stairs again.

They lurched, forward and up and lurched again. Selena took another shot while Cole quite literally covered her back. *Not what I had in mind, dammit.* His own back cramped, moments away from total seizure here on the once-bloodstained steps of the Berzhaani capitol. *Get off before you fall off.*

And cover Selena's back for real.

* * *

Selena had aimed the startled horse at the steps before it had time to think about what she was asking, before it had time to refuse. Cole clutched at the harness, hot against her back. A Suwan cop already lay dead at the base of the imposing steps. Another sprawled at the edge, halfway into the neatly groomed shrubs that hadn't been here the last time. She got a glimpse of statuary and understood, then, that the changes were a memorial for those who had died on these steps.

No memorials for you, she snarled silently at the Kemenis charging up the steps just ahead of them. The suicide charge, with one man already at the top of the steps and struggling with the door. A door he should have had no chance of opening without the access code.

With the horse making an honest, gallant effort beneath her, Selena overtook a straggler Kemeni and shot him down, giving the horse its head so it could flounder over the falling body. And then the man just ahead—but the horse stumbled and the bullet skimmed the man's neck—he reflexively threw himself to the side and Selena overtook him in an instant, leaving him at her back. At *Cole's* back.

Except Cole chose that moment to release his grip on the harness, his voice briefly in her ear. "*I'll cover you.*"

And then her back was cold and exposed—and ahead, the Kemenis gave an exultant group cry and shoved one of the massive double doors open.

Gunfire behind her left no doubt as to Cole's activities, and as three men and their Abakan assault rifles rushed into the capitol, Selena saved ammo by simply mowing down the man ahead of her—no longer trying to stop the several men left on the steps, but heading for the doors themselves. Once the Kemenis hit the fancy dining room, they could shoot down the entire assembly.

Gunfire behind her, gunfire ahead—the two-beat stutter of the Abakans interspersed with the weapons of the fast-arriving Berzhaani security, the powerful report of Cole's Browning behind her.

And here she was, riding a befuddled cart horse into the Berzhaani capitol for a bizarre reunion, caught up in the moment with her body and mind in full accord—no doubt, no hesitation, no regrets.

And so it was that she burst into the capitol with a fierce grin on her face and a whoop of intent filling the lobby right along with the horse.

A whoop cut short as she ducked, taken unaware by the newly positioned security arch. She pressed herself against the horse's neck and they blasted through it, but Selena's feet caught, forced back along the horse's flanks. The horse grunted in offense and switched to crow-hopping, buck-running past the dead security guard. Selena rode him through it, thighs jammed up against the harness saddle as they came up behind a Kemeni. Just rode, making no attempt to calm the animal—until they closed in. She pressed a rein against his neck, lifted the other slightly, and rubbed that heel across his ribs as though she had spurs on. And the horse, every bit as over the limits of personal endurance as she suspected, flung his hindquarters out in mid-hop and splatted the Kemeni against the wall.

The next closest man whirled to check on the noise, the hoofbeats, his expression primed for pure disbelief. Selena tucked the left rein around her right thumb and lifted her pistol, too close to miss. Too close altogether, for as the man went down the horse couldn't avoid him, and stumbled wildly before righting itself, its breath huffing audibly from more stress than effort.

But just one more...

One more, and they fail. *Again.*

The sound of gunfire lured her on as clearly as a trail of bread crumbs, and the screams jolted her into speed. She gave rein, urging the horse into the choppy canter it could manage in these halls, straight for the dining room—straight through the doorway.

As soon as she'd cleared it—as she found the Kemeni posturing to her left and the assembled staff and dignitaries to her right—she bailed. She sent the horse between the gunman and his targets, and she pulled a tuck-and-roll dismount, taking carpet burns regardless. Tuck and roll, until she stopped herself at the Kemeni's feet.

He towered over her, treelike, his attention so focused on the astonishing presence of the horse that she had plenty of time to bring her gun to bear, aiming straight up at his crotch—plenty of time to wait for just the right moment.

"Bang," she said. "Wanna die?"

Chapter 23

Security appeared as if from out of the woodwork—an actual possibility, unless that feature had been changed in the reconstruction—latching on to the Kemeni so roughly that Selena suspected he'd soon wish he'd taken her up on her offer. Outside, the gunfire had stopped, changing into rough shouts and nearly screamed demands for surrender.

God—Cole! The arriving security backup had found him and were screaming Berzhaani at him, orders he wouldn't be able to understand—not well enough to respond before he was shot.

Selena leaped to her feet, scanning the assembled men and women in their semiformal attire, ignoring the horse who'd found himself a corner to tuck his head in, trailing breeching straps and tracing and presenting his butt to anyone who might think about getting close to him. There—Razidae! In conversation with one of the arriving security guards, but she couldn't wait for that—he was the only one who could stop the confrontation on the steps. She ran to him, grabbing his arm even as his eyes widened with both affront and recognition; she caught a glimpse of Dante Allori not far away, reaching for his ringing cell phone—Aymal at work—one eyebrow arched high in exquisitely expressed *what have you gotten into now*. Only a few words later he headed for Davud Garibli, a man strangely apart from the others.

Later for that, too, and even as the security guard grabbed her, she said, "Sir, that's my husband your people are yelling at—he doesn't know Berzhaani and—"

Renewed gunfire cracked through the building from outside. A short spurt, and then silence. Selena dropped Razidae's arm and wrenched herself free from the guard.

And she ran.

Spotlights painted the stone steps in harsh light and brittle shadow, distorting the half-dozen dead and wounded Kemeni. It had indeed been a suicide charge. In such small numbers, they could not have hoped to survive. They'd simply been intent on causing their damage before they died—and they would have, had Selena not interfered.

Had Cole not interfered.

Heart thumping painfully in a manner oh-so-different than her reactive nerves, she hunted Cole. He'd gone off the horse about a third of the way up the steps, but then he'd fought his own battle. There was no telling where he'd ended up—

There. That abaya, crumpled off to the side and half-hidden in the shrubs. Capitol security slowly closed in, weapons aimed and ready and every single man looking as though it would take nothing more than *boo* to cause a full-bore volley of gunfire. All Cole had to do was twitch…

"*Stand down,*" she shouted, even knowing that a stranger's voice—a *woman's* voice—would have no authority. "He came to help! He is American, and has no Berzhaani!"

They didn't so much as glance at her, and she ran down several steps, aimed her pistol off to the side, and fired a shot into the sculpted dirt of the memorial garden. "You want a target?" She thumped herself in the chest for emphasis as they turned to this new threat, reflexively ducking, bringing their weapons to bear. "*Here's* your target, you fools!" Another two shots into the dirt and she had what she'd wanted—every gun on the stairs was pointed directly at her.

And it had seemed like such a good idea at the time...

Selena held her breath, remembered that she wore black over tan and hoped none of them would mistake tan for khaki in this light. She froze, and the only move she made was to open the trigger finger and thumb of the hand on her pistol, holding it precariously with her remaining fingers—the clearest, most concise gesture of harmlessness she could muster.

They didn't look convinced. *Oh, God, they don't look at all convinced—*

Except suddenly they'd altered aim, pointing their weapons slightly down and to the side, their expressions changing from wary, aggressive anger to something somewhat closer to abashed. Huh.

From behind her, Razidae's deep voice rang out. "Stand down. The Kemenis are contained. Hunt for stragglers and leave that man and this woman to me."

Selena's strength left her in a whoosh of relief; she almost sat down right then and there, at Razidae's feet. But her eyes sought out the stained and ragged abaya and the familiar shape of the body beneath it, and she couldn't bring herself to look away as she said to the prime minister, "Good evening, sir. I came to warn you that the Kemenis had something planned for the evening. I see my timing wasn't quite right."

"In fact, I consider your timing to be perfect," Razidae said, his commanding voice taking a distinctly dry note. "Considering I wasn't even aware of your presence in my country. But we will discuss that later. Go to him."

Selena spurted into motion. "Cole!" And then, as she slipped in her haste and literally skidded the few remaining steps to reach him, "*Cole,* dammit!" By then she was beside him, one hand heading for his shoulder, ready to shake him—

He stirred. He lifted his head and grinned up at her as he rolled over to almost-sit, a feeble half-assed sort of grin with the wry twist that said he knew it. No blood...she saw no blood anywhere. She patted him, careful of his back, unable to believe he hadn't been riddled with holes. "Are you all—"

"Hell, *yes,*" he said. "I'm *fine.*"

She snorted with utter disbelief—that he still had his humor, that he wasn't full of leaky holes. "I can't believe you weren't shot."

"Are you kidding?" Shaking with chills, burning with fever, his eyes not even beginning to focus, he still had the wherewithal to give a short laugh. "As soon as I realized they'd decided I was one of the bad guys, I decided to take a dive. A big, convincing dive."

"You were damned well *too* convincing," she snapped, and jerked her hand away from his shoulder to let him know he'd pay for scaring her, too.

For all of two or three seconds.

In the background, someone shouted about finding a

wagon, and finding an injured man. Selena closed her eyes, hoping they were in time. "Dobry is still alive," she whispered to Cole, shorthand translation.

Cole sighed with weary relief.

She opened her eyes to find him watching her—watching closely. The chills, the fever, the subtle jerk in his body that told of his strain. "But you're okay. You'll be okay."

He spared an arm from supporting himself and used it to pull her in close, to the kind of embrace where they stopped being individuals and became one being. One intense, grateful being, for the moment forgetting the circumstances also embracing them—the capitol steps in the aftermath of a terrorist attack with an injured comrade a block away.

Almost.

She was the one to pull away, taking all her willpower—and helped along by the commentary flying in the background, by those who'd forgotten she'd shouted out in their language. Helped, too, by the knowledge that one of them had already died, and that Cole was much sicker, much closer to that downward spiral, than he would ever admit.

Cole didn't let her pull back very far. Just far enough to meet her eyes and give her that wicked, wise-ass grin of his. "Okay?" he said. "Just *fine*."

She could have smacked him.

But she didn't. She leaned in to kiss him, and then to drag him away to safety.

Chapter 24

Days of worrying later, days of debriefing…days of explanations and international appeasement later, Selena found herself back at the ritzy Suwan restaurant—this time without Dante Allori. Without Dobry, who still slept in recovery from his wounds. But not alone, either. And not without a mission.

"You heard about the station house, right?" Selena spoke into the discreet earbud mike of her cell phone—the Agency phone, newly secure again—and nodded at the server who refilled her glass with tea. She spooned jam into it and almost wished Dobry was there to make a dour face at the habit.

But Cole's voice in her ear was a welcome relief after several days of IV antibiotics, a hyperbaric treatment or two, and one very bad second night when Berzhaan's best doctors thought the infection was winning the battle. He still tired far too easily, and his arms were stained with a fading rash of red dots that had been hidden by darkness and the abaya. But he'd wanted to "be here" for this, so Selena charged the phone battery to the fullest, pulled out the wireless earbud, and clipped the phone to the pocket of the gorgeous silk tunic she wore over loose black slacks. She sat at the same table where Ambassador Allori had once hosted her, and carried on a conversation with her husband, waiting for the final scene of the latest Kemeni tragedy.

"I heard about the station house," Cole confirmed. "TRAMMEL came by to act embarrassed about it. Seems the station security upgrade was the last job Betzer did for Hafford before taking his crew independent. Obviously a man who thought ahead, our Betzer. He left some strategically placed taps in place when he left."

"*Your* Betzer," Selena murmured.

"No one's Betzer anymore," Cole responded more soberly. "It's a good thing capitol security tracked down the surviving merc. He's been damned enlightening, from what I hear."

Not that tracking him down had been difficult. The man had managed to leave the wagon, but wasn't moving any faster than a crawl when Razidae's men caught up with him. And in acknowledgment of Selena's role in preventing a massacre at the private preview of the rebuilt capitol, they'd handed the wounded merc over to the embassy, where he proved very talkative when offered a deal that took the charge of treason off the table. "It's a good thing," Selena said, and nibbled a left-over breakfast pastry. "What a tangle. Betzer's group working to prevent Aymal's defection—"

"He made it to the States?"

"Touchdown yesterday afternoon, while you were sleeping. He's apparently been set to full babble ever since. There was a bombing planned for March Elementary

School in Webster, New York, but those school kids are completely safe."

His sigh of relief echoed through her own chest. "Okay, so Betzer was supposed to grab Aymal, and he knew about the thing with the capitol because he helped round up the Kemeni stragglers for his mystery boss, who was running a separate op—with Scott Hafford's inside information and driven by Davud Garibli—to get rid of Razidae once and for all."

"Or at the least, emasculate his leadership abilities by destroying the supposedly secure capitol." Not that they'd found out who that boss was—it was the one thing on which the wounded merc stood fast.

"Hey," Cole protested. "Watch how you use that word. It's a scary one. It could delay my recovery."

"You mean *emasculate*?" Selena asked, all innocence.

"The longer I'm in this hospital, the longer until we get back home…the longer it takes to get on with our lives." Cole's voice went suggestive, and Selena found herself glancing around, suddenly certain everyone in this conservative restaurant could hear. But she turned serious quickly enough, pushing the half-eaten pastry aside.

"I hear that," Cole told her. "That sudden silence into deep thought."

She made a face at him, quickly covering it with a fake sneeze as a dignified set of businessmen walked by, observing her unescorted presence with disapproval. "Brat," she whispered at him. But she recovered quickly, because he'd been right. And she didn't want to wait any longer for this conversation. "Here's the thing," she said, and took a deep breath. "I figured out something on this op. The whole I-am-what-I-am thing. And you're the one who said it…accept it. Use it."

"That I did," he agreed. "Something like that, anyway. But I don't get the feeling you're talking about the job anymore."

"No." She kept her voice low and watched her fingers tear off bits of innocent pastry. "I'm talking about us. About our family. I think we need to face facts…if practice could get it done, we'd be pregnant by now."

"If practice could get it done, we'd have quints by now," Cole said, his voice taking on an edge of fervency. "Oh, hold on—" He moved the phone from his mouth; his voice became muffled as he exchanged words with someone on his end. The receiver rustled against cloth, and finally he came back to her. "They were admiring my maggots."

Selena desperately muffled a snort, not willing to attract any more disapproving looks. Dobry had taught her that much. As a legate, it worked to her advantage to have a strong public personality, to be recognizable. Now that wouldn't always be the case.

Cole cheerfully continued. "We did a good job with that, they said. The things ought to come out tomorrow."

She cleared her throat, quite deliberately. "That's nice, dear."

"I know, I know…bad timing. Practice. Pregnant. Quints. And…?"

She couldn't help but lower her voice again, feeling very much as if she was walking out onto thin ice, the clear kind that showed every crack as well as the deep rushing water beneath. "So I think it's time we accepted that I am what I am. As much as we want a family—*our* family—I don't think it's gonna happen the usual way."

"No," he said, entirely sober. "It doesn't look that way."

"And we could go the whole high-tech route, or we could try to find a surrogate, or…"

Or the part she didn't have any idea how he'd respond

to. The part they'd never talked about, because until recently they'd never had the need.

But apparently they'd both been thinking about it somewhere along the way, for Cole's voice had gone soft, too. "Lena…you've seen what I've seen over the past handful of years. The toll terrorism takes…the number of kids it leaves behind…"

He knew.

He felt it, too.

Relief whooshed out of her lungs. "Yes," she said. "That's it. There's someone waiting for us, Cole. Someone *already* waiting for us. I don't care where she comes from, I don't care—"

"She?"

"She," Selena repeated, almost shyly. "To start."

"She," Cole repeated. "Yeah, I like the sound of that."

Don't cry in the restaurant, Selena, not even from happiness. Taz wouldn't.

Except she wasn't the Road Runner, and she wasn't Taz…she was Selena. Through and through.

"Lena?"

And just like that, she was back at work. For here came Scott Hafford, moving through the tables on the trail of the maître d'—glancing around as though he expected the world to come toppling down on him at any moment, but a man still going through the motions.

"Target's here," Selena murmured to Cole. She waited until the maître d' had gone past her table but Hafford hadn't, and she stood.

That's all she did. She stood and she waited, silent, one eyebrow slightly raised.

Hafford stopped in his tracks, his options crossing his face as he considered them—to fight, to run, to accept the inevitable. And eventually his shoulders sagged, and he nodded. In turn, Selena caught the eye of the CIA case officer who'd been stationed not far from her. The man stood, waiting to take custody.

"You knew," Hafford said, and waved off the maître d' who'd turned to check on him.

"We knew you were susceptible," Selena agreed. "And now we've got some people who will want to talk to you about Arachne."

Hafford went so pale she thought he might pass out; he steadied himself by gripping the back of an occupied chair, oblivious to the startled man seated on it. "You know," he murmured. "It's almost a relief."

Ignoring Cole's, "Arachne? Arachne who?" in her ear, Selena nodded. "I can imagine that's so. I can only hope it's also a relief that so few innocent people died because of you. That the capitol is opening today as planned even though you fed codes and bypass information to the Kemeni. That Razidae's government is strong and moving forward."

"I didn't want any of it to happen," Hafford said, a quiet but desperate plea for understanding. "I had no choice."

"Really?" she said coolly. "There's always choice, Mr. Hafford. And then you live with who you discover yourself to be."

"You'll see," he said, and if anything, that haunted look intensified. "You think your people are a target? You'll feel differently when you've faced what I have."

My people? The FBI, the CIA?

No. She knew who she thought of as *her people*. Who she'd have to warn. *Athena Academy*. She'd have to connect with Delphi…

But she'd finish here first. She gestured for him to precede her, and the local case officer stood to accompany them out of the restaurant, a casual move of which Dobry would have approved.

Outside the restaurant, Selena blinked at the bright sunshine and lifted her face to the unusually warm air of the fall day. Cole had been quiet for some moments. Now he said quietly, "Hey, you okay?"

And he meant *okay with all of it.* With what they'd been through together, with what they'd learned about each other together. What she'd learned about herself...and what they planned for their future. Even with the questions still unanswered about their future.

Okay? Selena took a deep, happy breath. "Hell, *yes,*" she said. "I'm *fine.*"

* * * * *

Experience the anticipation, the thrill of the chase and the sheer rush of falling in love!
Turn the page for a sneak preview of a new book from Harlequin Romance
THE REBEL PRINCE
by Raye Morgan
On sale August 29th wherever books are sold.

"Oh, no!"

The reaction slipped out before Emma Valentine could stop it, for there stood the very man she most wanted to avoid seeing again.

He didn't look any happier to see her.

"Well, come on, get on board," he said gruffly. "I won't bite." One eyebrow rose. "Though I might nibble a little," he added, mostly to amuse himself.

But she wasn't paying any attention to what he was saying. She was staring at him, taking in the royal blue uniform he was wearing, with gold braid and glistening badges decorating the sleeves, epaulettes and an upright collar. Ribbons and medals covered the breast of the short, fitted jacket. A gold-encrusted sabre hung at his side. And suddenly it was clear to her who this man really was.

She gulped wordlessly. Reaching out, he took her elbow

and pulled her aboard. The doors slid closed. And finally she found her tongue.

"You…you're the prince."

He nodded, barely glancing at her. "Yes. Of course."

She raised a hand and covered her mouth for a moment. "I should have known."

"Of course you should have. I don't know why you didn't." He punched the ground-floor button to get the elevator moving again, then turned to look down at her. "A relatively bright five-year-old child would have tumbled to the truth right away."

Her shock faded as her indignation at his tone asserted itself. He might be the prince, but he was still just as annoying as he had been earlier that day.

"A relatively bright five-year-old child without a bump on the head from a badly thrown water polo ball, maybe," she said defensively. She wasn't feeling woozy any longer and she wasn't about to let him bully her, no matter how royal he was. "I was unconscious half the time."

"And just clueless the other half, I guess," he said, looking bemused.

The arrogance of the man was really galling.

"I suppose you think your 'royalness' is so obvious it sort of shimmers around you for all to see?" she challenged. "Or better yet, oozes from your pores like…like sweat on a hot day?"

"Something like that," he acknowledged calmly. "Most people tumble to it pretty quickly. In fact, it's hard to hide even when I want to avoid dealing with it."

"Poor baby," she said, still resenting his manner. "I guess that works better with injured people who are half asleep." Looking at him, she felt a strange emotion she couldn't identify. It was as though she wanted to prove something to him, but she wasn't sure what. "And anyway, you know you did your best to fool me," she added.

His brows knit together as though he really didn't know what she was talking about. "I didn't do a thing."

"You told me your name was Monty."

"It is." He shrugged. "I have a lot of names. Some of them are too rude to be spoken to my face, I'm sure." He glanced at her sideways, his hand on the hilt of his sabre. "Perhaps you're contemplating one of those right now."

You bet I am.

That was what she would like to say. But it suddenly occurred to her that she was supposed to be working for this man. If she wanted to keep the job of coronation chef, maybe she'd better keep her opinions to herself. So she clamped her mouth shut, took a deep breath and looked away, trying hard to calm down.

The elevator ground to a halt and the doors slid open laboriously. She moved to step forward, hoping to make her escape, but his hand shot out again and caught her elbow.

"Wait a minute. *You're* a woman," he said, as though that thought had just presented itself to him.

"That's a rare ability for insight you have there, Your Highness," she snapped before she could stop herself. And then she winced. She was going to have to do better than that if she was going to keep this relationship on an even keel.

But he was ignoring her dig. Nodding, he stared at her with a speculative gleam in his golden eyes. "I've been looking for a woman, but you'll do."

She blanched, stiffening. "I'll do for what?"

He made a head gesture in a direction she knew was opposite of where she was going and his grip tightened on her elbow.

"Come with me," he said abruptly, making it an order.

She dug in her heels, thinking fast. She didn't much like orders. "Wait! I can't. I have to get to the kitchen."

"Not yet. I need you."

"You what?" Her breathless gasp of surprise was soft, but she knew he'd heard it.

"I need you," he said firmly. "Oh, don't look so shocked. I'm not planning to throw you into the hay and have my way with you. I need you for something a bit more mundane than that."

She felt color rushing into her cheeks and she silently begged it to stop. Here she was, formless and stodgy in her chef's whites. No makeup, no stiletto heels. Hardly the picture of the femmes fatales he was undoubtedly used to. The likelihood that he would have any carnal interest in her was remote at best. To have him think she was hysterically defending her virtue was humiliating.

"Well, what if I don't want to go with you?" she said in hopes of deflecting his attention from her blush.

"Too bad."

"What?"

Amusement sparkled in his eyes. He was certainly enjoying this. And that only made her more determined to resist him.

"I'm the prince, remember? And we're in the castle. My orders take precedence. It's that old pesky divine rights thing."

Her jaw jutted out. Despite her embarrassment, she couldn't let that pass.

"Over my free will? Never!"

Exasperation filled his face.

"Hey, call out the historians. Someone will write a book

about you and your courageous principles." His eyes glittered sardonically. "But in the meantime, Emma Valentine, you're coming with me."

COMING NEXT MONTH

#105 SPIN CONTROL by Kate Donovan

Defending FBI agent Justin Russo against a murder rap would take every skill in attorney Suzannah Ryder's arsenal. His top secret activities, his suspicious confession and disappearance before the trial—nothing added up. With Justin refusing to be straight with her—for her protection, he claimed—could Suzannah prove him innocent as the evidence mounted against him?

#106 DARK REVELATIONS by Lorna Tedder

The Madonna Key

Trapped into becoming an antiquities thief for the powerful Adriano family, Aubrey De Lune had given up her daughter, her career, everything. But when she stole a sacred 600-year-old manuscript attributed to Joan of Arc, Aubrey discovered the Adrianos' dirty little secret...as well as the key to *her* heritage, *her* power...and getting her life back.

#107 GETAWAY GIRL by Michele Hauf

Getaway car driver Jamie MacAlister had finally "gotten away" from her dubious past working for a clandestine rescue force at odds with Paris law enforcement. Or had she? When clues to her former mentor's murder lured her back to the fast lane, the chase was on...but could Jamie put the brakes on her attraction to the prime suspect?

#108 TOO CLOSE TO HOME by Maureen Tan

By day she policed a small Illinois town. By night, she worked for the Underground, rescuing runaway women and children from abusive men. But Brooke Tyler's two worlds collided when she discovered the remains of a woman who'd died a decade ago, exposing secrets and unleashing a killer who would test her like never before....

SBCNM0806